Letters for Lucien

by

Suzy England

Letters for Lucien

Cover Art by *Diana Carlile*

The Wild Rose Press, Inc.
PO Box 708
Adams Basin, NY 14410-0708
Visit us at www.thewildrosepress.com

Publishing History
First Edition, 2024
Trade Paperback ISBN 978-1-5092-5256-5
Digital ISBN 978-1-5092-5257-2

Published in the United States of America

His eyes traveled down to her hands and the fingers wrapped delicately around her mug. The large diamond on her wedding ring winked up at him. *Is she really mine?* It was a question he asked himself constantly. While sipping his coffee, his thoughts traveled back in time to a woman in a wheelchair. He'd only seen her twice, once in the hospital elevator and once in the park, but he knew, even that early on, that she was special. She'd changed him—just as easily as the seasons change, bringing with them a new beginning.

"You know what? I was wrong." He fixed his eyes firmly on her face.

"About what?" she asked.

"Remember when I told you my favorite season is spring? I was wrong."

"So, what is your favorite season?"

"It's fall."

"Oh, I think I love fall most, too. It's the change in the air. There's something about it that makes you feel so refreshed. I mean, it takes forever for fall to make it to Texas, but when it does, there's nothing better. Even the tiny bit we're getting right now." She breathed deeply, closing her eyes as she slowly exhaled.

"I love fall for a different reason. Your eyes remind me of fall."

"What about Pumpkin here?" She grinned, patting her belly.

"Well, yes. Naturally, the fruit of our labor is the best part." He placed his hand on top of hers.

"You know what's gonna happen when he gets here, don't you?" she asked.

"What?"

"You're gonna fall in love with spring all over again."

Praise from early readers...

"This book had my tear ducts working overtime!"

"Truly a treasure trove of life lessons and inspiration!"

"No words to express the beauty and depth of this piece of work. From the beginning to the end it was awesome!"

"You are an incredibly passionate storyteller and I feel blessed to have read this book."

"The letters and the lessons in them are incredible. I have learned a lot from this book. It's amazing, full of joy but painful too. Just wow."

"Touched to the soul by Sunny and Mathew's journey, I will now use this book as one of my references as I navigate this road called life."

"You put pen to paper and make it seem so easy."

"It's my favorite of all your books!"

There really are places in the heart you don't even know exist until you love a child.

—Anne Lamott

Chapter One

There will be good days and bad days.
Today's going to be a good one.
-Leo

Guarded optimism and a Post-It note of encouragement were all Mathew Ellis possessed when he walked through the main doors of his office building. His first day back at work after a life-altering three-week absence, his drive into downtown had been scored by a steady stream of silent prayers and the words from his closest friend. *Please just let me stay busy today. I'll take any and every corporate fire I can get—I'm not picky.* The silence that left him aching at home followed him inside the elevator, broken only by the sounds of twisted thoughts banging inside his head. The ascent to the fourth floor began and his stomach growled. A quick mental calculation confirmed he hadn't eaten a thing since lunch the day before. Things like food and sleep and even hygiene had fallen to the bottom of his list for a string of dark days.

I'll ask Brynn to run out and grab us something.

Brynn, his administrative assistant, stood waiting beside his desk. Her eyes widened with surprise and relief when he entered the office.

"The boss man is back!" she said, her face bright and welcoming.

1

"As promised," Mathew said, trying his best to mimic her upbeat tone.

"It's so good to see you. You've been missed."

"Thank you."

"How is Sunny feeling?"

"She's doing really well…and sends her love."

It was a lie. Probably the first of many that would fall from his lips.

"Please tell her I'm thinking about her."

They continued to exchange pleasantries until a call on her cell phone drove Brynn back to her workspace. Alone again, Mathew sank into his leather chair. Hoping to find stacks of files in need of his attention, the corners of his mouth turned down when he observed the sparseness of his desk. It was exactly as he'd left it the Thursday before Easter. The phone beside him showed no signs of activity. Not a scrap of paper or hand-scrawled message in sight. Three whole weeks had passed. Had no one noticed? Or was everyone hiding from him? Years of painstaking diligence in establishing his celebrated accounting firm—one of the largest in Houston—so it could thrive without him. It had been the end goal all along. But the man he'd become could not see the bigger picture. Mathew longed for distraction. He needed to feel needed. If not at home, then at least at work.

The last two days had been rough, following his father-in-law's departure. His wife's shell had become impenetrable, and her need to communicate in any form was unapparent. The ghost Mathew witnessed the day of the funeral had now taken up full-time residence and the home they shared at the desirable Bunker Hill address had become more like a prison. She hardly ventured downstairs, drifting silently between their bedroom and the nursery to pass the hours. His prayer that she protest his decision to return to the office and beg him to stay home had not been answered. She'd merely nodded when learning of his plans.

He reached into his wallet and found the business card Dr. Sumner had given him. Now smudged and wrinkled, he'd studied it intently for days on end, committing every letter to memory.

Dr. Emily McNichol, PhD, LPCC, FT
Psychotherapist/Crisis Interventionist

He tapped the card on his desk a few times, debating. After a minute, it returned to the safe folds of his wallet and he powered up his computer. Right hand on the mouse, he was greeted by his email. Not a single new message since his last login. Nothing new on his desktop calendar either. Disappointment coated him like the pollen he'd washed off his windshield earlier that morning.

What am I doing? Why the hell am I even here?

He surfed the web for a while, mostly reading up on financial news. After half an hour in deafening silence, his patience was shot. His finger pressed the intercom button, summoning Brynn.

"Could you come in here for a minute, please?" Mathew asked.

In less than thirty seconds, Brynn was back in his office, a tablet and stylus in hand.

"You don't need to take notes. I just want to talk." He motioned to a chair.

"All right," she answered, a touch of wariness in her voice.

"How long have you known me?" Hands folded

together, his elbows rested on his desk.

"Well, let's see. I started working for you about four years ago."

"In the four years since you've been working with me, can you ever recall a Monday morning when there was complete silence in this office?"

Brynn thought for a moment. "No, I don't think so."

"Correct me if I'm wrong, but I am Mathew Ellis, right? Head of this operation?"

"Yes, sir."

"This is my firm?"

"Yes, sir, it is." She nodded with a confused look.

"Then can you please explain why my desk is bare? Why isn't the phone ringing? And why I have yet to have one person knock on that door and apologize for interrupting me?"

"Well, sir…"

"How long do you think it's going to be like this?" His face wrinkled with frustration. "Everyone walking around on eggshells? Afraid to have a conversation with me?"

"Sir, I…" Brynn shook her head, a look of compassion in her eyes.

"Could you please find something for me to do? I'll organize files. I'll make phone calls. I'll order lunch for every single Ellis Consulting employee and deliver it personally. Just please give me something to do."

His tone was not harsh. Quite the opposite. Haunted eyes and the slump of his broad shoulders both conveyed a desperate need for direction.

"Well, my Buggati needs washing, and I really should pick up my vintage Valentino ball gown from

Celebrity Cleaners," she said with a smirk.

"Thank you. You have no idea how much I needed that." Mathew smiled; his first real one in weeks.

****

"Sunny! Lunch is ready!" Leo called from the bottom of the stairs but received no response. *A tray it is*, he decided after a moment, turning back toward the kitchen with Ivy, their Havanese, following closely behind.

Leo had spent the morning trying anything and everything to combat the unnerving quiet. Taken the dog on an extra-long walk. Spent an hour in the gardening shed. Watched two different shows on The History Channel. With Mathew back at the office and Sunny a recluse upstairs, he longed for some type of stimulating conversation. From the phone in the kitchen, the old man dialed, thankful when his call was answered on the first ring.

"Sunny?" Mathew answered his cell phone, an urgency in his tone.

"Sorry, it's just me," Leo responded.

"Is everything all right?"

"I tried to get her to come down for lunch, but no luck."

"Have you seen her at all today?"

"No. She slipped down and got some coffee, I think. But that's when I was out walking Ivy. I'm going to take a tray up to her in a minute. How're you? You must be swamped up there."

"Don't I wish? This office is no different than where you're standing right now. I've been begging Brynn for something to do, but even she's afraid to bother me."

"She'll come around. Everyone will come around, you'll see."

"I sure hope so. Otherwise, I might as well stay home."

"You get my note?"

"I did. I'm looking at it right now. I stuck it on the corner of my monitor—and I really appreciate it. It means a lot, Leo. Thank you."

A tiny smile formed on Leo's thin lips. "Just wanted you to know I was thinking about you. Want to come home for lunch?"

"No, I better stay here, just in case. And there's something I need to do later, but I shouldn't be too late."

Chapter Two

It was sprinkling by the time Mathew made it to his car. Despite the bleak skies above, his outlook was positive, thanks in part to Brynn's touches of humor throughout the day and her efforts to help him find some much-needed normalcy. Every comedic exchange they'd shared had been a boost, and for the first time since his father-in-law had returned home, Mathew inched closer to being his true self again. Sliding behind the wheel, he took a cleansing breath and cleared his mind.

The traffic en route to his destination was heavy, with rain following suit. He'd quietly debated whether or not to call first, but decided arriving in person would be more of a challenge. A challenge was needed. A personal victory. A chance to mark a very big item off his To-Do list: *Make an appointment with a therapist.*

A red light at an intersection near the park forced him to stop. As the rain increased dozens of would-be parkgoers ran for cover underneath make-shift umbrellas of jackets and blankets. One couple caught his eye, and immediately those brief feelings of optimism he'd experienced vanished. A young man stood in the rain, drenched from head to toe, but happily holding a blue plaid umbrella over the head of his very pregnant companion. Their expressions were lighthearted and genuine. As the light changed, Mathew could not bring himself to move the car forward. His gaze stayed focused on the couple, his hands in a death grip on the steering wheel. The rain washed away their image and replaced it with one of himself and Sunny, kissing in the rain on a sandy beach. The car behind him honked several times, pulling him back to reality. Slowly, his foot eased away from the brake and the car inched through the intersection. His gaze shifted back and forth between the road ahead and the rear-view mirror, watching the couple until they dissolved behind a soggy gray veil.

****

Leo tiptoed up the stairs, tray in hand and dog in tow. Outside the bedroom door, his weight shifted back and forth while listening for signs of life within. If Sunny was sleeping, waking her was not the play. Days and nights had swapped places, and she hardly closed her eyes during the nighttime hours. After conferring a moment with his faithful companion, he tapped lightly on the door and waited for a reply. Again, nothing. Leo drew a deep breath, quietly turned the doorknob, and peeked inside.

Sunny sat on the edge of the bed, papers scattered everywhere. She was wrapped in Mathew's robe—a large *E* monogrammed on the pocket on the left-hand side. Leo's thoughts turned to that of Hester Prynne, and of all the things that single letter now stood for: evasive, empty, emotionless. Sunny's hair hung in damp strings around her pale face. *Well, at least she found her way to the shower*. In his heart, Leo couldn't fault her for anything. Not the silence nor the need to hide. He'd walked a similar path once upon a time and ached for Sunny to return to them.

"Sunny?" Leo said, startling her.

"Oh, Leo. I didn't hear you." She quickly folded the paper in her hand, tucking it back into Mathew's bedside table. The tears were visible, and she made no attempt to wipe them away.

"You must be feeling better if you're up to a little spring cleaning." He eyed the surrounding mess.

"Just going through some old things. Things I need to get rid of." She gathered the items off the bed and floor in hasty fashion before dropping them into the small wastebasket beside the desk.

"I brought you some lunch."

"Thanks, but I'm really not very hungry."

"But you skipped breakfast..." He couldn't hide the argumentative tone in his voice.

"I had coffee."

"Coffee's not enough. Now I want you to get comfortable because this tray's heavy." He walked toward the bed, determined not to take no for an answer.

"All right." She sighed and accepted the tray, her gaze falling on an envelope tucked underneath the linen napkin.

"Can I bring you anything else?"

"No. Thank you." She avoided his eyes as she reached for the glass of juice in front of her.

Leo stood beside the bed, waiting for a sign that maybe she needed a shoulder or a friendly ear. But it never came. So, with a nod and a look of defeat, he conceded and left the room.

****

Sunny studied the tray, noting the special effort Leo made to offer several treats she enjoyed. Chicken salad on a fresh croissant. Her favorite pasta salad. A bowl full of sweet strawberries with a dollop of whipped cream. Just like Mathew, Leo always went the extra mile. Took the extra step to make sure everything in her world was just right, even when he knew it wasn't.

She slipped the mysterious envelope from under the napkin, and at once the mystery disappeared. There was no need to look at the return address or postmark. She recognized her father's handwriting immediately. It was messy. Almost childlike. A wild combination of print and cursive letters. The envelope was heavy, indicating a letter of some length contained within. Was it a sermon or a eulogy? A little of both? Whatever it found, a large piece of his heart surely accompanied the words he'd penned. She'd been waiting, knowing it was just a matter of time. All those things he'd wanted so desperately to say to her before he turned and waved one last time as his car eased out of their driveway. With a heavy sigh, she opened the envelope.

Chapter Three

Mathew found a parking space on the street across from the entrance to Dr. McNichol's office. The rain intensified, and he sat immobile inside his car for several minutes, gripped by apprehension. While he believed Dr. McNichol would be nothing short of professional, Mathew had always been an immensely private person. Knowing Dr. Sumner had recommended her helped ease his mind somewhat. But it was still his private world. His devastation. His anguish. Could he trust the darkest moment of his life to a stranger? Would it be easier that way?

His hand rested on the phone, tapping it lightly with an index finger. *Should I call Sunny? Tell her what I'm doing? Will she tell me she needs me to come home?* He craved a sign—something to give him the go-ahead or, conversely, something to summon him back home, putting off his To-Do List for yet another day.

Watching the main doors of the professional building, he established a game plan. *Five more minutes. If someone walks out those doors in the next five minutes, then I'm going in.* It was cowardice, and he knew it. It wasn't a game plan. It was nothing more than Liar's Poker. For weeks he'd been an ace liar–to himself and everyone around him. He'd kept the emptiness hidden, trying to find Sunny and losing

11

himself in the process.

A sudden break in the rain allowed an elderly couple to emerge from the front of the building. Mathew glanced at his watch. Fate called his bluff—with only a minute to spare. True to the promise, he drew a deep breath and exited the car, jogging and jumping puddles until safely inside the building.

The lobby was dark and quiet, but not entirely unwelcoming. Though he'd visited his dentist in that same locale for several years, he'd never noticed the benches or plants or artwork. He paused at the large directory hanging on the wall behind a glass case. There it was, in the top right corner, the fifth name from the top. *Dr. E. McNichol, Suite 110.* His heartbeat increased, but his feet continued forward, moved by a force of their own toward the large oak door of her office.

Unlike the lobby, Dr. McNichol's waiting area boasted bright and cheerful decor. Mathew quickly sized up the bodies in the room. A gentleman in a business suit sat in the corner reading a magazine. The man never looked up, completely aware of Mathew's entry. A woman sat beside him, quietly engrossed in a novel. She looked up for a moment but quickly returned to her reading. A receptionist sat behind a small desk just to the left of the entrance and smiled pleasantly at him.

"Good afternoon," she said softly.

"Hello," Mathew whispered, trying not to disturb the couple across the room. "I'd like to make an appointment."

"Is this for yourself or a family member?"

"For myself. And my wife. Well, I don't know if

she'll come, but…" He stopped, unsure what to say.

"Have either of you met with Dr. McNichol before?"

"No, ma'am. We were referred by Dr. Wade Sumner."

"May I ask the nature of your experience?"

"I'm sorry?" The question puzzled him.

"Are you interested in bereavement counseling?"

"Uh, yes, ma'am."

"I have a couple of forms I'll need you to fill out." She shuffled through a drawer for a moment, then produced the necessary documents.

"Sure. Thank you." He selected a pen from the cup on her desk.

"You can take them with you, or if you have the time, you can fill them out here."

"I've got time. I'd like to see Dr. McNichol as soon as possible—today, if she's available."

"Fill those out, then we'll take a look at her schedule." She handed him a clipboard.

Mathew took a seat on a chair by the door. He filled out the first sheet quickly, giving all the rote yet pertinent information about his life. Name. Address. Phone numbers. Insurance. The second sheet proved to be more challenging. The first side was easy enough— his complete medical history. Hospitalizations. Surgeries. Former and current medications. Nothing he couldn't answer, though dates were somewhat hazy, forcing guesses on a few. Flipping over to the backside, the questions became exponentially more difficult. Mathew paused and read each one several times, unable to continue.

Whom did you lose?

What were the circumstances of the death?

How long ago did the death occur?

Describe the circumstances of the death and how it's affected you.

Why did you decide to take part in therapy?

While the first three questions could be satisfied with fairly short and straightforward answers, the final two questions were beyond his grasp. The amount of space given was limited, making the task that much more daunting. *How the hell can I possibly explain the effects of his death? In twenty words or less?*

He filled in the first three blanks despite an overwhelming feeling of helplessness. The lightheaded sensation he'd experienced at the funeral returned. On shaky legs, he returned the clipboard to the receptionist. She spoke to him, but he couldn't hear anything over the ringing in his ears. Shaking his head, he turned to the door with a promise to come back another time.

Chapter Four

How Mathew got there, he didn't know. The car had somehow read his mind, stopping at the closest watering hole. He and Sunny were frequent guests in the restaurant, but this trip was aimed at finding liquid comfort inside the bar. A familiar face offered greetings just inside the door.

"Mr. Ellis?" The man looked surprised.

"Hi, Antonio." He nodded.

"You're a little early for dinner." The man eyed his watch.

"I'm just here for a drink."

"Of course. Will Mrs. Ellis be joining you?"

"Not anytime soon, I'm afraid."

"Well, enjoy." The gentleman motioned toward the bar.

For being so early in the day, the bar was surprisingly full of patrons. Trying to secure the last remaining open bar stool, he collided with a woman and his shoes paid the price–an entire highball giving them a whiskey bath.

"Oh, my God! I am so sorry!" She looked up with eyes full of embarrassment.

"It's okay. Don't worry about it." He inspected the damage.

"I'm really, really sorry."

"It's fine, I promise. I had them Scotchgarded."

"That was bourbon," she teased.

"I was afraid you were going to say that. Would you like another drink?"

"It was my fault entirely. You don't need to–"

He motioned to the bartender. "Could you set her up with one more? And I'll have a Dos Equis. Exactly what are my feet bathing in?" He glanced down at his shoes for a moment before meeting her gaze again.

"Maker's Mark and ginger ale."

"Interesting combination."

The bartender placed a fresh drink in front of her, then turned and popped the top on a beer. Mathew pulled a wallet from his back pocket and slid a fifty-dollar bill across the bar top.

"You don't need to do this. I should be buying *your* beer, as an apology," she said.

"It's no big deal. Pay it forward later." He clinked his bottle against her glass. The bartender returned and offered Mathew his change. As he silently counted the bills, the woman beside him continued to speak, trying to engage him in conversation. Though he didn't really feel like talking, she persisted…everything from Astros baseball to her online horoscope. Mathew focused on the flat screen above the bar, giving nothing but an occasional nod. She never got the hint and just kept talking.

"I read an interesting article in Cosmo. Did you know that couples who meet in bars have the lowest divorce rates in the country?"

"Don't believe everything you read in Cosmo." He avoided her eyes and took another sip of beer.

A minute of silence passed before she said, "Are you waiting for someone?" Her hopeful expression and meaning were obvious to him.

Though she was young and beautiful, there was no temptation. Not her dark hair falling across her shoulders. Not her perfectly manicured nails. Not her tasteful, expensive wardrobe. His heart belonged to Sunny, and no degree of physical beauty from another woman would change that. But emotions are funny things, whispering in one's ear to play devil's advocate. Maybe these were the signs. A kind face. A willing listener. A vacant corner booth. It wouldn't be the first time two strangers shared cocktails and confessions, leaving their burdens at the bottom of empty glasses. Maybe he didn't need Dr. Emily McNichol. Maybe the company of another lonely soul was all he needed.

"No, but someone's waiting for me." He downed his beer and placed the bottle firmly on the bar. "If you'll excuse me, please."

Another band of showers followed him through the parking lot, and by the time he reached his car, he was soaked. Heart pounding fiercely, reality hit. Twice that day he'd been given the opportunity to share the pain– both on paper and in a crowded bar. Twice, he'd run away.

Mathew started the car, unsure where the road would take him, but he needed to drive. To empty his mind of the day's events. He wanted to run home to Sunny and bolt himself inside her innermost room. But the ghost standing guard at that secret door would only stare through him with hollow eyes and deny him entry. He'd read the books. He'd caught glimpses of the talk shows. Leo even spelled it out on a Post-It note that very morning. *There will be good days and bad days.*

He drove in silence, his thoughts moving in time

with the windshield wipers. Back and forth. Past and present. His subconscious mind took control, driving along the route he and Sunny loved to cruise on Sunday afternoons. A familiar guitar riff of an old Gordon Lightfoot song on the radio added to the mood. Over the volume of the radio, the sound of the rain was barely audible. He pressed the gas pedal harder, driving recklessly on the slick road. The rain pounded the windshield, the wipers now moving at max speed. Thousands of tiny dots were wiped away, then instantly replaced by thousands more in a vicious cycle that seemed without end. Be it rain or tears, the road ahead blurred until the center line became a distorted yellow ribbon on the asphalt. Signaling, the car pulled onto the shoulder and stopped. Mathew stared out into a world he no longer recognized. The wiper blades continued to move across the windshield.

Think of something happy. Think of something happy.

Images appeared. A chapel. A ring. A promise. The layers of her hair across a pillow. The look in her autumn-hued eyes on their first night as husband and wife. Her look—one reserved just for him. One he might never again behold. Mathew sat for a long time with his forehead resting against the steering wheel.

The rain stopped, but his tears didn't.

Chapter Five

Mathew waited in the driveway for several minutes, letting both the engine and his mind idle. Most of his thoughts had been washed away with the downpour and now only questions remained: *Do I even bother going inside, or sleep in the casita? Fall into bed beside a woman who isn't truly there, or stave off this helplessness for another night by myself? Either way, this day is gonna end in silence and defeat.*

He slipped the key into the backdoor, careful not to make a sound. With the twist of the doorknob, he exhaled and prepared to embark upon another lonely night. His eyes strained to read his watch in the faint patio light. It was after midnight. *So much for being home early.* Steps into the kitchen, he froze at the sight of Leo sitting at the island.

"What are you doing up?" Mathew's voice was soft and calm. He locked the door behind him, dropping his damp raincoat on the kitchen counter.

"I couldn't sleep," Leo whispered.

"You were waiting for me, weren't you? I'm sorry I kept you up. Go on to bed. I'm gonna have a drink then I'm going up myself."

"Would you like some company?"

It was more of a request than a question. Mathew studied the old man's eyes, full of gentleness and truth but stained with sorrow. In all their years together, he'd never seen him look more distraught. He knew that just as his father-in-law, Huck, ached for Sunny, Leo's hurt was the same for him. They'd been best friends and the strictest of confidants. They'd traveled the world, nursed each other's hangovers, shared birthday and holiday dinners. And now, thinking back on the last twenty-one days, he realized that he'd done to Leo what Sunny had done to him. Distance. Avoidance. Protecting himself, but at someone else's expense. Mathew paused for a moment.

"I'd love it." He patted his dear friend's shoulder.

The living room was dark, except for the tiny lights that lit an enormous bookcase, one which filled an entire wall. Mathew noticed a crystal glass of amber liquid sitting on the table beside his favorite chair.

"A couple hands of gin?" Leo fumbled inside a sleek ebony box on the coffee table that held the television remotes and a deck of cards.

"No, I don't think so." Mathew took a sip of cognac, allowing the distinct combination of fruit and spice to warm him.

"How 'bout chess? We could start a game?" he asked.

"Not really up for games of any kind tonight, Leo."

"I understand…"

Leo shuffled across the room to the bookcase and returned with something Mathew hadn't seen in a while—an exquisite hourglass encased in handcrafted cocobolo wood.

"Where'd you find this?" Mathew asked, examining the lost treasure.

"It's been right there on that shelf ever since we moved in."

Leo gently flipped the timer upside-down. Instantly, grains of sand made their hasty descent to the bottom of the glass bulb. Mathew's gaze turned from his drink to the smooth wood grain that encased the hourglass. He leaned forward and ran a hand lightly along the top, focusing on the rich color of the wood. The deep red, highlighted with streaks of gold and amber, reminded him of the golden highlights in Sunny's hair. Without realizing it, he rubbed his thumb and forefinger together and the subconscious feel of her hair against his skin calmed him even more.

The two men shared many nights in the presence of the timer, engaged in a raucous debate or merely pondering life's mysteries. The grains of sand equaled only a quarter-hour, but they'd been able to solve many of the world's problems in less time. It had served them well over the years, their fifteen-minute confessional timer, as Leo had dubbed it. Most nights, it had been a timer of truth, and Mathew knew the reason it suddenly resurfaced.

"We haven't conversed in the company of this in a while." He gave the timer a tap.

"Not since the night we officially declared hardcore political topics off limits—at least when Sunny's in the room."

"Remember that night we filled out the entire NCAA basketball bracket, backward, in less than ten minutes?"

"What about that night we rewrote the lyrics to that Beatles song? Hey, Prude?" Leo flashed a big grin.

"I don't know if it was the margaritas or the jetlag, but man, we were on a roll that night." Mathew laughed.

The room quieted. Mathew took another sip of his drink, continuing to watch the grains of sand fall through the narrow strait of the hourglass. Shifting his gaze, he found Leo's eyes. Gray eyes, soft and caring, and ready for whatever Mathew needed. Feelings of shame filled Mathew—for his recent actions or lack thereof. The words were there, but saying everything that needed to be said would be like jumping off the cliff. And for three long weeks, he'd managed to teeter on the edge. Letting go required a degree of bravery he didn't yet possess.

"There's something I have to tell you, Matty. Something I've been meaning to say for a while." Leo finally spoke, looking into Mathew's eyes with fatherly kindness.

"Please, Leo…" Mathew raised his hand in protest, shaking his head.

"No, let me finish," the old man pleaded.

Mathew sighed and nodded but made no verbal response.

"You and Sunny mean everything to me. Everything. I know it never will, but I want things to be the way they used to be. Just tell me what to do and I'll do it. If you want me to leave you alone, then I'll leave you alone. If you want me to just leave…" Leo's voice trailed off, and Mathew noticed the uncertainty in his eyes.

"Aw, Leo…"

"Just say the word. I'll do whatever you want me to do. No questions asked. I can be on a plane back to Seattle first thing tomorrow. I've already cleared it with Dr. Walsh. Nora and Jake are fine with me living there year-round. I'm strong enough now."

"Of course we don't want you to leave. We need you. *I* need you now more than ever. You being here is more comforting to me than I can even express." Mathew extended his hand and gripped Leo's tightly.

"I wish I could say that I know what you're going through, but I don't. I don't know what it feels like to lose a child. I only know how I felt when I lost Patty. It was the lowest point of my life."

Leo never talked about Patty, his wife who'd been struck and killed by a car just a month after they were married. He hadn't mentioned her name in years. His courage was more than just a nudge.

Mathew sat back heavily and shook his head. "I don't even know what I feel anymore. I went to Dr. McNichol's office today but bailed at the last second. Then, I drove around for a while. Ended up across town at Antonio's place and had a drink in the bar."

"Is that where you've been this whole time?"

"No. I've been burning a tank of gas just driving around in the rain. Driving and thinking." He swirled the last few drops of cognac around the bottom of the glass.

"Sometimes the road is the best therapist."

"Sometimes," Mathew agreed.

Another quiet moment lapsed before Leo spoke again. "Mr. Yates called." Reaching into his pocket, he produced a folded piece of paper and slid it across the coffee table.

"He did? What'd he say?" Mathew glanced at the note. It was just a phone number and time written in Leo's casual hand.

"The headstone is finished. They're delivering it tomorrow, if you'd like to be there when they place it."

"Does Sunny know? I mean, did you tell her he called?"

"Nope. Haven't seen her since lunch. She's been very quiet today. I left a tray outside your bedroom around six, but she hasn't touched it. She got a letter today from Huck. I guess she was too upset to eat."

Mathew examined the note. "You wanna know something crazy? I don't even remember what it looks like." He could see himself standing with Huck, trying bravely to make decisions as to granite colors and fonts, but the image of the headstone was nothing more than an out-of-focus photograph.

"It doesn't matter. We remember Lucien...and that's all that matters."

Hearing his son's name made Mathew's heart pound. It was the first time Leo had said his name out loud in weeks. Tomorrow, a piece of stone would show the world that on Easter Sunday of that year, a baby boy had come quietly into the world and left the very same way. But the love he'd created from the moment they'd learned of his existence still echoed loudly inside them all.

"I once asked you how you dealt with Patty's death. You said you sat in the dark for a long time. That's exactly how I feel. Like I've been imprisoned in a room of total darkness. And it's not just because we lost Lucien. I've lost Sunny now too."

"But I also told you that when God turns out the light, He sends you a flashlight."

"I don't think there'll be a flashlight for us, Leo." Mathew quietly traced the rim of his glass.

"Maybe it's not your job to wait for a flashlight. Maybe you have to be Sunny's flashlight now."

"I've been trying. She won't even look at me."

"Maybe your light's not strong enough yet. Maybe she can't look at you because the pain in your eyes is too much for her right now. I bet if you work on making your light brighter, then you can show her the way." He gave Mathew a hard look, then turned his attention back to the hourglass. The last grains of sand fell to the bottom of the glass bulb. "Looks like time's up for tonight."

"I know I don't say it often enough, but I love you, Leo."

"I love you too, Matty." This time, Leo reached for Mathew's hand. He gave it a firm and caring shake.

"We're both up way past our bedtime. Let's call it quits." He gave Leo's hand a final pat before releasing it.

"You head to bed. I'll shut everything down." Leo picked up Mathew's empty glass.

"No, I'll close up shop tonight. I've got something I need to do first."

Mathew made a sweeping motion with his hand, urging Leo to go. His gray-haired friend disappeared, and Mathew was once again alone. He stared at the timer in amazement. *Well, he's done it again. That simple wisdom that rivals the world's most renowned thinkers. And once again, he did it in under fifteen minutes.*

He flipped open his wallet, retrieved Dr. McNichol's business card, and dialed her office number on his cell. Her machine answered on the third ring, advising him to follow the standard drill after the beep.

"Uh, hello. My name is Mathew Ellis. I was referred by Dr. Wade Sumner. I'd like to make an appointment."

Chapter Six

Upstairs, Mathew found Sunny asleep in their bed. It surprised him. Most nights she bypassed their bedroom altogether and sequestered herself in the nursery. He closed the door as gently as possible, trying not to wake her. Ivy looked up at him from her spot under the window, but quickly returned to doggy dreams. Quietly, he slipped off his shoes and tiptoed around to Sunny's side of the bed. The light from their bathroom fell in a narrow sliver across her face. He studied her, relieved to do so without the fear of her running away. This is what their marriage had become: Sunny imprisoned inside an invisible cage while he observed her from a safe distance. Would she ever wake up from her seemingly comatose state? And if so, then what?

He yawned and undressed, eager to slip into bed beside her. As was routine, he emptied his pockets onto the dresser—spare change, the phone message from Leo, and a tiny sterling silver heart. Heart pounding, his thoughts returned to the design of the headstone. He hadn't been to the cemetery since the day they buried Lucien. Mathew had driven by there twice that evening, but couldn't bring himself to turn in. Tomorrow, his fears would have to be faced. Would Sunny want to go? She hadn't left the house since the funeral. Maybe this would be the first step.

He eyed the little silver heart lying among the shiny coins. While not expensive, it was priceless in terms of sentiment. A gift from Sunny, he carried it everywhere. Especially in those first days following the funeral, still hiding from the world in a t-shirt and bathrobe. It provided unseen comfort whenever his hand dipped into his pocket.

Maybe she needs it now. Mathew turned it over between his fingers, but it slipped from his grasp and fell noiselessly to the floor. Bending to pick it up, his gaze snagged on something else. The wastebasket beneath Sunny's antique desk—overflowing with a mass of papers. Papers that hadn't been there that morning. His curiosity kicked into overdrive. Mathew retrieved both the pocket heart and the wastebasket and tiptoed out of the room.

The door to the nursery down the hall was closed but light glowed from underneath it. Mathew pushed it open with his foot. A night light beside the crib filled the room with soft pink warmth. He settled himself on the floor in the middle of the room and dove into the trash can, eager to dissect its mysterious contents. Some pages were wadded up in tight balls. Others, it appeared, were merely dropped into the receptacle without a thought. There were pages and pages, written on all manner of things—monogrammed stationery, the kitchen notepad, sheets of plain white copy paper, even lined notebook paper. *She's been writing letters this whole time...*

Mathew sat on the floor, wearing only his suit pants and socks, and read every word his wife had written. Every line was composed of the all-encompassing love that could only come from a mother. The letters were both beautiful and heartbreaking, and Mathew ached with the realization that Lucien would never know the beauty of his mother's face, the warmth of her kiss, or the calming nature of her hands upon his skin. The tears he cried on the side of the road earlier returned, and he didn't try to stop them. When he finally wiped them away, he wondered if he'd experience those same blessings again himself.

He yawned again. It was late and time to stash Sunny's letters out of sight. On the shelf inside Lucien's closet, he located an empty basket, probably earmarked for small toys or extra diapers. Mathew placed the stack of letters inside and pushed it silently to the back of the shelf. At the door, he turned for one final look. He studied the mural of The Little Prince on the wall, noting the boy's regal expression. With a nod, he closed the door.

When he returned to their bedroom, Sunny's side of the bed was vacant. The sound of running water echoed from the bathroom. *Should I go in there…or just wait here for her?* But the decision was made for him as she rounded the corner, stopping cold when she saw him.

"You're home?" she asked.

"I've been home a while."

"Where've you been?"

"I couldn't sleep. I was in the other room—reading. I didn't want to wake you."

"Oh." She nodded.

"Leo said you didn't eat much for dinner. You want me to go down and get you something?"

"No. I'm not hungry."

29

"Something to drink? I could get you some juice or something."

"I don't need anything," she said, her tone despondent.

Yes, you do! You need me! Say it! You need me, Sunny, just like I need you. Please don't do this to me. I can't live like this. I don't want it to be this way.

"All right, but if you change your mind..." He sighed, staring with helpless longing, though she made no further response.

With conversation at a standstill, Mathew retreated to the bathroom to complete his nightly ritual, fully expecting to find an empty bed upon his return. To his shock, she was back in bed, curled up, facing the wall. His heart shot up into his throat. Was it a sign? Doubtful. Too many times he'd thought that maybe— just maybe—she was coming around. But it always ended in disappointment and hopes were always severed. Crawling into bed, he turned onto his left side to face her. *If I could hold her, even for a minute, maybe then she'd come around.* His hand found the edge of her pillow and the tips of his fingers brushed against her hair. It wasn't much, but it was enough. Just the feel of a few wisps of her golden hair relaxed him in a way he couldn't describe.

"Mathew?" she whispered.

"Yes."

"I'm glad you're home."

"Me too." He reached out and stroked her head, letting his fingers run softly through her hair.

She didn't respond, but she didn't pull away either.

Chapter Seven

Ten months earlier

My Little Prince,
You're probably going to be so disappointed that I'm writing letters to a little boy throughout this journey and it turns out you're a girl. But it won't matter to me, because I already love you in a way that I can't even describe. Your father and I haven't been to see a doctor yet, but we know. We don't need to see you swimming around inside me to know you are real. You. Are. Real!

Speaking of your father, let me tell you right off the bat how blessed and lucky we are to have him in our lives. I met your father in an elevator at a hospital here in Houston. I saw his eyes and immediately felt a connection. I have a strange feeling that you will have those very same eyes–honest and playful and the most amazing shade of green.

I know that you will be brilliant because you are your father's son. And I won't have to explain the math. I was already expecting you when your father and I married, only we didn't know it. We were on our honeymoon and I wasn't feeling well. I took a pregnancy test. Two tests, actually. I'm a left-brain person and thus, a stickler for hard evidence. I'm sure none of this matters much to you, but it might someday.

I wouldn't be telling the whole story if I didn't mention how surprised and excited we were—and are!

You have only one living grandparent—my father, Harland Hayes Porter. Everybody calls him Huck, and honestly, no one knows how that nickname came about. He's a brilliant man, and you are so lucky to have such a cool grandfather. He's what folks call "an old hippie." He still lives on the same two hundred acres outside of Austin in the house where I grew up. You're going to love it there! Get this—he was a professional motorcycle racer for years. Now that he's retired from racing, he designs and builds custom bikes, trains young racers, and travels all over the globe. He's still a pretty big deal in the racing world. Grandpa Huck doesn't know about you yet. In a few weeks, he'll be visiting us, and we'll tell him then. I can teach you everything you need to know where he's concerned. I know all the right buttons to push to get exactly what you want from him. But you won't have to push hard because he's going to be crazy about you from the word go.

My mother, Daphne Davidson Porter, passed away when I was nine. She's the most beautiful person I've ever known. She was a free spirit, just like your Grandpa Huck. She left us much too soon, but I know she loved me very much. For the first time in my life, I truly understand just how deep her love was for me because that's how I feel about you. Many times she'd say that she loved me more than I would ever know. But now, because of you, I know. Without a doubt, I know.

Your father was raised by a man named Leo Silva. Now there's a character. You'll learn loads from that man. Leo was everything to your father and still is.

Your father grew up in the foster care system in Phoenix, never knew his parents, and was never adopted. After aging out of the system, your dad met Uncle Leo in the parking lot of a casino of all places. Leo became like a dad to your father, and they've been best friends and partners in crime ever since. Leo has a heart of pure gold. I know there's nothing he wouldn't do for your father and me, and for you. So really, when you think about it, it will be like having two grandfathers because Leo is family too. He'll be the one to teach you to play cards, grille perfect baby back ribs, and take you to your first major league game (Go Astros!). Like I said, he's quite a character.

What can I tell you about your father without writing an entire book? Falling in love with him was the easiest, most natural thing I've ever done in my life. Uncle Leo and I were patients in the same hospital, and that's how we met. Leo had suffered an aneurysm and I was having a tumor removed from my spine. Your father nursed us both back to health. We actually met in a hospital elevator. We had a short conversation, and I couldn't stop thinking about his eyes. Later, we ran into each other in the park across from the hospital, and then not long after that, he asked me out to lunch. That was the beginning of our love story—one that's now brought you to us.

Your father is a very smart and savvy businessman, and runs one of the largest and most successful accounting firms here in Houston. It's one of the most respected firms in the whole country. The best part is that you'd never know it. He's down to earth and kind to everyone. I'm sure he's tough when he has to be, but fortunately, I never have to see that side of him. I know he'll want to spoil you and this will be my biggest challenge as a parent—keeping him in line. I wasn't quite sure what his reaction would be when I told him about you. We never discussed having children. Especially since we're both past what most consider the child-rearing years. Your dad was overjoyed. I've never seen him look happier than when I showed him my positive pregnancy tests. I took a picture and I can't wait to show it to you. He loves you very much, and you are blessed to have him as your father. He's a good man. Good in every sense of the word. Honest. Loving. Devoted. Loyal. Generous. Selfless. Mathew Ellis— your father, my husband. The greatest gift we could ever hope for.

Two things (because I know you're thinking it):

1. No, your father doesn't have a middle name.

2. No, his name is not misspelled. If you ask why, he'll tell you the same thing he told me on our very first date: "Why bother with two t's when one does the trick?"

Yes, he's snarky like that. That's part of what roped me in.

Well, I've hit the key players for you except for me. Oh, and Ivy. Yes! We have a dog! She's the most precious ball of fluff. She and Leo are big buddies. Your father gave her to me as a birthday present. He's always giving me presents and is already planning to buy presents for you. He has a list of favorite children's books written out. I think he's planning to read some of them aloud to you. We both love books, and that's initially what started up our conversation at the hospital. When I was a kid, I wanted to be a book illustrator. Turns out you have to be an artist and I can barely draw a stick figure. I'm actually something you'd never expect–a meteorologist. I mean, with a name like Sunny, what else could I do but work on figuring out the weather? I have both my bachelor's and master's and was thinking about working toward my PhD...until your father came along and turned my world upside down (in the best way!). I was an atmospheric researcher at NASA for nine years and I loved it. Then, the business with the tumor started. I've taken an indefinite leave of absence, but the powers that be have assured me I can return to NASA at any time.

I want you to know something right from the start: I promise to always be completely honest with you, no matter what. There have been things in my past that have been painful and ugly and have led me to make some poor decisions where trust is concerned. I don't want there to be any secrets between us. And I want you to know that you are loved beyond measure by so many people. Your father has taught me so much about love and trust. They're the most valuable lessons I've learned to date. I want to share all this and more with you. That's what family is all about—love and trust.

More later, precious one!

Love,

Mommy

(I can't believe I just signed my name like that!)

****

Sunny stared out the window of the plane, lost in thought. Aside from morning sickness, their honeymoon had been magical, but she was both anxious and excited to be returning home. The brand-new journey of their married lives now had an unexpected stowaway and all thoughts centered on the tiny little life growing inside her. She looked over at Mathew, brow furrowed and fully engrossed in his political thriller. Before long, he stopped and locked eyes with her.

"What?" he asked with a grin.

"Nothing. Just trying to settle an internal debate about you."

"A debate about me? I can only imagine."

"I can't decide if your lips are so delicious because I'm in love with you, or if I'm in love with you because your lips are so delicious."

"Really? What a coincidence. I've been trying to figure out if you're so incredibly beautiful because you're pregnant, or if you're pregnant because you're so incredibly beautiful?"

Sunny bit back a grin. "Interesting. Do you have any theories about this so-called dispute?"

"Not yet. But I'm sure that whatever the answer, it'll require lots and lots of research." His lips pressed against her cheek as his hand pressed against her flat stomach.

"Now listen, Leo will be waiting for us, and I know we've discussed this already, but I have to say it again." Sunny's voice was low and serious.

"I know, I know…" Mathew rolled his eyes.

"You and I both know that a secret of this magnitude is really pushing it where you're concerned."

"I can handle it, I promise. In fact, I promised at the hotel. I promised in the elevator. I promised in the taxi. I promised at the airport, on the runway, in this very cabin…"

"Then say it again."

"I promise I won't tell Leo or your father or

anyone else until we've been to see a doctor. Happy?"

She cocked her head to one side and gave him a hard look. "You'll never make it."

"Wanna bet?"

"Of course. Just give me a minute to think about what I want when I win because I want it to be something really good."

"Well, I've already won. I have you and her."

"You mean him. It's a boy, Mathew. God help me, but I'm gonna have two of you to wrangle."

"You keep saying boy. What makes you so sure?" Mathew asked.

"Call it a mother's intuition."

"You've been pregnant now for what? Ten minutes? And already you're acting on intuition?"

"Just wait. You'll lose again."

"No, I won't." He rested his forehead against hers. "I have you and this beautiful little baby—boy or girl. No way can I lose now."

****

The sun was setting as they made their way home from their ten-day honeymoon in the south of France. Sunny had pulled double duty—planning their wedding and preparing their new home–a stunning modern farmhouse in the desirable Bunker Hill area of Houston. Mathew had given her free rein, but she'd solicited his help and keen eye for the classic, tasteful, and refined. Leo made few requests, as he only lived with Mathew during the winter months. The rest of the year, he resided in Seattle with his only living blood relative, his niece, Nora, and her husband. All the bedrooms were large and luxurious, but they agreed to give Leo the primary suite downstairs. He'd argued relentlessly, but

Mathew and Sunny remained united, refusing to give in.

The few remaining items from Mathew's Uptown apartment were delivered without incident during their honeymoon. Leo and Ivy had been living in the new house for the past week with his lady friend, Barbara, to keep them company. Leo was walking around, managing without his walker most of the time. Driving still was not an option. Perhaps by Christmas, his doctor had said.

When they pulled up to the front door, Leo and Ivy were outside waiting for them. Sunny reminded Mathew of his promise one last time before they exited the car.

"Welcome home, Mister and Missus!" Leo hollered, dog in his arms. "Man, have we missed you two!"

"Leo!" Mathew clapped his arms around the old man. "You look great! Getting stronger every day."

"You look sunburned." Leo studied Mathew's face.

"He's like a five-year-old when it comes to applying sunscreen. Nothing but whining." Sunny hugged Leo.

"Can I help you with your bags?"

"No, no, we got it." Mathew collected their things from the trunk.

"You think you were busy before the wedding? You should see the loot that's waiting for you. I've never seen so many wedding gifts in all my life. Looks like Santa's workshop in there," Leo said with a laugh.

Sunny sighed. "Well, it'll have to wait a couple of days, at least until we're back on Central time. I'm too tired, even for presents."

With Barbara's help, Leo surprised them with a wonderful dinner. Though he'd set the table for two, she and Mathew insisted he make another place for himself. Sunny watched Mathew's eyes carefully—certain that he'd slip any minute and reveal the news of her unexpected pregnancy. But he never did. They laughed, sharing stories from their travels, reliving the wedding, progress on the house, and Ivy. Sunny watched as Mathew slipped the dog scraps of food from his plate and stroked her head with loving affection. *If he's this good with a dog, he's gonna be wonderful with a baby.* Sunny reached for his hand and gave it a loving squeeze.

They sent Leo to bed and cleaned up the dishes before heading up themselves. It wasn't late, but they both were exhausted. Ivy followed behind them, as if this had been her routine for years. She found a spot underneath Sunny's most prized possession—an escritoire she'd inherited from her grandmother. Curling herself into a perfect little ball, she closed her eyes.

"Well, someone feels right at home." Sunny nodded toward the dog.

"As long as she's not on the bed. That's for you and me only."

"Until I have a large protruding belly between us."

"An incredibly sexy belly." Mathew pressed a kiss to her stomach.

"You say sexy now, but you might not think so when it looks like I've swallowed a watermelon."

"A watermelon or a monster truck, you will still be sexy."

"We'll see," she said, one eyebrow cocked.

They crawled into bed and curled into each other's arms, listening to the sounds of their new bedroom. It was silent, aside from the sound of a dog barking nearby. Sunny took a deep breath and exhaled slowly. The room smelled of new paint and freshly stained wood.

"Of all the wedding gifts, I bet you never thought you'd get a baby, huh?" Sunny asked.

"I can't stop thinking about it–him, I mean. Or her. Could be a girl."

"He's gonna look exactly like you, I just know it." She lightly drew circles on his chest with one finger.

"I dunno. *She* might look just like her mother."

"I never thought this would happen, Mathew. I didn't think I would ever have a baby."

"Why not?"

"I'm thirty-nine years old, for crying out loud. I'm supposed to be prepping for hot flashes, not pumping breast milk."

"If it makes you feel better, I'm not exactly young, Sunny."

"Yes, but it's different for men. You, becoming a dad at forty-nine? No one will give it a thought. But me, becoming a mom at thirty-nine? People will swear I'm way too old. You wait."

"I think you're worrying for nothing."

"I've also never really seen myself as very maternal. I don't cook, or bake, or any of those traditional mom things."

"And how many moms do what you do professionally? Not many. You're anything but traditional, and your mothering will reflect that in the most amazing way possible. You'll also be the hottest mom at the playground, I have no doubt."

Sunny laughed. "Hottest mom? You think I should aspire to be the hottest mom?"

"What? Some moms cook in the kitchen, some moms cook in the bedroom."

"God, you're a mess, Mathew Ellis." She sighed.

He rolled his body onto hers. "I know...and you wouldn't have me any other way."

Chapter Eight

"Well, Mr. and Mrs. Ellis, you are indeed pregnant. I'd say just beginning your eleventh week," Dr. Sumner announced as he entered the exam room.

"Wait. Eleven weeks already?" Mathew looked at Sunny. "That would mean…"

"That you were sampling more than just wine during that surprise weekend trip to Napa." She gave him a playful look.

"You've missed two periods, is that correct?" the doctor asked.

"Yes, but I also had major surgery, built a house, and planned a wedding all within the last several months. I thought initially that I skipped because of stress or my age. Then I started feeling extremely tired."

"That's the classic first symptom. Now today, we'll do a full workup. Complete medical history, full exam, and an ultrasound. The urine test provided us with the proof, but we'll also need to draw blood to confirm things like your Rh factor, certain immunities, and so forth—all standard procedures. And don't shoot the messenger, but because of your age, yours is considered an advanced maternal age pregnancy."

"Advanced maternal age? But she just turned thirty-nine." Mathew's eyes widened with surprise.

"Hey, it's better than the previous term—geriatric

pregnancy," said Dr. Sumner.

"Makes me sound like Sarah, from the Bible." Sunny laughed.

"I agree, it sounds pretty awful. In this office, we actually call it 'thirty-five plus pregnancy.' The only difference between you and my younger patients is that you'll have a few extra appointments here and there, and a couple of extra ultrasounds. When you come back for your nineteen-week appointment, we should be able to determine the baby's sex if the fetus is cooperative and you two have the desire to know."

"I'll already know." Mathew shot Sunny a look.

"Making wagers already? I must tell you, I've been in this business for thirty-two years and the moms beat the dads two to one on guessing the sex. So just be prepared." He gave them a good-humored wink.

"Do you have children of your own?" Sunny asked him.

"Yes, I have four daughters."

"And did you and your wife make any bets along the way?" she asked him again.

"We sure did, and I lost every time. The last one really cost me—a no-holds-barred-spare-no-expense week in Maui."

Once the physical exam was complete, Mathew helped Sunny up and they strolled down the hall to wait for the ultrasound. Dr. Sumner would join them after the results were ready, but the actual procedure would be with a technician. They sat alone and waited, neither saying a word. After several moments, Mathew spoke.

"Is this really happening?" His eyes and tone matched, both filled with excitement.

"I still can't believe it!" she squealed.

The technician entered, introducing herself with an extended hand. She sat down on a small rolling stool beside the examination table. "Any questions before we start?"

Sunny shook her head and looked at Mathew. "I'm good. You?"

"No, I'm ready."

The technician turned the lights down and typed information into the ultrasound machine. Mathew laced his fingers with Sunny's.

"Now I want you to try and relax as much as possible. Just keep breathing."

Sunny watched the monitor intently, unsure exactly what she would see. Then, she saw it—a tiny, moving mass. The technician talked them through what they saw on the screen.

"How big is he?" Sunny asked.

"About an inch long, weighing just a few grams. A tiny little peanut."

"It's so strange to watch all the movements because I can't feel anything."

"But you will before you know it, and the first flutters are the best."

"Does everything look good? Healthy, I mean?" Mathew asked.

"Everything looks great. Let's print out some pictures. Never too early to start that photo album." She continued to enter more information into the machine and within moments, several black-and-white images emerged. Just as they were done printing, Dr. Sumner entered.

"How does everything look?" he asked.

"Just as you predicted. Right on target with your

due date." She handed the scans to the doctor.

"These look good. What a photogenic baby you have. I'm sure the Easter Bunny will have a special treat for this baby." He smiled warmly. "You're the picture of health, Mrs. Ellis. I think you have an uneventful, textbook pregnancy ahead of you—the best kind to have."

"Even at my age?" She raised an eyebrow.

The doctor laughed. "Yes, even at *your* age. As I mentioned before, I'll schedule a few extra visits and tests, but I'm not anticipating any hiccups."

Mathew extended his hand to Dr. Sumner. "Thank you so much. We're really excited."

"Be sure she takes her prenatal vitamins, gets plenty to eat, and plenty of rest."

"I'll see to it." Mathew nodded.

"My receptionist, Gena, will give you a goody bag filled with all sorts of information on your way out. The do's and don'ts of the next few months. Please read over everything and give us a call if you have any questions. And if ever something doesn't feel right, call us. You know your body better than anyone, so listen to what it has to say."

"I will. Thank you, Dr. Sumner." Sunny shook his hand.

****

Hand in hand, Mathew and Sunny walked through the parking garage. They spoke no words but shared the sweetest conversation with their eyes. As she reached for the car door handle, he caught her hand and turned her around to face him.

"I have never been happier than I am at this moment in my entire life. I am so in love with you,

Sunny Porter Ellis, you and this baby, and I'm telling you right now, you can have the bet. I just want to tell everyone."

"I love you so much, Mathew."

"And I love you…both." He touched her cheek.

"This baby is so lucky to have you."

"We're both lucky because we have you."

Mathew took several steps back. He continued to hold her gaze, lifting his arms and shouting a joyful declaration to the surrounding city, his voice reverberating off the concrete walls of the parking garage.

"I am so in love with this beautiful woman and now we're having a baby!"

Chapter Nine

Mathew drove straight to their favorite local bookstore to pick up a pregnancy book and calendar after leaving Dr. Sumner's office. Sunny pretended to shop, but it was more fun to watch her husband. It was a kid-in-a-candy-store moment. Mathew was a voracious reader. Their very first real conversation revolved around Zane Grey and Larry McMurtry and their shared love of Westerns. But this shopping trip wouldn't include his customary genres. Sunny made one selection—a historical fiction novel. Her husband, on the other hand, walked out with four pregnancy guides, two calendars, three baby name books, and a stack of children's books.

"You know, there are apps for all this. We can track everything on our phones."

"I'm not trusting our baby's progress to an app. I prefer the old school methods, like physical books and paper calendars, thank you."

"Any excuse to spend money. And you call yourself a CPA. I'd scold you, but what good would it do?"

"You can spank me later…if that will make you feel better." Mathew winked, offering a devilish grin.

Anticipating a driveway full of cars, Sunny and Mathew traded confused looks when they arrived home and found only Barbara's Buick present.

"I thought Leo was hosting poker night with his buddies?" Sunny said.

"I thought so too. Where is everybody?" Mathew asked. "Maybe he canceled?"

"No, he definitely mentioned the game this morning. Maybe they moved the time back."

They entered the house via the front door and found it eerily quiet. It was dark, save for one lamp lit in the living room. Mathew and Sunny traded looks.

"You don't think...that Leo and Barbara are..."

"Having sex?" Sunny's eyes widened. "Good God, of course not."

"He's old, Sunny, but he's not dead."

"They're probably out back playing chess or cards or something."

"Or maybe they're in his bedroom playing Hide the Sausage."

"Mathew Ellis!" She shrieked. "You're awful."

He carried their shopping bags upstairs and Sunny continued on through the house. She spied Leo and Barbara outside on the patio —sub sandwiches and a deck of cards between them. Barbara was a regular fixture around their house, helping take care of Leo post-aneurysm. Now, in addition to being his part-time nurse, she was one of his dearest friends and most ruthless poker buddies. Her eyes lit up when she saw Sunny joined them and the two women shared a hug.

"How was your honeymoon?" Barbara asked.

"It was wonderful. We had a fantastic time."

"Well, it must have been because you look beautiful."

"What time are the guys coming over? Are y'all feeling lucky?" Sunny asked.

"I canceled the game. Barbara and I are just going to hang out and watch TV and work on our bridge strategy. We're playing in a tournament in two weeks," Leo said.

"I hope you didn't cancel just because we're home."

"Cancel what?" Mathew strolled outside, picking up the end of the conversation.

"Leo canceled poker night," Sunny answered.

"What's wrong Leo? Feeling a little light in the wallet?" He shot a smirk at Barbara.

"It's not that. It's just that...you know. The guys...you know how they are." Leo shook his head.

"Well, Barbara's not a guy..." Sunny said.

"Thank you, Sunny."

"You're welcome." She nodded at Barbara.

"Leo, what's up? You haven't canceled a poker game in years. Maybe ever—aside from being hospitalized, I mean." Mathew looked confused.

"Well, I thought that maybe you and Sunny might like some privacy. You know, peace and quiet."

"Leo, this is your house. We want to continue with your poker games just like always. Just because we're married doesn't mean anything really changed–except my last name." Sunny reassured him.

"Well, I thought that under the circumstances..." Leo's voice trailed off and he looked at Barbara.

"What circumstances?" Mathew asked.

Leo let out a sigh. "Dr. Sumner's office called this morning right after you left...to confirm your obstetrical appointment."

Mathew and Sunny traded looks. Neither could contain their laughter.

"Why is it that I never get the chance to surprise you?" Mathew asked Leo, shaking his head.

"So, are you two?" Leo pointed his finger back and forth between the two of them.

"Yep." Sunny smiled. "We're having a baby, Leo."

"That's wonderful! Congratulations!" The old man stood and gave each of them a big hug.

"Now listen. My father does not know yet. He's coming to visit soon, and we want to wait and tell him in person." Sunny cautioned.

"My lips are sealed," Leo promised, pretending to lock his lips with an invisible key.

"Congratulations, you two." Barbara hugged them affectionately. "What a lucky little baby to have you for his parents."

"Did you say *his*?" Mathew gave Barbara a look.

"Oh yeah. Y'all are having a boy. No doubt."

"I'll take that action. I say they're having a girl." Leo looked at Barbara.

"You're on." She offered her hand, and they shook firmly.

Chapter Ten

"Good morning." Mathew strolled into the kitchen.

"How'd you sleep?" Leo sat at the breakfast table, working on his second cup of coffee.

"Fine."

"How's Sunny?"

"She's great. I just came down to get her some juice and a piece of toast. I don't want her passing out while she's in the shower."

"Morning sickness?"

"No. She's only been sick one time."

"Well, that's good. I can't believe you're having a baby."

"I still can't believe it myself."

"So, you're okay with it?"

"Okay? Have you seen my wife? What man wouldn't be okay with it?"

"That's what I thought. I just never heard you talk about children."

"We didn't."

"This was a surprise for both of you, huh?"

"Well, yeah…"

"You're gonna be a great father." Leo's face shone with pride.

"I know I am. I had a great role model."

"You certainly did," Sunny added.

"I was gonna bring up some juice for you."

Mathew turned around quickly at the sound of her voice.

"I'm all right. I'm not an invalid. Tell him, Leo."

"She's right. Could beat both of us in a footrace on her worst day."

"Okay, I get the hint." Mathew threw his arms up in a sign of surrender.

Sunny whipped up her one and only signature dish—omelettes. Leo and Mathew traded sections of the newspaper. The three enjoyed breakfast together, though Leo was more quiet than usual. So much so that Mathew and Sunny traded looks several times during the meal.

"Listen, there's something important I need to talk to you about," Leo said.

"Of course." Mathew glanced at Sunny, her face full of concern.

"I just want to tell you both one more time how happy I am for you. This baby is so lucky."

"We think we're the lucky ones." Sunny reached and held Mathew's hand.

"I've been thinking a lot about it and I think it's time for a few changes around here."

There was a sudden authority in Leo's voice that Mathew knew well. One that said, 'arguing is pointless.'

"What kind of changes?" Mathew asked.

"I think it would be better for everyone if I moved into a senior living facility."

"Leo—"

Leo raised his hand, cutting Mathew off. "Let me finish. Barbara and I have talked about it and there's a wonderful complex not far from here."

"You and Barbara?" Mathew gave Leo a look.

"You're newly married and starting a family and the last thing you need is an old man taking up space. I've got no children to be a burden on, and I'm certainly not going to be a burden on you—not with a baby on the way."

"But we don't want you to go. We love having you here. This is your home, Leo." Sunny looked to Mathew for support.

"You've been very sweet, but I think you and I both know that you'd rather have your husband and your home to yourself."

"That's just not true. You're a part of this family. I knew that from the word go. If my father and I had lived together, it would be the same situation. Mathew would've gotten a package deal," Sunny stated.

"But the situation is different now," Leo said.

"Do you want to leave? I mean, are you making this decision based on what *you* want or what you think *we* want," Mathew asked with a serious tone.

"Well…" the old man hesitated.

"If we thought this wouldn't work, we'd tell you. You know me better than that. And I know you're a big boy and could take it. We don't want you to leave—unless it's what you absolutely want."

"We want you here…with us," Sunny added.

"We're going to respect your wishes no matter what, Leo. But I can promise you, the idea of having you move has never been breached by Sunny and me. Not one time."

Arms folded across his chest, the old man fell silent and dropped his gaze to his lap. Sunny locked eyes with Mathew. The tiniest movement of his head sent a signal of caution, to let the silence remain until Leo was ready to respond. A full minute passed before Leo brought his eyes up to meet Mathew's—eyes filled with fatherly devotion.

"I've been watching some diaper changing videos on YouTube. I'm not saying I'll be an expert, but I think I'll get the hang of it."

A beat of silence was followed by raucous laughter. Mathew reached out and gave Leo a gentle punch on his shoulder.

"Oh, Leo…we don't need you for diaper changes." Sunny brushed laughter-induced tears from her eyes.

"Yeah, there are more important jobs we need you to take care of." Mathew winked at his wife.

"Like what?" Leo looked puzzled.

"Like how to make the perfect margarita and whether to hit on sixteen," Mathew said with a nod.

"And who better to teach him than his dear old Uncle Leo?" Sunny touched his arm with affection.

"Are you sure?" Leo asked.

"We've never been more sure of anything," Mathew reassured him.

As Sunny cleared the breakfast dishes, Mathew excused himself. Leo remained steadfast in his chair, sipping his coffee and eyeing the sports section. Mathew returned to the kitchen momentarily and resumed his spot at the table. He placed a stack of books in front of him.

"What's all this?" Leo asked.

"Some books I picked up yesterday."

"They're all the same book."

"Yes, I know." Mathew grinned.

"And why do you need three copies of the same

book?"

"One for you, one for me, and one for Sunny."

"Lemme see that…" Leo held out his hand for a copy. He pushed his glasses higher up on his nose and read the title aloud. "The Complete Book of Baby Names."

"Here's yours." Mathew handed a copy to Sunny. "Now, here's what I'm thinking."

Sunny and Leo traded looks, both rolling their eyes.

"What?" Mathew asked. "The most important gift we'll give this baby is its name. It's the first thing people will judge our child by. It's got to be the perfect name. I want each of us to study the names, alphabetically, of course, and come up with a short list for each letter. A list of boys' names *and* girls' names."

"So, I just look for the name that speaks to me? The name that sounds like a winner?" Leo asked.

"Exactly!" Mathew said, his voice full of enthusiasm.

"Just like picking a racehorse." He opened the book and began thumbing through.

"I say we pick out our top three for each letter of the alphabet. That'll keep it simple." Mathew looked at Sunny.

"With you, nothing is simple." She rolled her eyes again.

Chapter Eleven

Dad's Advice: There's no substitute for good manners. That means opening doors for others, pulling out chairs, using the right fork, etc. I'm sure your mom will have more to add later. But the bottom line is: be a gentleman and treat everyone with respect.

I just finished reading up on your progress from our weekly calendar. I can't believe we're already at fifteen weeks! It says that you're now almost four inches long and weigh about as much as a letter. You've grown so much since we first saw you moving around on the ultrasound four weeks ago. It says that your bones are beginning to get stronger and harder and that a fine coating of white hair is beginning to cover your skin. What? Well, now you have something in common with Ivy. It also says that your thyroid gland is fully formed and there's a good chance that you might be sucking your thumb. You are just an amazing little being, you know that?! We're going back to see Dr. Sumner this afternoon, and then we're picking up your grandfather at the airport. He still doesn't know that you exist, and I only have to hold my tongue for a few more hours. I think Mommy is proud of me for keeping you a secret. But I have a confession to make. I did tell someone—Brynn, my assistant. I didn't mean to tell her. It just slipped out. I know she won't tell anyone. Brynn has been instrumental in helping me with lots of surprises for your mom, so I'm not worried that she'll slip up. Of course, she said that if you happen to be a girl, you're to be named in her honor. But that's not gonna happen, is it? That's another little secret I've been keeping from Mommy. I've known you were a boy from the start. But, I like playing devil's advocate. Actually, I just like playing the devil where your mother is concerned. But in a good way. Uncle Leo is in on it with me. He doesn't think you're a girl either.

I wish you could see how beautiful a vehicle you're riding around in—the Rolls Royce of pregnant bodies. I thought your mother was radiant before, but every day she glows more and more. She should be the Goodwill Ambassador for Pregnancy. I think she's kind of upset that her clothes don't really fit her the same way. She has exceptional taste in clothes, but the woman hates to go shopping. I've never known a woman who hated to shop more than she does. But from what I've read, over the next couple of weeks, she won't have a choice. I think there's a maternity shop in River Oaks that makes house calls. I'll ask Brynn to check on that for me.

Well, your mommy is beginning to stir, so I better close and stash this out of sight. These letters are another one of my little secrets. Hey, I'm getting pretty good at this secret business, huh? But there's one thing that I'll never hide from you or your mom or the world and that is how much I love you both. I can't believe that in twenty-five weeks or less, I'll be holding you in my arms. And even though I can't imagine feeling more pride or joy than I do at this very moment, I know I will.

I love you!
Daddy

Mathew slipped the letter inside a leather notebook, storing it away in the bottom drawer of his bedside table. He crawled back into bed beside Sunny and kissed her cheek.

"Good morning," he whispered.

"Good morning. You're up early."

"I had some work to do. How did you sleep?"

"Fine." She yawned, stretching her arms above her head.

"Today's the big day."

"I can't wait to see his face."

"He's going to cry, which means you're going to cry, which means I'm going to cry."

"I'll throw some extra tissues in my purse."

"How did your mother tell your father she was expecting you?"

"You know something." She sat up in bed. "I don't know. That's one Porter story I've never heard."

"Well, we'll have to ask him."

"You made the dinner reservations, right?"

"Yes, for seven o'clock. Is that too late for you?"

"No, I'll just eat a snack after we leave Dr. Sumner's office."

"The little patisserie downtown, *mon chéri*?"

"How did you know?"

"I'm a mind reader…and in French, no less. And I'll do whatever it takes to impress you." He pressed his lips against the spot on her neck that made her squirm.

"What time is our appointment?" She tried not to laugh as his lips tickled her.

"Not until two-thirty."

"What time is it now?" she asked.

"Eight-thirty."

"Aren't you going into the office?"

"Not when I have unfinished business here." He shucked his t-shirt and boxers and tossed them on the floor beside the bed.

****

"Mrs. Ellis, if you could just step on the scale for me…" The young nurse motioned to Sunny.

"I hate this part." She huffed and looked at Mathew. She slipped her shoes off and stood on the large scale.

"It looks like you've gained…seven pounds so far." The nurse eyed the scale before making the notation on Sunny's chart.

"Is that too much?"

"That's fine, Mrs. Ellis."

"What's the norm?"

"You're fine, Mrs. Ellis, really," the nurse insisted.

"You're not going to tell me, are you?" She followed behind as the nurse led them to an empty examination room.

"The doctor will be in soon." She smiled and turned, softly closing the door behind her.

"What's with these nurses being so tight-lipped? I must be monumentally off target if she wouldn't tell me. I'm a cow. Just say it."

"Sunny, you are anything but a cow. You're barely showing. And think about how thin you were when you started this journey. I'm sure seven pounds is nothing. But if it'll make you feel better, let's ask Dr. Sumner."

Sunny looked around the small examination room, studying the various charts and posters on the wall.

"I wonder if he's sucking his thumb?"

"Who? Dr. Sumner?"

"No, genius." She pointed to a poster on the wall, one that showed various stages of fetal development. "I'm talking about our tadpole."

"Ellis men do not suck their thumbs. We carry blankies instead. Nice, clean, dignified blankies." He raised his chin and spoke with an air of snobbery.

"Oh, right. I forgot. Cashmere blankies, no doubt?"

"What else?" He winked just as someone knocked on the door.

Dr. Sumner entered, dressed in scrubs and a surgical cap.

"Good afternoon, Ellis family." He shook hands with both of them. "Please excuse me. I had a delivery earlier and no time to change."

"No problem." Sunny smiled.

"Sorry you've had to wait a bit, but when your turn comes, I promise to give you my full attention as well." He glanced at Sunny's chart, silently reading over her information. He shook his head in disappointment. "Now, now, Mrs. Ellis. Seven pounds? You're only fifteen weeks and already you've gained seven pounds?"

Sunny traded looks with Mathew. "I asked the nurse, but she said…" Her voice trailed off.

"I'm only kidding you. Seven pounds is perfect. Morgan, my nurse, told me you were concerned. I'm just teasing you a bit."

"Thank goodness." She let out a huge sigh.

"You look fantastic. No morning sickness, blood pressure normal, urine looks good. Let's find the baby's heartbeat. Lie back and we'll take a listen."

Mathew stood beside her, holding her hand, and watched as the obstetrician placed a Doppler stethoscope on her stomach, rolling it around in a sea of clear jelly. Within seconds, they could hear it. It was stronger than he expected and sounded like a rush of a bird's wings flapping in a rapid, synchronized rhythm. Sunny squeezed Mathew's hand.

"Good strong heartbeat. One hundred thirty beats per minute."

"So that's good, then? One-thirty is good?" Mathew asked.

"The normal range is between one hundred twenty and one-sixty. Right on the money. I'll see you back in four weeks. I realize we won't be at the magic twenty-week mark, but maybe Baby Ellis won't be camera shy and we can find out just who's swimming around in there. I'm sure you're anxious to find out."

"Yes, we are." Sunny nodded, smiling up at Mathew.

"You still have the wager?"

"Of course." Mathew extended his hand as the doctor stood to leave.

"You're a glutton for punishment, aren't you?" Dr. Sumner shook Mathew's hand.

****

The little patisserie near Dr. Sumner's office was closed, so they settled on a snack from Starbucks after the appointment. Sunny was a giant ball of nerves, constantly wiggling around in her chair and obsessively checking her phone.

"You are making me crazy, you know that?" He stuck his fork into her slice of lemon pound cake.

"I'm sorry." Sunny released a heavy sigh.

"You have nothing to be nervous about."

"It's not that I'm nervous exactly. I just feel

61

guilty."

"Guilty? For what?" Mathew asked.

"Well, because I'm already fifteen weeks, with this nice little bump, and we haven't told him yet."

"It's not like you've *known* for fifteen weeks. We just got official confirmation a month ago. It hasn't been that long. And you were adamant that you didn't want to tell him over the phone."

"I know…" She pinched off a piece of cake.

"But?" Mathew pressed.

"Well, maybe we should've driven up there and told him as soon as we got back from the honeymoon."

"Sunny, what do you honestly think is going to happen? '*Hey, Pop! Guess what? I'm pregnant.*' To which he'll reply, '*Damn it, Sunny! Why the hell didn't you tell me sooner?*'" Mathew's imitation of Huck was dead on, and she couldn't help but laugh.

"You're right."

"Once he hears the word pregnant, he's done. You'll see." He gave her a reassuring nod.

"I hope so." She took another bite of her cake.

The ride to the airport was quiet. Sunny's hand rested gently on his. The stereo was turned off and Mathew hummed a song softly.

"I think you'll like the automatic transmission in this one better than the standard shift of the convertible."

"I still cannot believe that you bought another car."

"All the hottest moms cruise around in big SUVs these days."

"But do we need three cars? Four, if you count Leo's?"

"When it comes to you and our baby, I'll do

whatever it takes. The convertible is for when you want to go shopping or out to lunch with your friends. When you're in full baby mode, you can take this."

"But we agreed we'd trade in the car. I don't need two cars, Mathew."

"So, I had a weak moment at the dealership." He laughed.

Huck's flight arrived right on schedule, and Sunny didn't realize how much she missed her pot-smoking, liberal, renegade father until he hugged her.

"My God, Sunny! You look fantastic!" He beamed, pulling her in for a tight hug.

"I've missed you so much!" Her eyes filled with tears.

"Mathew! How the hell are you?" Huck extended his hand to his son-in-law.

"I'm great, sir. It's wonderful to see you."

"How was LA, Pop? The race? I can't believe you flew straight here."

"Aw, baby girl, I'm just sorry I couldn't get here sooner. I'll tell you all about it at dinner."

The restaurant was crowded for a Thursday evening, but their table was waiting. Mathew ordered draft beers for the men and cranberry juice for Sunny. The three of them were like bees—buzzing and talking all at once. Sunny could not stop smiling, amazed at the way Mathew and her father fell back into conversation as though not a day had passed between them. Their laughter was contagious, and it wasn't long until Sunny's cheeks began to ache from sheer happiness. She'd tried to remain calm but kept exchanging nervous glances with Mathew. He, however, was the picture of relaxed, acting as though nothing were out of the ordinary. They'd decided beforehand to wait until after dinner to share their news. Mathew would casually reach into his pocket for the ultrasound photos, telling Huck he'd begun work on a new project. It would then be up to Huck to decipher the images in the photographs. They had a small side wager on how long it would take Huck to catch on.

The waiter cleared their dinner dishes, and Huck ordered a Coke. He always ended dinner with a soda. Sunny gave Mathew a light tap on the leg under the table, letting him know it was time.

"Is now the time?" Huck asked them as the waiter set down his drink.

"The time for what?" Sunny asked.

"The time when you tell me that I'm gonna be a grandfather." Huck fought back a smile.

Mathew shot Sunny a look and waved his arms in frustration. "I give up! I absolutely give up!"

"Pop! But how—" She looked back at Mathew.

"It's so obvious. Your face–it's fuller. Your waist– it's fuller too. Your new car is practically a bus. You're drinking cranberry juice–straight up. It's obvious to anyone who knows you, baby girl."

"So that's it? You're just going to be all Sherlock Holmes about the whole thing?" Sunny huffed.

"Of course not!" He stood and took Sunny's hand, helping her to stand. "My beautiful baby girl is going to be a mom. I am so happy. So very, very happy." He hugged his daughter in the middle of the crowded restaurant. After a moment, Huck released her and made his way around the table. "Mathew, I couldn't be more thrilled. This is incredible news." He shared a warm hug with his son-in-law.

"Thank you. We're very excited."

Huck sat back down, and the buzz started all over again. The ultrasound pictures were examined, and Grandpa Huck was brought up to speed on everything that was happening in utero.

"You know, I think I'm due an Oscar. I made it through the entire dinner without once letting on that I knew."

"You're amazing. I can't believe you figured it out." Sunny shook her head.

"I knew the minute I saw you at the airport. You just have that glow. And then, when I saw your new ride, there was no doubt."

"All that planning...wasted." Mathew looked at Sunny.

"I'm sorry if I ruined your surprise, but I couldn't resist putting the surprise back on you," Huck said.

"You're not mad that we waited to tell you?" Sunny asked.

"Of course not. I'm glad you waited to tell me in person. You can't hug someone over the phone." He reached and gave Sunny's hand a squeeze.

"How did Daphne tell you about Sunny?" Mathew asked.

"Yes, I don't think I've heard this story," Sunny added.

"Aw, hell! That was a long time ago. We never told you that story?"

"If you did, I don't remember it."

"Well, your mother sent me on a little scavenger hunt one evening after I came home from the track. She had these little notes hidden all over the house. You know how she used to love to leave us notes? She had me looking all over the place. I searched for all these clues for at least half an hour."

"What sort of clues?" Sunny asked, her eyes locked on her father.

"She had these little riddles. I can't remember exactly. But riddles that led me to specific places in and around the house. The last place I went was upstairs, to our bedroom. Your mother was waiting for me there. I had no idea she was even in the house. She scared the living shit out of me. Well, here was your incredibly beautiful mother, lying on our bed, waiting for me. There was a box on the bed too, with a big yellow bow on it. I still could not figure out what had gotten into her. But when a gorgeous woman is lying in your bed, you don't ask questions, am I right?" He gave Mathew a look.

"I agree with you there—one hundred percent." Mathew nodded.

"We had some sort of verbal exchange, I can't recall exactly what was said. Then I opened the box and found a tiny pair of baby booties inside. And that's how your mother told me that you were on the way." Huck looked away for a moment, a slight blush on his cheeks.

"Pop! That is a great story. I can't believe you never told me."

"Well, I guess I was supposed to wait until this moment. So, Mathew, how did Sunny tell you?"

"She took two pregnancy tests at the hotel while I was out trying to run down something for her headache. When I came back up to our suite, she was standing there in a hotel robe with her hands in her pockets. She asked me to pick one of the pockets because she had a surprise for me. Never entered my mind that she would be pulling out a little white stick."

"And since you'd done two tests, it didn't matter which pocket he selected." Huck grinned.

"Precisely." Sunny nodded.

"Smart girl." He took a sip of his soda. "So, when will my grandson be making his appearance?"

"April," Sunny answered.

"What makes you think it's a boy?" Mathew asked.

"I don't know. It's just what came to my mind when I hugged her at the airport. And after sitting here and watching you both, it's for sure going to be a boy. But, if it happens to be a girl, well, you know how I feel about baby girls." Huck eyed his daughter, his expression full of love.

"Dr. Sumner said we'll have the ultrasound and hopefully find out exactly what we're having at my next appointment–and that will definitely be cause for a phone call."

"Well, I think a toast is in order." Huck raised his glass. "To my grandchild—the perfect reflection of the love between the two most important people in my life."

****

My Little Prince,

Here you are, fifteen weeks along. I can't believe how much you are growing. I still haven't felt you, but I know you're in there. Daddy and I heard your heartbeat today. Dr. Sumner said your progress is right on target and, of course, I'm not surprised. You're an Ellis! I've gained seven pounds so far but I'm not going to complain. I'm preparing my body to be a healthy haven for you, and gaining weight is part of the deal. I plan on doing everything in my power to make sure you are strong and healthy so you can arm wrestle your father from the get-go.

Daddy is downstairs playing cards with Pop and Uncle Leo and some of our friends. We were so excited to finally tell him face-to-face about you, but he figured it out before we had a chance to tell him. I told you— he's a sly one. Your grandfather can string clues together in ways I can't even describe. Oh, was he smug at the dinner table! I know we'll laugh about it for years to come. The general consensus is that you are a boy and I've never thought otherwise. Daddy still thinks you're a girl. Or does he? I overheard him talking with Uncle Leo and they were using words like 'him' and 'he' and 'his,' so I think this whole 'girl' thing is just to give us a topic for debate. Your father always picks out the most bizarre girls' names from our books too, just to toy with me. Well, maybe two can play that game.

Mommy is tired, so I will end my letter here. I know I've told you many times today, but I never tire of saying it—I love you with all my heart!

Night-Night!
Mommy

****

Dad's Advice: When buying a car, there are some general rules to remember. First of all, the car salesman, despite what he says, is not your friend. He's going to flatter you, build you up, compliment you, etc. because he's there to close the deal and get a check. They may tell you that they're giving you the best price and that they're losing money on the deal all in the name of friendship but that's not true. Second item to note: Do NOT fall in love with the car. If you do love it, do NOT let the salesman know. Trust me on this.

Mommy got up early this morning, so I only have a few minutes to write before she comes looking for me for breakfast. She's downstairs with Uncle Leo and Grandpa Huck right now. We've had a very busy weekend, and your grandfather is flying to a race in Florida later this afternoon. This was the big weekend when your mother and I were going to tell him all about you. And we did—only it wasn't a surprise like we planned. Instead, your crafty grandfather beat us to the punch. Said he figured out Mommy was pregnant from the moment he saw her in the airport. I'm now 0-2 in the surprise department. But it doesn't matter because you continue to surprise me every day.

Dr. Sumner will do an ultrasound on our next visit. You'll be nineteen weeks then. Almost halfway through the ballgame. I am so proud of your mother. Everyone is in awe of how beautiful she looks. We just finished writing all the thank-you notes for the wedding gifts, and I guess we'll be starting over with baby gifts soon. I'm not supposed to let you know this, but your grandfather already informed your mother and me that he's building you a custom mini-motorcycle. I know, I know. What's a baby going to do with a motorcycle? I asked your mother the same question and she replied, without batting an eye: "Learn to race, of course!" So, in addition to your faithful dog, Ivy, you will also come into this world with your own set of wheels. I'm sorry for ruining the surprise. That's happened to me a lot lately too.

Mommy is hollering for me to hurry up. You think she knows what we're up to? With our little conversations? I'll tell her one day, but for now, I'm

happy keeping this our little secret.
    Daddy loves you!

Chapter Twelve

"Mathew, any last-minute declarations?" Dr. Sumner asked as he applied the clear jelly to Sunny's ever-expanding stomach.

"All bets are in." He looked down at Sunny and squeezed her hand.

"Sunny?"

"It's a boy." She gave Mathew a grin.

He placed the ultrasound transducer on her, gently rolling it across her belly.

"Oh, look at the spine, Mathew…"

"And is that a foot?" Mathew pointed to the monitor.

"Yes, that's a foot. Now if this baby will cooperate and move the other foot…" Dr. Sumner entered more information into the machine.

"It's just incredible." Sunny marveled at the image on the screen as the doctor narrated all the various visible parts of Baby Ellis.

"I'm going to take some measurements." His fingers clicked on the keyboard. "By measuring the femur, along with several cranial measurements, we can make sure that everything is right on track."

"Look at those tiny little hands." Mathew squeezed her hand again.

"He's looking right at us. Look at his little eye sockets!" She couldn't hide the excitement in her voice.

Stealing a quick look up at Mathew, she was moved by the tears in his eyes.

"Sunny, this baby is the picture of health. Growth is right on target. I think we'll stay with the original due date."

"Oh, thank God." She sighed.

"Everything looks good, then?" Mathew asked.

"Everything looks great." He removed the transducer and wiped the clear jelly away with a tissue. "And you look great, Sunny. You could even gain a little more weight, actually."

"Wait. You're giving me permission to double up on dessert?"

"Let Mathew double up. You stick with something healthy." He stood and flipped the light switch.

"Thank you so much, Dr. Sumner." Mathew said.

"Wait! I haven't told you what you're having."

"Oh my gosh. I almost forgot. I got so caught up in looking at all the little parts," Sunny said with a laugh.

"Before I tell you, just what exactly is the reward for the winner?" the doctor asked.

"Well, we took a cue from you. A week in Maui." She smiled at Mathew.

Dr. Sumner grinned, shaking his head. "Well, Mathew, I hope you like the beach because you're having a boy."

****

Mathew held his hand on the small of her back while ushering her into the elevator.

"We're parked on Level Two, right?" he asked.

"Yes."

The doors closed, and he hit the emergency stop button, just as he'd done the first time he kissed her in the elevator at the hospital.

"Not again…" She sighed and rolled her eyes.

"Do you have any idea…" He tucked a loose strand of hair behind her ear. "Any idea at all how much I love you?"

"Well, I have a little bit of an idea," she teased. "But pregnant women can be very forgetful, so I might need a little reminder."

With her back against the wall of the elevator, he slipped one arm around her waist, resting his other hand on her stomach. "I have never been happier to lose a bet in my life." He kissed her deeply. Her arms disappeared under his jacket, pulling him closer. He moved from her lips to her neck, humming as he kissed her—a song that had been on his mind for days.

He stopped and looked into her eyes. Their exact color was still a mystery, and they looked inside him with an intensity he couldn't define.

"I love you, Sunny."

"I love you too."

Inside the SUV, he wasted no time, eager to share the news of Baby Boy Ellis.

"It's me. Hold on just a minute while I put you on speakerphone." The cell phone was placed on the dash mount as Mathew pulled out from the parking garage. "Are you there?"

"I'm here. How'd it go?" Leo asked.

"Everything looks great." Mathew looked at Sunny.

"We're having a boy, Leo!" Sunny's eyes sparkled.

"A baby boy! Congratulations! Wow, this is incredible. But I'm not surprised. I've been saying it was gonna be a boy for weeks."

"Yeah, right." Sunny laughed. "You two owe me big."

"What do you mean we owe you?" Leo asked.

"Oh, c'mon, Leo. Are you telling me you forgot our bet?"

"Did we have a bet?" he asked innocently.

"Very funny." She laughed again.

"Listen, Leo, we're gonna give Grandpa Huck a call and give him the news. Not that he'll be surprised."

"All right. I am so happy for you both. I'm happy for all of us. A little boy. This is great. And the best part is that we no longer have to look up any girls' names."

"You got that right. Hey, we'll talk to you later."

"Congratulations, Sunny."

"Thank you, Leo. Bye."

Mathew ended the call. He opened his mouth to speak but Sunny cut him off.

"You two think you're pretty smart, don't you?" Sunny asked, her tone laced with sarcasm.

"We don't think. We know."

Mathew smiled at his wife, his expression one of both gratitude and disbelief. A dream he'd carried in his back pocket, wrinkled and worn like an old receipt, was finally coming true. He'd spent his entire childhood longing for a family. And now, after half a century of searching, his fortunes had reversed, almost overnight. With Sunny and their baby, he finally had the complete package.

"Are you okay?" Sunny asked.

"I am the best I've ever been. Let's call Grandpa Huck."

Mathew pressed the button and Huck answered after just half a ring.

"Huck Porter."

"Hi, Pop. It's us."

"I've been waiting by the phone all day. Are you finished with the doctor?"

"Yes."

"And I suppose Mathew is thrilled to be having a boy?" Huck spoke with a smug tone.

"Yes, he is." She bit her lip, gently patting Mathew's thigh.

Mathew listened while Sunny did all the talking. Her hands were working overtime, gesturing wildly as she shared every detail of their appointment. Every few seconds, he glanced her way. Her smile was as wide as he'd ever seen. It made the surprise he'd planned that much sweeter.

"Pop, Mathew just missed our exit, so I better go and help him concentrate on the road." Sunny pointed out the window of the Suburban.

"Maybe he did, and maybe he didn't."

"Huck! You're gonna ruin the surprise." Mathew said.

"She's so smart, she's probably already figured it out." Huck laughed.

"What are y'all talking about? What surprise?" Sunny asked.

"You two have fun. And congratulations! Love you!"

Huck hung up. Sunny shot Mathew a look.

"We're not going home, are we?" she asked.

"Nope." He continued to stare straight ahead.

"I knew you and Leo were up to something this morning. All the whispering and running around."

"We're taking a little trip."

She thought for a minute. "Plane, train, or automobile?"

"Automobile."

"A three-hour tour?" she asked playfully, hinting at their exact destination.

"More like four, but you guessed it."

****

They stopped for a late lunch at their favorite restaurant en route to their weekend get-a-way. Side by side they sat, studying the pictures of their baby boy from the ultrasound. Time got away from them as they talked and dreamed of the baby that would be joining their family in just a few short months. Stories and laughter of Leo and his baby bets and Grandpa and his mini-motorcycle project filled Sunny with joy. She watched Mathew's eyes light up as he continued to examine the pictures. The way his hands held the photos themselves, she knew he would be nothing but tender with their son. They were the same expressive hands she'd watched tell stories that afternoon when they had lunch together for the first time. She reached over and placed her hand on his, her eyes filled with memories and tears.

"What's wrong?" he asked.

"Nothing. Nothing at all," she assured him.

It was breezy and cool when they arrived at their ranch in the Texas Hill Country. Sunny offered to help carry their bags inside, but Mathew refused. From the moment she'd moved into maternity clothes, he hadn't let her do much of anything—which would appeal to some women, but not Sunny. She loved being part of the action and was not a casual observer. She did convince him to build a fire while she put away their groceries.

"Glass of wine?" she called from the kitchen.

"Just bring the bottle."

When she entered the living room, a tray of assorted cheeses in hand, she found Mathew wearing nothing but boots and boxer shorts, lying on a mattress in front of the fire. He wore a grin as big as the Texas sky beyond their door.

"What are you doing?" Sunny asked, fighting to stay composed.

"Getting comfy and waiting for my wife."

Though Mathew wasn't a native Texan, he adopted a certain drawl every time they visited their ranch. Being away from the city and the demands of his firm, he allowed himself to let go and embrace his most silly self. She never called him out on it, because she loved this side of him most.

"Is that the mattress from our bed?" She cocked an eyebrow.

"It might be."

"Mathew, there are two full-size sofas in here."

"And yet, it's hard to fully curl up with a pregnant woman on a couch." He patted a spot on the mattress beside him, his twang in full gear.

"Listen, Matthew McConaughey, I need to take a shower first."

"*Alright, alright, alright.* How 'bout some company?"

He was up and out of his boots before she could answer. Sunny unbuttoned her blouse and dropped it on the floor.

"I still have traces of that sticky jelly all over me." She inspected her belly.

"Wait! Don't move," Mathew cautioned.

"What?" She looked up at him.

"No, no, no, just stay right there. No! Don't!" He ran into the bedroom and returned in seconds with his cell phone.

"Mathew, you've already taken a bazillion pictures of me this week."

"And I plan to take a bazillion more this weekend."

"Mine has to be the most photographed pregnant mass." She rolled her eyes as he snapped photos of her from all angles.

"That's because yours happens to be the most beautiful pregnant mass. As excited as I am to see our baby, I will miss this sweet belly." He bent down and kissed her belly button.

"I'm gonna miss it too. Some days I look at it and I can't believe it's mine. And it's going to get bigger. It still amazes me every day."

"You still amaze me every day." He unhooked her bra, and it fell to the floor beside her blouse. "Everything about this body amazes me." He ran his hands across her breasts. "And these just happen to be two of my favorite fringe benefits."

****

Well, it's official. Dr. Sumner checked out all your hardware and you are definitely a boy (not that I ever had any doubts). Your mother and I are thrilled. So are your grandfather and Uncle Leo. Of course, we all knew you were a boy, but it was fun to play around with your mom for a few weeks. I have to admit though—I think she was onto us. She's incredibly smart, and it's hard to keep anything from her. I think she gets that from Grandpa Huck. The best news of the day, though, was when Dr. Sumner confirmed that you're healthy and growing right on schedule. So, the Easter Bunny should be bringing you right on time.

Mommy and I are up at the ranch. You're going to love it up here. I surprised her with a trip to celebrate YOU! She's taking a shower right now, and when she gets out, I have a few more surprises for her. Uncle Leo and Grandpa sent her gifts, and I have a few of my own. I also have a very special surprise planned in the morning. I came up with a few clues for her. We'll see if she figures it out. Like I said, your mom is so smart, I won't be surprised when she does.

I better go for now. I have a towel, nice and warm from the fire, to wrap around her when she steps out of the shower. I have been taking tons of pictures so you can see just how beautiful she looks during this time. Just when I think she can't possibly look more radiant, she surprises me again. I know what it is. All the love she feels for you shines through more and more with each day that brings us closer to you. Blackjack and we're there (21 more weeks!).

I love you,
Daddy

****

While Sunny finished up in the bathroom, Mathew further fluffed the cozy love nest in front of the fire with the addition of pillows and their favorite plaid blanket. In the center, three beautifully wrapped gifts waited.

"Hurry up! It's time for presents!" he hollered.

"Matthew Ellis!" She entered the room, wrapping a towel around her hair. "This is so sweet. But I feel bad. I didn't get you anything."

"We can work out some sort of trade later." He winked.

"Which one should I open first?"

"This one." He handed her the largest box first. "It's from Leo."

"From Leo?"

"Yep. And there's a card too." He pulled a small envelope from under the bow and handed it to her. She opened it and read it aloud.

Dear Sunny,

I must admit that I haven't spent a lot of time around pregnant women in my life. But I know for a fact that you happen to be the prettiest one I ever saw. This baby is so lucky to have such a special Mom.

Congratulations!

Love,

Leo

"Oh, Mathew!" Sunny's voice cracked. "That's the sweetest thing Leo has ever said to me."

"And cue the waterworks..." he said, feigning annoyance.

"Listen, for the record, you've cried way more tears today than I have." She shoved his shoulder.

"That's because I'm deeply in touch with my emotions."

"You are deeply full of shit."

"Come on...let's see what he got you." Mathew pushed the box closer to her.

Sunny opened the gift, laughing when she pulled out a book. "*Babies on Hips, Great Meals on Lips: Easy Recipe Planning for New Moms.* Wow! Is that a hint or what?"

"That's a great gift. Not that you'll ever use it—but

it's the thought that counts." He took the book from her and placed it on the coffee table. "All right, on to gift number two." He handed her a smaller box, complete with a blue bow.

"Is this from you?"

"Nope."

"There's no card."

"I think the card is inside."

Sunny opened the second gift. Under several layers of tissue paper, she found a tiny pair of baby booties. They were old. Their leather was worn, and the grosgrain ribbon bows and flowers that adorned them had faded. They were tied together with another piece of ribbon, stained and frayed.

"Where did these come from?" She stared at them. They seemed too tiny to belong to a real baby—perhaps a one-time prized possession of a doll. They reminded Sunny of something one would find hiding inside an old trunk in an attic. Checking the bottom of the box, she found a letter.

Baby Girl,

Congratulations on giving the world a precious gift—my grandchild! What a blessing for our family. I couldn't be happier for you and Mathew. You are both passionate, caring souls—deeply committed to each other. I can't think of two people more deserving of such a blessed experience.

And now, on to the shoes. Yes, you probably don't recognize them. These are the shoes! The shoes your mother gave me the day I went on the most special scavenger hunt that brought me the news of you—my baby girl on the way. Your mother told me you were a girl from the beginning and I never doubted it. She was so incredibly beautiful throughout her entire pregnancy. And once again, it's like seeing her all over again with each picture I see of you. You continue to glow, lighting everyone's heart with a joy I can't even begin to describe. How fortunate I feel to be able to bask in the glow of your happiness. It's my greatest blessing to date (until I hold another little blessing in the spring).

You never wore these booties, I'm sorry to say. But your mother fastened a pink ribbon on them (yes, that ribbon was pink at one time) and hung them on a tiny wooden stake in her garden. And there they hung for years, drinking in the sun and rain. Your mother said she left them there in case any garden fairies came along in need of something to put on their tiny feet. I don't know if you will remember them hanging in the garden or not. They were swallowed up by Lantana and Plumbago by the time you were big enough to roam around. I'd forgotten about them myself until I told you that story last month. It took some time, but I was finally able to locate the box where they've been hiding all these years.

Once again, your father has proven himself to be a sentimental old fool. But if loving my family so deeply means I'm a fool, then I'm happy to be found guilty.

With all my heart, I love you and that precious boy inside you.

So much love,

Pop

As much as she wanted to read it aloud to Mathew, her throat closed, holding her words hostage. Chest heaving, she could barely see the lines as tears stung her eyes. When she finished, she dropped the letter and slumped against Mathew, completely overcome with a dozen emotions. The love for her father. The ache for her mother. The fear of something happening to Mathew…or their baby.

Mathew held her, whispering soft reassurances that she was completely safe.

"My father should know better than to write something like that to me. I'm just one big emotional hormone." She took a deep breath, wiping tears from her eyes with the cuffs of her pajama top.

"So, these are the famed shoes?" Mathew held them up, hoping to lighten the mood. "Did you wear them into battle?"

Sunny couldn't help but laugh. "It sure looks that way. No, my mother kept them in her garden."

"What? To scare away the birds?" he said teasingly.

"No! They were for the garden fairies. Just read the letter…"

"And your father kept them all these years?" He whistled in amazement and placed them on the table beside the cookbook.

"He tries to pass off his sentimentality by claiming he's a pack rat. That man never could throw anything of nostalgia out."

"Think you're up for one more?" He placed the final gift in front of her—a white box tied with a tasteful pale blue bow. "This one's from me."

"Did you wrap this?" she asked, taking the box from his hands.

"All by myself."

"Is this gonna make me cry?"

"I don't think so. Just open it."

She untied the bow and removed the wrapping, having absolutely no idea what could be hiding inside. Mathew excelled in everything and surprising her was no exception. Removing the lid, she was immediately baffled. She reached inside and pulled out two items.

"A travel alarm clock…and a carrot?" She gave him a confused look.

"Do you like them?" he asked with a smug grin.

"They're…unique."

"Well, today was a big day. I wanted to get you something really special," he said proudly.

"They're certainly different."

"There's a card too." He motioned to the box.

Sunny opened the small card. Seeing Mathew's handwriting instantly triggered a smile. It was the exact opposite of her father's. Font-like and precise, like the millions of spreadsheets that have crossed his desk throughout his career. She cleared her throat and read his words aloud.

In the morning, I'll chime at the appointed time. The carrot? A key. A journey awaits you and me.

"Mathew, this makes no sense." She looked up at him.

"That's because it's a riddle."

"Well, the clock part makes sense. *In the morning, I'll chime at the appointed time*. But the carrot is a key? A key to what?"

"I guess you'll have to sleep on it, and when the alarm sounds, maybe you'll have it figured out."

She reread the riddle, still perplexed. "You came up with this by yourself?"

"Yep."

"How 'bout a little hint?"

"Do you think your mother gave your father any hints on their scavenger hunt? Nope, no hints. Just think about it. You're a smart girl, as your father says."

"The carrot is a key..." She fanned herself with the card, trying her best to decipher the code.

"In the meantime, I think there might be one more gift around here." He reached under the blanket, pulling out a small, slim rectangular box, wrapped in the signature black and white striped paper of her favorite local jeweler.

"Now this box is smartly dressed."

"This is just a little something from me to you." He placed the box in her hands.

"Another treat?"

"What can I say? I'm a hopeless case." He shrugged.

She gave the box a shake. "Marbles?"

"Open it..."

She ripped the wrapping without hesitation. Inside, she found an elegant strand of pearls. "Oh, Mathew..." She shook her head as she did every time he surprised her. "These are magnificent."

"Let's try 'em on. Here, let me help you." He secured them around her pale neck.

"How do they look?" She held her hair up, striking a model's pose.

"Even better now that they're on you."

She ran her hand lightly across them. "They're beautiful, but you have got to stop with all these gifts. Really. A new car and a strand of pearls in two months?"

"The car is a necessity. You have to have transportation. And the pearls? Well, I cannot allow you to give birth without them."

"What? Why not?" She laughed.

"All the greatest TV moms wore pearls. Carol Brady. Mrs. C, from Happy Days. I think even Marg Simpson wore pearls. You're gonna be right up there with the best."

****

My Little Prince,

Indeed! You are NOT a little princess. Not that I ever thought you might be. Daddy and I are overjoyed that we have a healthy baby boy on the way. Dr. Sumner checked out all your parts and said you are the picture of health. I can't believe that we're halfway there. It won't be soon enough. I wish I could hold you in my arms right now. We called Uncle Leo and Grandpa Huck as soon as we left the doctor's office to share our good news. Of course, they both knew you were a boy all along—they just like to tease me.

Daddy kidnapped me and brought me up to our ranch. It is so beautiful and peaceful—I know you will love coming here. And the best part is only Uncle Leo and Grandpa know how to reach us. This way, I can have your father all to myself without someone from his office tracking him down. I am very proud of your father's business success but sometimes I'm selfish and don't want to share him with the rest of the world. I wish you could see how excited he is about you. I was watching him today and the way he looked at the new ultrasound photos of you. I hope you have your father's hands. They are strong and expressive, yet gentle. I think I fell in love with his hands first. And I know when I see his hands holding you I will fall in love with them all over again.

Well, you won't believe it, but we decided on a name for you. A first name, anyway. Still haven't tackled a middle name, but I have a couple of ideas. We've decided not to tell anyone. We'd like for one part of this journey to be a surprise. We have spent days going through our baby name books with no luck. But tonight, alone with your father here in the cabin, we found it. Daddy opened the baby name book he's been studying for weeks. I closed my eyes, and fate led my finger right to your name. The more I say your name and think about its meaning, the more sure I am about it. Daddy feels the same way. We hope you will be proud of your name and will appreciate the nature in which it was given. Your name picked us, not the other way around. Your father and I have seen fate do a great many things—and giving us the perfect name for our son is obviously no exception. I do plan, however, to still call you my "Little Prince" because that's my special name for you. Also, I wouldn't want to write your name down and have someone uncover our secret. As you know, your father is getting better at keeping secrets, but he's a work in progress.

It's two o'clock and I need to get some sleep. I was just up on my nightly trip to the bathroom and wanted to write down these thoughts while they were fresh on my mind. Daddy has some sort of surprise planned for me—an alarm is sounding at seven o'clock and I'm supposed to use a carrot (yes, a carrot!) to unlock something. I have no idea what. If you have any ideas, feel free to wake me up and let me know. But I know Daddy. I will love it no matter what. And I will always love you no matter what!

Love,

Mommy
XO

Chapter Thirteen

While Sunny dressed, Mathew loaded up the Suburban, ensuring every detail was letter perfect. A fully stocked picnic basket. Thermoses filled with hot beverages. Their favorite plaid blanket, snatched from the makeshift bed in front of the fire. Back in the cabin, he gave the interior a final glance, satisfied that he hadn't overlooked anything. A check of his watch prompted a sigh of relief. Plenty of time before his buddy would be ready with the surprise—one that had been weeks in the making. Pulse racing with anticipation, he wiped his sweaty palms on his jeans. Today was not just about surprising Sunny. Today was a test of his own faith.

Sunny emerged from the bedroom, hiking boots unlaced and jacket slung over one shoulder. Her footfalls were heavy. She stopped and locked eyes with Mathew. Immediately, he detected trouble.

"What's wrong?"

"You're making a pregnant woman get up at the crack of dawn to go hiking? Really? And what's this supposed to be? Breakfast?" She held up the carrot.

"What's the deal? Ten minutes ago everything was fine."

"Ten minutes ago I hadn't registered the fact that we'll probably be miles away from a restroom. I'm not squatting behind a bush, Mathew."

"A little faith, please? I promise that if and or when you need to pee, I will escort you to a real toilet."

"What about breakfast?" she asked, her eyes narrowing with suspicion.

"It's all taken care of. Now then, Mrs. Ellis, shall we?"

Windows down, they drove down through the hills of the property, taking in the scenery. A cluster of does in a field. Twenty head of cattle gathered around salt licks and feeders. A bevy of baby goats, their cries sounding eerily humanlike. Several times Sunny shielded her eyes as the rising sun's rays bounced off the hood of the SUV. Mathew dug around inside the center console for a moment, then pulled a pair of sunglasses into view.

"Here, take these."

"You've certainly thought of everything," Sunny said, taking the sunglasses, her tone still a touch sharp.

"Actually, I just realized I forgot something important. Toilet paper. For when you need to duck behind a tree."

"Haha, very funny."

"A handful of leaves will work just fine—just be sure you're not wiping with poison ivy."

Sunny stuck her tongue out at him. They crossed a cattle guard and drove through an open gate. The landscape changed to rocky inclines lined with clusters of dense trees.

"So help me God, Mathew Ellis, if you scratch my new ride on a tree branch…"

"I don't know how on earth I went to bed with my sweet wife last night yet woke up with Beth Dutton."

At that moment, the trees parted to reveal a

clearing beside a gorgeous stream. The morning light reflected off the dew, and the treeless expanse shimmered like an ocean. A reply to her husband's comment would have to wait. This scene was much too beautiful for snark.

"Mathew…where are we? Is this our property?"

"No, this is Reagan's place. Remember when we drove through the gate? That's when we crossed over."

"It's stunning."

"The perfect spot for a breakfast picnic. I've got a basket in the back with all your favorites, including hot chocolate with almond flavoring, just the way you like it."

"Mathew, this is really sweet of you, but I still don't understand what the carrot has to do with a picnic."

"That's because this is not the surprise. Food first, then the surprise."

The minutes disappeared, along with the morning dew on the grass, as they enjoyed breakfast and each other in total solitude. The air was invigorating, and fall wrapped its inviting arms around them. Mathew couldn't help staring at her. The rays of sunlight moved through her hair, creating a halo around her head. His eyes traveled down to her hands and the fingers wrapped delicately around her mug. The large diamond on her wedding ring winked up at him. *Is she really mine?* It was a question he asked himself constantly. While sipping his coffee, his thoughts traveled back in time to a woman in a wheelchair. He'd only seen her twice, once in the hospital elevator and once in the park, but he knew, even that early on, that she was special. She'd changed him—just as easily as the seasons change, bringing with them a new beginning.

"You know what? I was wrong." He fixed his eyes firmly on her face.

"About what?" she asked.

"Remember when I told you my favorite season is spring? I was wrong."

"So, what is your favorite season?"

"It's fall."

"Oh, I think I love fall most, too. It's the change in the air. There's something about it that makes you feel so refreshed. I mean, it takes forever for fall to make it to Texas, but when it does, there's nothing better. Even the tiny bit we're getting right now." She breathed deeply, closing her eyes as she slowly exhaled.

"I love fall for a different reason. Your eyes remind me of fall."

"What about Pumpkin here?" She grinned, patting her belly.

"Well, yes. Naturally, the fruit of our labor is the best part." He placed his hand on top of hers.

"You know what's gonna happen when he gets here, don't you?" she asked.

"What?"

"You're gonna fall in love with spring all over again." She leaned forward and kissed him.

Mathew glanced at his watch. It was time. He casually began repacking the picnic basket, glancing over his shoulder every few seconds.

"What are you looking for?" Sunny asked, scanning the trees behind them.

"Well, the surprise should be here any minute."

"The surprise is coming to us?" Her eyes widened with curiosity.

"You've got the carrot, right? Because it might not start without the key." Mathew teased.

"I left it in the car."

As soon as the words left her mouth, she saw them. Mathew's good friend, Reagan, emerging from the trees, leading two beautiful horses—all saddled and ready to go.

"Oh, my God." Sunny pushed herself up before Mathew could offer her any assistance.

"You must promise me. No horsing around. We're going to go for a serene and peaceful ride."

"I wouldn't do anything to put myself or this precious cargo in danger. You have my word."

"Yeah, well, when your father-in-law is the Texas equivalent of Evel Knievel, you gotta spell it out nice and clear."

Reagan gave Sunny a leg up. Her face glowed with sheer joy as he adjusted her stirrups. After pulling the reins over the horse's head, he offered Sunny a few insights on the animal's temperament, but assured her the horse was gentle.

"Thanks for getting up so early to do this for us. Let's meet back here in an hour," Mathew said to Reagan.

"Just an hour?" Sunny frowned, her tone echoing disappointment.

"It's an hour more than you ever expected. I'm thinking solely of your bladder. Also, you haven't ridden for a while. Let's not push it, okay?"

The men mapped out a route for the ride. Sunny stroked her horse's neck, leaning forward as much as her belly would comfortably allow. Once Mathew was up in the saddle, Reagan gave his horse a friendly slap on the backside then turned and walked toward the SUV.

"The carrot is a key! Of course. It makes perfect sense. Very clever, Mr. Ellis. And very sweet."

Sunny held out her hand to him. While he couldn't see her eyes behind the dark tint of her sunglasses, he was certain they sparkled with gratitude. He took her hand and pressed a kiss to the back of it.

"Now don't get too comfortable in that particular saddle. I might just have a carrot to start *your* engine later." Mathew winked, quoting a well-known image from his favorite Larry McMurtry novel.

"Promises, promises," she answered.

****

Dad's Advice: It's the little things.

My greatest desire for you in your life is to spend your days with someone that you love beyond words. Life is not measured by the size of your bank account— believe me, money cannot buy happiness. I know that for a fact because I spent years trying. It can't buy you health, true friendship, or peace of mind. Loving someone who loves you can bring you the greatest joy in the world. And that's why you have to treat the people who share your life with you completely differently than you treat the rest of the world.

You can be tough in business and fearless in competition, but with those you love, you have to show them something that no one else ever has. Fortunately, when you find that special someone, that's all you'll want to do. And that's why it's important for you to remember how much the little things count. Now, I'm not referring to manners like I discussed earlier. I mean taking time, putting forth extra effort. I love showing your mom that she's different and more special than all the rest of the women in the world. I surprise her with funny cards and sentimental gifts. Sing her silly songs and dance her around the kitchen. Wake her up early and take her horseback riding. It's important to me to show her how lost I'd be without her.

We're still here at the ranch. Mommy is asleep. She's worn out. We were up late last night, and then up early this morning. After lunch, we went into town to do some shopping. Then, we tried a bit of fishing. But no luck. I should just tell you now that your old man is not a very good fisherman. But there's something relaxing about fishing that makes it all worth it, even if I come home empty-handed nine times out of ten.

I surprised your mom with a horseback ride this morning. She hasn't been on a horse since her accident. Not long ago, she was thrown from a friend's horse into a metal gate and injured her back. She walked away but continued to have a lot of pain. She eventually got to the point where she couldn't walk, so she got it checked out. Your mom is not a fan of doctors, needles, hospitals, or medicine in general. Thank goodness your grandfather is the type who won't take no for an answer. He loaded her up and took her to see a specialist. Turns out that fall was the best thing to happen to her. Doctors discovered a large tumor on her spine. Thank God it wasn't cancerous. She's made a full recovery. Now the only affliction she suffers is me.

We finally decided on a name for you. And we're not telling anyone—especially that sly grandfather of yours! It's about time your mother and I had something to surprise everyone with. The jury is still out on a middle name. What do you think about the name

James? I've always been a big Jimmy Stewart fan. Mommy is still undecided. Uncle Leo really wants us to name you Mathew, but I don't know about the whole father-son-pass-the-name-down thing. Mommy and I talked about it for a long time and decided that you should have your own name. I don't want people making judgments about you based on having my name. You will be your own man. And I know you will make a name for yourself in this world. Just make sure that you do so with honesty, integrity, and virtue.

Listen, it's almost dinnertime. I better wake Mommy up. I can never decide if she's more beautiful asleep or awake.

I love you!

****

My Little Prince,

We're home! We had a wonderful weekend. Daddy is downstairs taking care of some urgent business that came up while we were gone. He said it was nothing but I could tell from his expression that it was something important. Your father is the king of keeping the office at the office. But sometimes, it can't be avoided. His firm handles huge accounts with big, scary numbers. I prefer something less scary—like sending astronauts into space. (wink!)

We're only home for a few days, and then driving to Austin to have Thanksgiving with Grandpa Huck. He hasn't seen my belly in weeks (except in photos, which your father insists on taking around the clock). I know he will be thrilled to see the progress we've made in person. We wanted Uncle Leo to come with us, but he's flying to Seattle to spend Thanksgiving with his niece, Nora. We're still undecided as to where Ivy will be spending the holiday. I guess we'll let her flip a bone to decide who she's going with.

I almost gave away our secret last night. Daddy gave me a very special book. It's called "The Little Prince." Sound familiar? My mother read that story to me hundreds of times when I was a little girl. That's why I'm calling you my Little Prince. It's kind of like having a special connection between my mom and you. I've been thinking about her a lot lately. I wish she could be here with me right now. If I close my eyes and try really hard, I can almost feel her hands on my belly—just the way she used to move her hands through my hair when I was a little girl. I talked to Daddy about it last night. He has the most amazing way of helping me see things in a new and wonderful light. Your father is my candle.

We went horseback riding yesterday. It was glorious! I haven't been riding since my accident. Your father was very apprehensive about me getting back in the saddle. We've talked a lot about fear this weekend. He worries about us; I worry about us. It's a perfect storm of worry around here. I'm not saying I'm waiting for the proverbial shoe to drop, but I worry. All. The. Time. Guess it comes with the territory. I asked Daddy if he ever feels that we're living a charmed life–like things are so good, maybe they're too good. His response was simple yet profound: Lives are blessed, not charmed, because charms wear off, but blessings can last forever. He's so smart, that Daddy of yours.

Well, my little love, it's time to turn in. As much as I love being in the Hill Country, it's nice to be back home and in our own bed. Hopefully, your father won't be too much longer on his conference call.

I love you, my angel.
All the love I can give (and a little bit more),
Mommy
XOXO

Chapter Fourteen

Getting out of Harris County the day before Thanksgiving was a hair-pulling nightmare. Road construction and two different accidents added a full hour to their drive time. A stop at Buc-ees to gas up and use their immaculate restroom facilities tacked on and additional fifteen minutes. Sunny squirmed in her seat, filled with nervous anticipation as she sipped a Dr. Pepper Icee and texted her father constant updates. Mathew remained silent in an effort to combat any additional stress. Ivy never made a peep either, sleeping the entire trip.

"He's waiting for us."

Mathew pointed to a dark dot on the landscape—Huck, sitting on his Hog next to the fence. When their vehicle got close, the enormous metal security gate slowly opened. Huck turned sharply and took off like a shot, the motorcycle kicking up a cloud of dust in its wake. The SUV followed along the winding dirt drive. From the corner of his eye, Mathew saw Sunny sit up a little straighter when her childhood home came into view. From the outside, it didn't look like much—a two-story limestone obscured by mature oaks. Inside, it was something straight out of Architectural Digest. The exact opposite of what one would expect from a man who spent hours each day with his hands inside greasy engines. Had he not found success in the racing world,

Huck Porter would have made quite the interior designer.

The car was barely in park before Sunny was hopping out and racing into Huck's waiting arms. Mathew took his time getting out, giving father and daughter a moment to savor their reunion. After a minute, he released Sunny and hustled around to the driver's door. Huck pulled Mathew out of the vehicle and then wrapped him in a tight bear hug.

"It's about damn time," Huck teased and clapped Mathew on the back.

"I'm glad we made it. Your daughter was going apeshit."

"Patience has never been her virtue." He shot Sunny a look.

"Pop!" Sunny protested.

The two men managed to get all their luggage into the house in one trip. Mathew took Ivy on a short walk while Sunny unpacked. Once settled, they met Huck out back by the pool. A nearby firepit crackled, the distinct scent of mesquite wood in the air. A tray with all the makings of s'mores waited, along with various beverage options. Sunny parked herself on a chair between them, dog in her lap. Within minutes, she and Mathew fell under Huck's spell, as he spun one crazy tale after another.

"You know, baby girl, when you hopped out of the car, I thought for sure I was hallucinating—which isn't possible since the only mushrooms I consume these days are on a Mr. Gatti's pizza. My god, Sunny, you are your mother reincarnated. It's incredible how much you look like her."

"She looks great, doesn't she? The toast of her Ob-

Gyn office. All the nurses can't stop bragging about her."

"Mathew, I don't know what you've been doing, but don't stop. Our girl here looks fabulous."

"Well, I wish I could take the credit. But this is all you and Daphne. She was a vision long before I ever got my hands on her."

"She certainly was." Huck turned his happy face back toward Sunny. "Listen, I've been cooking for two days straight, getting all your favorites ready for dinner tomorrow."

"I'm sure it will be delicious. And since you've done all the prep, Mathew and I will handle all the cleanup."

"Oh, I insist." He poked her rib playfully.

"We appreciate everything you've done, Huck," Mathew added.

"Don't thank me yet. It might taste like shit on a shingle." Huck laughed and slapped his forearm with force. "C'mon, you two. Let's get inside before we're eaten alive by mosquitos. I have a trip planned."

"A trip? But we just got here." Sunny looked at her father, confused.

"I assure you that the commute is minimal." He gave her a wink.

****

"Just give me a minute…" Huck said, as he removed his glasses from his pocket and examined the projector.

"Pop, this is wonderful. Where did you find these?" Sunny was balancing a box filled with old photos on her lap.

"Well, when I went looking for the baby booties, I

came across a few other treasures that we haven't seen in a while."

"And the home movies? I haven't seen these in years." She carefully placed the box on the floor beside her.

"I finally get to see a Sunny Porter I've never seen before," Mathew said, grinning. "And on an actual 8mm reel. This is a first for me."

"Everyone was using camcorders back in the eighties, but I think old school is the way to go. You don't get this look on a tape. When it doubt, go vintage."

"I'm gonna print that on a t-shirt for you for Christmas," Sunny said.

"Mathew, would you get the lights?" Huck asked.

"Certainly." Mathew crossed the room and flipped the switch.

Within seconds, the wall of the living room came alive with grainy images of a girl sitting on a tiny dirt bike. Her golden hair was pulled back in a ponytail; her crooked grin instantly pulling on your heart. She looked to be about ten years old. Fiery. Adventurous. Purple and silver metallic helmet tucked under one arm. The image changed and Mathew stood frozen at the light switch, remembering a faded photo that Huck had given him while Sunny was in the hospital—a shot of his daughter in her early twenties, carefree and striking in a white tee and jeans. Casual elegance, even back then.

Sunny motioned to him, and he joined her on the couch. The minutes disappeared as the movies and stories carried them away to another place. Huck narrated the trip back in time, with Sunny making playful comments and corrections. Mathew tried to focus on the pictures on the wall but found his eyes moving back to the woman beside him. Watching the interactions between father and daughter was much more intriguing to him than the movies themselves. He marveled at her hands—so delicate and expressive. They could tell a story all by themselves. Mathew was shocked when he glanced at his watch and found time had slipped away. He stood and stretched, which prompted Ivy to announce her need for another walk with a loud bark.

"I guess Ivy's had about all she can take," Huck said.

"Me too, I'm starving," Sunny added.

"Mathew, I hope we didn't bore you with our trip down memory lane." Huck patted his son-in-law's arm.

"If it involves your daughter, there's no way I could be bored. I'm ready to watch more later, just say the word."

"Can't. I don't know if Sunny told you, but we have a few Porter family traditions around here that we observe each Thanksgiving."

"Actually, no." He looked at his wife.

"Sunny and I always kick off the Thanksgiving holiday with a game of Monopoly—loser does the dishes tomorrow. Of course, win or lose, you and Sunny have already volunteered for that chore. Tomorrow morning, a light breakfast. Turkey and trimmings will be served around one o'clock. After that, football and naps all around. Before retiring, my world-famous turkey sandwiches with homemade bacon jam."

"Sounds good to me." Mathew nodded and flashed him a *thumbs up*.

****

"Two, three, four, five. Marvin Gardens. I'll take that one as well." Huck moved his horse and rider marker around the board.

"Pop! You're killing us." Sunny looked down at the few bills in front of her.

Mathew took the dice and shook them in his cupped hands. They danced on the surface of the game board for a moment. Once they settled, Mathew eyed the board and moaned, then moved his top hat marker into position.

"Welcome to Park Place." Huck's eyes gleamed with amusement.

"I'm getting the family discount, right?" Mathew asked.

"I don't have to tell a sharp businessman such as yourself the rules of mixing business with family." Huck held out his hand, eagerly anticipating his payment.

"That leaves me with fifty bucks." He gently fanned himself with the fake bill.

"Great." Sunny rolled her eyes and picked up the dice. Frowning, she moved her Scottie dog along the board, landing on another Huck-owned property.

"Boardwalk." Huck smirked and finished off his second beer.

"But I'm your flesh and blood."

"Cough up the dough, baby girl." He held out his greedy hand toward his daughter.

Sunny counted out the last of her bills, shaking her head in playful disgust.

"What's that leave you with?" Mathew asked.

"I got ten bucks." She held up the last of her

currency.

"Let's see. For sixty bucks, I can put you two up for the night on Baltic or Mediterranean. Of course, it's not the best part of town. And you'll have to bring your own sheets."

"But I want to stay on Boardwalk with the eight hundred thread count Egyptian cotton linens," Sunny whined.

"It's a dollar for every thread." Huck winked.

Mathew checked his watch, ready to call it a night. "We can handle it for one night." He snatched Sunny's ten and handed it to Huck, along with his fifty. "We'll take your best room, sir. After all, my wife is with child."

Huck laughed. "Listen, if Jesus can sleep in a barn, you can handle one night on Baltic."

****

Sunny checked the alarm clock beside the bed and then slipped her hand under the pillow. *All set.* She could hear Mathew humming and brushing his teeth down the hall. She hummed along while she changed into her pajamas.

"Do you need anything?" Mathew asked once back inside the bedroom.

"Just you."

"What a great night." He sighed and pulled the sheet back, slipping in beside her. "Your dad's a shrewd Monopoly player. He's also an amazing cook. How come you aren't?"

"Very funny. For the record, I help send humans to space. My dad can't do that."

"Touché." Mathew bowed his head.

"Listen, there's something you need to know about

tomorrow. It's about the turkey."

"What about the turkey?"

"My father carves the turkey. He's very methodical about it."

"Okay," Mathew said, looking puzzled.

"I just don't want you to be offended if he doesn't offer to let you carve it."

"You're forgetting that I've celebrated Thanksgiving with a master birdman for years. Leo never lets me carve the turkey either."

"Really?"

"He tried to teach me once, but he's not the most patient person." Mathew took his phone from the nightstand. "I guess he and Barbara made it to Nora's. I thought he would've called."

"I'm sure they're fine. We would've heard from Nora if they'd had any problems."

"You're right." Mathew put the phone back on the bedside table.

"Are you okay?" Sunny asked.

"Of course. I'm fine. Why?"

"Well, you just seem out of sorts. Since we got here, I mean."

Mathew paused for a moment. "Have you ever been driving somewhere, completely engrossed in thought, and then realize that you haven't been paying attention to the road and then suddenly wonder how you arrived at your destination?"

"Yes. I do that all the time."

"That's how I've been feeling today."

"What do you mean?"

"Before we left the house, I was thinking about the first Thanksgiving I spent with Leo. I was just a kid then. Now, fast-forward to today and I'm spending Thanksgiving with you and your father and we're going to be parents in just a few months. How did I get here? How did it go by so fast? And before we know it, our little guy will be spending Thanksgiving somewhere with his family and Leo will be watching me butcher a bird from somewhere above."

"You know, you always hear people say, 'they grow up so fast' and it really is true. I can remember those times from the movies we just watched like they were yesterday."

"About those movies…" He snuggled up to her, pulling her body close to his.

"They were pretty silly, huh?"

"Silly? They're fantastic."

"I know it made my father happy to be able to relive all that with us here."

"He is so proud of you, Sunny."

"I know he is. And every day that goes by, I understand his love for me more and more." She placed her hand on her pregnant belly.

"Seeing you back then and the way the sun bounced off your long ponytail. There's a tiny part of me that secretly wishes we were having a little girl. Is that bad?"

"No, it's not bad. Maybe next time." She smiled up at him.

"Really?" He sat up. "Just a few nights ago, you were telling me that you didn't know if you could do this. And now you're ready to be a baby factory?"

"Hold up, Slick. I never said *factory*. But maybe one more."

Chapter Fifteen

Sunny's body jerked, and instantly she was awake. Sweat covered her face, neck, and chest like a wet blanket. She lay in the darkness of her childhood bedroom for several minutes, trying to calm her breathing without waking Mathew. *It's just another crazy dream.* Like a detective, she tried to piece together the conversations that had occurred over the past few days. *Everything in my dream was white. What does that mean? All the broken baby things? No clue. Lost inside an auction house? Could mean anything. The dove flying into the clouds? We talked about the turkey and Leo being a master birdman. Who knows?*

With less than an hour until the alarm was set to ring, she slid out of bed and quietly dressed. Mathew was deep in dreams, his snore echoing off the walls. He looked so handsome it caused a serious hesitation–to scrap the whole plan and climb right back in beside him. Without a sound, she placed the clues on the bedside table, grabbed her boots, and tiptoed downstairs.

Light from the living room caught her eye. There sat Huck, asleep in his favorite chair. A pair of wire-rim glasses balanced on the end of his nose. A stack of papers rested on his lap. On the floor beside him, she spied a pen, lost as his grip gave way to rest. His late-night attempt at writing had failed, as sleep had taken over his body. Sunny pulled a wool camp blanket from the back of the couch and walked to her father. Gently, she removed his glasses and placed them on the small table beside his chair. Reaching for the papers, she stopped when she saw the name of the recipient on the first line: *Beautiful Boy*. Curiosity gave way to the rules of privacy, and Sunny sat on the floor beside her father's chair and read the words he'd written to her unborn son.

Beautiful Boy,

I know it will be years before you are old enough to read the words of an old hippie. However, being that I'm your only living grandparent, I feel that it's my responsibility to get my thoughts down before my time expires. I am Huck Porter, and I am blessed and honored to be your mother's father. I must admit that this is now my third attempt to write down something meaningful to you. I may fail again miserably. But for the sake of argument, and for the sanity of an old man, let's agree to allow the rules of gift-giving to apply in this case and say, "it's the thought that counts."

I could bore you with all the details of my life and my upbringing, but I won't. In fact, my first two letters consisted of just that—a complete history of the Porter family. Factual. Straightforward. Dull. It finally occurred to me today to tell you about something much more exciting and important to me than where I came from and that's where you came from: your amazing and beautiful mother.

Your mother and father told me several weeks ago that they were expecting you. Actually, I guessed that you were on the way. Your mother was glowing. I knew it the moment I saw her when I arrived in Houston.

Now, it's Thanksgiving, and your parents are here in Austin visiting me, and I can't believe the change that has occurred in just a few short weeks. The evidence of your residence is now apparent to me for the first time, and your mother is absolutely stunning. From the moment she stepped from the car, it occurred to me that I can literally refer to every phase of her life as her "most beautiful." She was the most beautiful baby. The most beautiful young girl. The most beautiful teen. The most beautiful young woman. The most beautiful bride. And now, the most beautiful expectant mother. Am I biased? Hell yes! You bet I am! But I'm also honest and know thousands who can substantiate these claims. But you'll know it too. She'll be the most beautiful Mommy, I have no doubt.

When your mother was about six years old, I knew exactly the type of person she'd grow to be. They say a person's character is fully developed by the time they start school, and I agree. We had been out riding one morning, just the two of us. From the time she was about four, your mother was zipping all over the place on a tiny little dirt bike that a good friend of mine built her. Motorcycles never scared her. I don't think anything scares her, now that I think about it.

Sunny checked the remaining sheets, but all were blank. Smiling, she placed them on the table beside the glasses. As quietly as possible, she turned off the lamp and exited, wiping traces of tears from her eyes.

****

"Sunny, will you turn that off?" Mathew whispered in the darkness. Receiving no response, he turned over to find her spot empty and cold. The alarm clock continued to sound incessantly, and he had no idea how to turn it off. After pressing all buttons and flipping all switches, he relented and turned on the lamp. A few seconds passed as his eyes adjusted to the light. He quieted the alarm and laughed when he saw a carrot and a note on the bedside table.

It is said that turnabout is fair play
So it's up before the sun
On this Thanksgiving Day.
My secret spot you have yet to see.
The Swiss Army will ensure it's forever you and me.

Mathew flipped the paper over, surprised to find a neatly drawn map of the Porter place on the other side—an arrow and the words *Start here!* pointing at Huck's shop. Suddenly, the playfulness of her riddle turned his stomach and a wave of fear ran through him. He scrambled into jeans and boots and grabbed a jacket, bolting out of Sunny's old bedroom and taking the stairs two at a time. Once outside the front door, his gait turned to a full sprint toward the large metal building where his father-in-law built some of the fastest motorcycles in the world. It was still dark outside—a fact that made him even more fearful. *Maybe she's waiting for me*. The light in the shop burned bright, but his gut told him she wasn't there.

A bright red 4-wheeler sat parked in the center of the shop–a fresh bunch of carrots on the seat, their leafy green tops spilling over the side. The first light of dawn was just beginning to break on the horizon. He forewent the map, relying on his memory of Sunny's secret spot by the pond. Huck had driven him down there back in the early summer. He pushed the carrots onto the shop floor. Swinging his leg up over the seat, he started the machine and took off in what he felt was the right direction. The sky would soon tell him if his instincts were correct.

Damn it, Sunny! Why the hell would you do something this stupid and this dangerous? I cannot understand why you would pull a stunt like this. What the hell are you thinking? You're damn right I'm upset! I will not calm down! Do you realize the danger you've put yourself in? Or our child?

Mathew ran through the various phrases he felt would surely fly from his lips the moment he found her. The more he thought about what she'd done, the angrier he became. He'd never lost his temper with her. Sure, they had disagreements, but never a fight. But this time she'd gone too far.

Light continued to grow around him. Up ahead, there was a ridge and his memory kicked into gear. He turned to the east and rode through the dense woods. *It's just up ahead. On the other side, there should be a clearing.* The low-lying branches brushed against his shoulders, and he flipped up his collar to protect his face. It was cold, and the wind found its way through his jacket. He hadn't bothered with a shirt. There hadn't been time.

As if a veil had been lifted, the trees thinned and disappeared behind him. Once in the clearing, he filled himself with a much-needed breath, certain that he'd barely breathed upon bolting from the bed. The air was chilly and burned his insides, like tiny needles piercing his lungs. Squinting, he could just make out her silhouette in the distance on the far side of the pond. Leaning forward, his hand pulled back on the throttle. When Sunny finally came into sharp focus, she was standing and waving, her face radiant with excitement. Beside her, a 4-wheeler in the same shade of red. Mathew eased up on the throttle, slowing the machine to proceed with caution. When his eyes met Sunny's, her happy expression vanished like a stone dropped in a muddy stream. Mathew knew she'd read his expression.

"Mathew, what's wrong?" she asked, her tone filled with alarm.

He didn't respond. Relief for her safety mixed with rage at her reckless behavior. Mathew parked and killed the engine, mentally loading the jumble of accusatory bullets he was set to fire.

"What is it?" she pleaded again.

"You know exactly what's going on!" Mathew hollered.

"Oh, my God! Is it my father?" Her hand shot to her mouth.

"No, it's not your father. What the hell are you thinking?"

"What are you talking about?" Her brows furrowed, eyes dark with confusion.

"I'm talking about you, Sunny. What in the hell do you think you're doing?"

"I was waiting for you…"

"So that's it? You were just waiting for me, is that it? Wrong! Try again."

"You're scaring me, Mathew. What's wrong?"

"You mean to tell me you don't know?" he hollered again.

"If you could just calm down for a min—"

"Calm down? You want me to calm down? You sneak out of the house, climb up on a 4-wheeler, take off by yourself, pregnant, and in the goddamn dark!"

"Now wait just a minute!" She shook her head defensively, offended by his tone.

"Wait a minute for what? So you can tell me how good a rider you are? How you've been riding around here since you were a baby? What about *my* baby? Does my baby get a choice? Hell no! He's just a passenger. Did you ever stop to think about the danger you might be putting him in? Of course you didn't. You took one look at that goddamn machine and you were gone. Forget me. Forget our son. Forget your own well-being."

"I don't have to stand here and listen to this." She pushed past him, heading around the edge of the pond toward the house.

"Sunny!" he hollered, but she continued to walk.

Within moments, she disappeared in the fall foliage across the clearing. Mathew picked up a rock, hurling it in anger across the pond.

I can't believe her! After all that talk at the ranch. After all the promises. 'I would never do anything to put myself or our baby in danger.' To hell with it! To hell with her promises!

He sat down and reached for another rock, turning it over in his hands several times before tossing it out into the pond. It hit with a small splash, leaving a wake of ripples behind. The unseasonably cold wind continued to blow. When the heat of his anger wore off, the thin jacket and lack of a shirt would send him back to the house. *You can run, but you can't hide, Sunny. You're going to hear me out on this. You are dead wrong on this one.*

The sun climbed higher. The ire he'd felt had subsided some, and now exhaustion took over. Rock after rock continued to break the surface of the water. With shame, he recalled the look on Sunny's face—one of genuine fear. The sound of a motor coming from behind him jarred him back to reality. An old white work truck pulling a flatbed trailer was headed his way. Mathew stood, dusted off his jeans, and walked toward the approaching vehicle. *So, she's decided to come back...*

"Hey, Mathew! Happy Thanksgiving!" Russell called as he stepped out of the truck.

Russell was Huck's business partner-in-crime and Sunny's second father. Together, they were the definition of motley crew. Still, Mathew was shocked to see him early on a holiday morning.

"Hey, Russell. I thought you were Sunny."

"Sunny? I thought she was here with you?" Russell glanced around, mentally taking inventory of the 4-wheelers at the scene.

"She didn't send you down here to get the bikes?" Mathew asked, confused.

"No. She forgot something in the truck when I brought her down here this morning." He reached down into his pockets, searching for something.

"You brought her down here?" Mathew asked, his eyes wide with surprise.

"We met in the shop early this morning. She's been planning this for a while. She wanted to get down here to surprise you. So, I loaded up one 4-wheeler and hauled her down here, then unloaded it so she could wait for you. But she left this in the truck, and I think it's pretty integral to the surprise part."

He held something shiny in his left hand and offered it to Mathew. Reaching out, he took a silver pocketknife from Russell's hand. On one side of the knife, he read Sunny's initials. On the other side, the words *Swiss Army*. Mathew's gaze dropped to his feet. He turned the knife over several times, his stomach twisting into a tight knot.

"Do you know what she was planning to do with this?" He mustered all his pride and raised his eyes to meet Russell's.

"Well, I hate to be the one to spoil a surprise, but I believe she wanted to carve your initials in her favorite tree. That one down there." Russell pointed to the large shady oak tree about fifty yards away.

"I was afraid you were going to say that." Mathew turned his guilty eyes back toward the house.

Chapter Sixteen

The wind continued to blow, sending crisp leaves swirling beneath his feet. Mathew pulled his jacket tightly around him to retain some heat. With hands thrust deep into his pockets, he dragged his feet along the ground, winded and tired. The terrain was forgiving for the most part, but the sheer distance from Sunny's secret spot to the house was lengthy. He could have hopped in Russell's truck for a lift back, but somehow, forcing himself to take every step his pregnant wife had taken seemed more appropriate.

His angry thoughts and words had fully dissipated, and now only a desire for forgiveness remained. Would he be able to find even one meaningful word of remorse to interest her? His case rested upon two things: a sincere declaration of his love, and a forthright apology.

The white truck was parked beside the shop. Mathew could make out Russell's frame in the distance, but didn't see Sunny. An adult game of hide-n-seek between them was not on his Thanksgiving Day to-do list. *She's gonna make me work for every ounce of forgiveness. And I don't blame her. Poor Huck. I bet she stormed into the house and unloaded on him. I owe him an apology too.* Huck had shared tales of heated arguments between himself and his daughter. The inevitable scene would go only one of two ways. Huck would keep his nose out of it at all costs or bravely defend his baby girl. Either way, Mathew prepared to stand alone.

Russell unhitched the trailer, pausing briefly to offer a wave. Mathew responded with a slight nod of acknowledgment before continuing to the house, his mind racing as he braced for an icy atmosphere. Just steps inside the front door, he paused and listened. The house was quiet. A check of every room on the first floor caused his heart to start pounding. No sign of Sunny or Huck anywhere. A scan of the patio produced the same result. *She must be upstairs.* Thoughts of her lying on the bed, her eyes red and wet with tears filled his mind. *What have I done? I've ruined our holiday. Our first holiday together as a married couple...and I've ruined it.* Reluctantly, he climbed the stairs, still uncertain of the first words he'd say when their eyes met.

The door to their bedroom was closed. He stood in the hall for a minute, collecting his thoughts and his pride—two things in short supply. After a deep breath and a prayer for luck, he knocked softly and waited for her reply. Nothing.

"Sunny?" he whispered and knocked again. "Sunny, may I come in?"

Mathew pressed his ear to the door and listened but heard nothing. When he turned the knob and peeked inside, he found it as empty as the rest of the house. Sunny's boots and jacket lay in a rumpled mass on the floor. A heavy sigh escaped from his chest, and he turned and walked back downstairs. With each step, he went through a mental checklist of hiding places. He paused a moment at the glass sliders that led outside, uncertain where to go first. A heavy hand on his shoulder startled him, and he turned around sharply.

"She's not here," Huck said calmly.

"Do you know where she is?" Mathew asked, his voice barely a whisper.

"Gone."

"Where?"

"She wouldn't tell me. She came in, stomped straight upstairs, changed clothes, grabbed the car keys, and left."

"She left? But the Suburban is still parked out front."

"She took her horse."

"A horse?" Mathew's blood pressure and voice began to rise.

"Her *metal* horse–her old '68 mustang."

"Well, I've got to find her." Mathew started to walk past his father-in-law, but Huck grabbed his arm.

"You won't find her. She doesn't make it that easy. You're better off just waiting here. She'll be back."

"With all due respect, sir, I just can't sit here waiting."

"And just where exactly do you intend to go?" Huck gave him a hard look.

Mathew paused, knowing he didn't have an answer. "I'll call her then."

"You can try, but she won't answer." He motioned for Mathew to follow him. The two men walked in silence to the living room. The fireplace was alive with a warm glow, and Mathew realized for the first time just how cold he was.

"You know I'm not the type of man to meddle in the marital affairs of anyone. And my daughter is no exception."

Mathew nodded.

Huck sighed before giving him an encouraging nod. "She's driving around, letting off steam, and cursing your name to the Heavens as we speak. But she will return. She always has and she always will. But that's not to say that there won't be a substantial cold front that hits when she walks back through the door."

"I'm really sorry that I've ruined your holiday, Huck."

"You haven't ruined *my* holiday."

"I'm afraid I have, sir."

"May I ask you a question?"

"Of course."

"Did you happen to bring any work along with you? Anything from the office? A good book?"

Mathew gave him a confused look. "No. Why?"

"It's going to be a long morning, I'm afraid. Sunny might not return for hours. I was hoping you might have something to keep you busy."

"I'd really like to take a little drive around, if you don't mind."

"Suit yourself."

"If you could just point me in the general direction."

Huck looked at Mathew. His eyes were a mix of empathy and sympathy. "I wish I could. Fate will have to be your compass, I'm afraid." Again, he patted Mathew's shoulder with fatherly reassurance.

****

With care, Sunny climbed the metal bleachers at the stadium. The *Home of the Spartans* had been a safe retreat in her teens, and without thinking, the bottle green Mustang had driven her there once again.

Whenever she needed some time away to think, she found herself sitting alone on the fifty-yard line. There was something about the immaculately maintained field and the expertly drawn white lines on green grass. It was orderly, and something to focus on when her thoughts weren't. She never attended even one game during her high school years, but logged hours in the stadium, just sitting and thinking. It was the one secret spot that even her father didn't know about. Right under his nose. She bit her lip and smiled for the first time since seeing her husband's face in the early morning light.

This place used to seem so big. There was a time when she dissected her childish dilemmas in what seemed like a vast space. Now, her issues had grown substantially while the space around her had diminished. The juxtaposition of viewing the world through two sets of eyes: those of a young girl, and those of a woman.

She slipped her hands inside the silk-lined pockets of her coat, cradling her pregnant belly within. Eyes closed, she thought of Mathew. His face. His mischievous grin. His bright eyes. But those images had been replaced with a face full of rage. A severe stare. Words filled with a hateful tone. It wasn't her Mathew. It was someone else. Not the man in the elevator. Not the man lying beside her in her hospital bed.

Forget me. Forget our son. Forget your own well-being.

His words were like arrows, leaving her heart full of holes. *Does he really think that little of me? Does he really think I'd hurt our baby?*

"When in doubt, I play the trust card." He'd said

that to her at the cabin when they'd discussed their collective fears until the wee hours. Those words now echoed loudly in her head.

"Of course you do," she said, her tone dripping with sarcasm.

****

The road into the small Austin suburb where Sunny grew up was virtually deserted, the bulk of holiday travelers surely settled at their destinations. Mathew knew he was at a disadvantage in his pursuit. This was Sunny's old stomping ground, and fate was doing little to help him locate his wife. He'd driven through the town twice but the vintage Ford Mustang was nowhere to be found. Huck promised to call if she returned home. He checked his cell phone again. No calls. No messages.

Where the hell is she? Surely she didn't drive all the way to Austin. Or did she? If finding Sunny in the quiet suburb was likened to the proverbial needle in the haystack, then driving into the state capital was completely out of the question. He turned down a side street, still fingering the buttons on the radio in search of something to listen to other than his guilt, banging like a bass drum in his head. He was met with a rash of sad breakup songs. The men of Player, begging Baby to come back, followed by Peter Cetera's desperate plea— convinced that if she left him, she'd take away the biggest part. *All right, all right...I get it.* A faint hint of a smile crossed his lips. The relationship he'd shared with the radio over the years had become almost clinical. Time and again, it provided the lyrical medicine he needed to get his mind clear and thoughts back on track. Mathew softly hummed along, nervously tapping his fingers on the steering wheel in time with the music as he glanced up and down alleyways and in and out of parking lots.

Please, Sunny...please come home. I'll do anything.

****

LP,

Happy Thanksgiving. I have to say I've been happier. Daddy and I are here with your grandfather for the holiday. Uncle Leo and Barbara flew to Seattle to spend time with Nora and her family. This is the first official holiday that your father and I have spent together as husband and wife.

Sunny stopped writing and stared at her last sentence. *Our first holiday. We'll forever remember this day of thanks for hurtful words and hurt feelings.* With a sigh, she continued…

For whatever reason, it hasn't quite turned out the way I envisioned. I planned a surprise for your father, but it backfired. And now I find myself sitting in the parking lot of my old high school, listening to the radio and writing these thoughts to you. But you were there so I'm not telling you anything you don't already know. I'm sure you could hear Daddy shouting. It doesn't matter now. I sat in the stands, staring at the football field for a while, and felt nothing, except a numbness inside. Who was that man? Did you recognize him? I surely didn't. And by the look in his eye, he certainly has no idea who I am. I never thought I'd confront these words, but I'm writing them now and I wish they weren't true. Your father doesn't trust me. All the talk of love and trust is nothing more than talk. He doesn't know me, and I guess I don't really know him. How can we be this happily-ever-after if he thinks I would put you in danger? Doesn't he know that this family we've created is the most important thing in my life? The shouting I can live with. The harsh words and tone? I'm a big girl. But the lack of trust? Bottom line: No trust? No hope.

She paused again, rereading the lines before her. No trust? No hope? Chewing on the end of her pen, she mulled over the final thoughts on the page. Strong words. Unforgiving. And she knew in her heart of hearts, untrue. Replacing the cap on her pen, she dropped it in her purse. The page of her journal was ripped clean from the binding, wadded up in a tight ball, and stuffed inside the glove compartment. She checked the rear-view mirror. Red, puffy eyes gazed back, confirming feelings of disappointment and hurt.

She closed her eyes and leaned back against the headrest. Hall and Oates sang softly on the radio and suddenly Sunny felt warm. Quickly, she unbuttoned her coat and cracked the window, bringing the cool autumn breeze inside. She checked her watch. Still a few hours until her father's turkey would find its way to the large table in the dining room. As much as she wanted to make Mathew sweat it out, she didn't want to leave her father hanging—a holiday casualty left to do all the work by himself. She placed her hand on the gear shift and eyed the mirror once more. Just as she was beginning to back up, she felt it. As if a butterfly whispered inside her...

The gear shift returned to Park, and Sunny placed her hands on her belly. She sat completely still for a moment, focusing with breathless concentration. Seconds passed, then she felt it again. *Oh, my God!* She was overcome with opposing emotions of joy and sorrow. Tears poured from her eyes as the first movements of the baby inside her were felt…and the pain in knowing that the man she loved above everything wasn't there to share the milestone.

****

Dad's Advice: Crawling is a skill you'll need long after babyhood.

Well, it looks like I have screwed up what might have been a beautiful Thanksgiving holiday. Your mom and I drove up yesterday to spend a couple of days with your grandfather. This is the first time Mommy and I have spent a real holiday together since our wedding. And I've ruined it. I viciously attacked your mom with an onslaught of lethal verbiage that, at the moment, I can't even recall the majority of. I was an absolute asshole. Your mom took off and frankly, who can blame her? I drove all over looking for her, but never found her. Your grandfather told me that would happen, but for whatever reason, I can't seem to listen. So now I'm sitting in Grandpa's living room in front of a nice fire, trying to get my head right.

What the hell was I thinking? I have never been so out of line in my life. And your beautiful mother has paid the price. I didn't even give her a chance to explain. I just ran over her like a Mack truck. I've never done that before. Except for some minor disagreements, we've never fought. I guess technically I can't even call it a fight. It can only be deemed as such if both parties contribute equally. I certainly didn't allow her to do that.

What am I going to say to her? How can I make her understand how truly sorry I am and how horrible I feel? I was operating purely out of love for her and for you, and I came across as anything but loving. I bet I know exactly what's going through her mind right now. The trust card. I've just made a liar of myself and I'm praying that I'll be able to find the words to show her that trust wasn't really the issue. I'm afraid. I am afraid of losing your mom. It's a battle I've fought from the moment I fell in love with her. There's a part of me that lives in fear of losing the best thing that's ever happened to me. We even talked about it at the cabin. I hated lying to her, but sometimes a lie is necessary if it protects someone you love. Do I suffer from irrational fear? I guess I do. I didn't want to tell your mom that because she worries about you. And worrying about me is the last thing she needs right now. So, I held my tongue, reassuring her that I'm not waiting for that good old shoe to fall. Loving your mom should be the most freeing feeling in the world. And it is—to a point.

God, if anything happens to her while she's out there somewhere, I don't know what I'll do.

He stopped writing, allowing his gaze to pass over the paper before him. Every sentence spoke the truth and made him wonder. *Is it possible to love too much? Too deeply? Love isn't love when it becomes debilitating, is it?*

He tore the page from the notepad and walked to the fireplace. Staring into the flames, he ripped the letter into small pieces and tossed it inside. Within seconds, the tiny yellow scraps of paper were consumed, drifting weightlessly up inside the flue like feathers in the wind. Hearing a noise behind him, he turned to see Huck. He stood just inside the doorway, holding Mathew's jacket out in front of him.

"Are we going somewhere?" Mathew asked.

"No, but I thought you might need this." He tossed the jacket to his son-in-law.

"Why?"

"The cold front just blew in."

"She's back?" Mathew's voice was filled with relief.

"She just pulled up."

"Thanks for letting me know."

"Don't start thanking me just yet."

****

Mathew stood outside the sliding glass doors on the patio. This was his litmus test. The patio was visible from almost every room in the house, and there was no way Sunny could make it upstairs without seeing him. From the corner of his eye, he caught Huck's silhouette inside the kitchen. Huck looked up at that exact moment and flashed him the thumbs-up sign just before flipping the blinds closed. *Either she'll come out here, ready to talk, or I'm in for the quietest Thanksgiving holiday of my life.*

****

"I'm back." Sunny stuck her head in the kitchen.

"Are you okay?" Huck stopped stirring and gave her the once over.

"I don't know." She looked at him with hollow eyes.

"Well, I think someone is waiting for you outside on the patio."

"I know. I saw him. But I really don't want to get into this right now. I'm tired and I want to lie down for a while. If you can give me twenty minutes for a power nap, I promise I'll come back down and help you finish up."

"Other than this dressing, everything is done. Can I get you anything?"

"No," she said, running a hand through her windblown hair.

"I'll call you when the turkey is on the table then. How does that sound?"

"That'll be fine." Sunny turned to leave but spun back around. "Hey, Pop?"

"Yes?"

"Thanks for understanding."

"I understand all too well. I've been right there myself. A wise man once said, 'This too shall pass.' You'll see. Everything will be fine, like it never even happened."

"I'll see you in a bit." She blew a kiss to him.

"Wait. Before you go, I just have to ask. How did it look? Still pristine as ever?"

"How did what look?" Sunny asked.

"The old Spartan football field."

Sunny lowered her head, shaking it back and forth as she looked down at her feet. When she caught her father's eye again, she couldn't help but grin.

"You're something, you know that?"

"So I've been told." He smiled back.

****

Sunny stood directly under the oversized shower head, allowing the water to wash over her. She'd taken her time getting upstairs and undressed, certain that Mathew would be in quick pursuit. She'd noted his performance on the patio from her bedroom window. The sorrowful way he stood, shoulders slumped and his hands tucked in his pockets, fully aware of his bad behavior and ready to make amends. Eyes on the bathroom door, she fully expected him to slip in and join her—which would make staying mad at him a near impossibility. She remembered the shower they took together at the cabin, and the playful look in his eyes. Mathew could melt her with just one look—and he knew it. They both knew it. But his signature playful expression had turned cold and steely in the predawn hours…and it was an image she couldn't shake.

Sunny stepped from the shower, dripping water across the floor, as she located a fresh towel. She wrapped it snugly around her, tiptoed to the door, and listened. *Mathew is sitting on the bed waiting for me, I just know it.* She rested a trembling hand on the doorknob. *Please, God, no more shouting. I cannot do the shouting. I know I said I'm a big girl, but not today.*

She swallowed her fear and opened the door. The bedroom was empty, exactly as she'd left it. Except for one thing. A small white envelope rested against her pillow. Her bare feet padded softly across the wood floor, and she dried her hand once more before reaching for the envelope. She slipped back over to the window, pulling the sheers back before peeking down on the patio. No Mathew. Returning to the bed, she dropped the towel to the floor and pulled the sheets back. The cold bedding against her slightly damp body chilled her. With a shaky hand, she pulled a note from inside.

Sunny,

Your father told me you'd returned, and I waited for you on the patio. I thought that maybe you'd be ready to talk about what happened this morning. I know you're probably exhausted and you should definitely rest. I'm so thankful that you are home and safe. I promise not to bother you, but I hope that at some point today, you'll allow me to explain myself.

    M.

Trying to gauge his exact tone, she read the note a second time. She focused on the single initial. It just sat there all alone on the page. No *love* or *I love you* in front of it. Everything was summed up right there—in his closing.

****

All of her father's culinary diligence prevented her from falling into a deep sleep, as the tempting scents of Thanksgiving dinner found her nose. Now fully dressed and ready to go downstairs, she applied lip gloss with an unsteady hand, her anxiety at its zenith. With each step she whispered affirmations, anticipating the moment her eyes met Mathew's. *No matter what happens, I will not ruin my father's holiday. He's worked too hard for this.* At the bottom of the staircase, she made a detour to the large mirror in the entry where she practiced a smile. *Not very convincing but it'll have to do.*

She continued to the dining room, still practicing her smile. The first to arrive, she inspected the elegantly set table. Her mother's favorite china looked as beautiful as ever. Two large bouquets of fresh mums, in a colorful array of autumnal hues, graced the center of the table. Several antique candlesticks held slender, flickering tapers and cast a warm glow around the room.

"Didn't your old man do a bang-up job on the table?" Huck entered the dining room, dressed in clean blue jeans, a starched white button-down shirt, and cowboy boots. "I clean up pretty good too."

130

"Pop, it looks beautiful, and you look beautiful too." She pressed her lips to his cheek.

"Four little letters—HGTV. You can learn a lot from those shows."

"Where's Mathew?"

"Well, I'm afraid it will just be the two of us."

"Mathew's not coming?"

"No, I don't believe so."

"He's not eating Thanksgiving dinner with us?"

"No, baby girl. It's just you and me. Just like old times."

"What the hell's going on?"

Huck sighed. "Mathew asked to be excused. What was I going to say? No? He's a grown-ass man."

"Where is he?"

"He left."

"And you just let him leave?" Sunny raised her voice.

"Yes, Sunny, I let him leave. Just like I let *you* leave."

Huck's eyes narrowed, forcing Sunny to look away. Her father excelled at many things—and twisting a situation around for her personal re-examination was no exception. Head down, she studied her feet, noting a chip in the polish on her left big toe. Mathew had actually painted her toes a few nights before…and had done a surprisingly good job.

Mathew is good at just about everything. He's also human.

Sunny raised her head and met her father's gaze with glassy eyes. "I know this was not how you envisioned spending your holiday."

"No, I have to admit it wasn't. But like I told you earlier, everything's going to work out. It always does."

Chapter Seventeen

Sunny stared out the kitchen window. Huck's dinner was just as she predicted: perfectly delicious. Looking around the kitchen, in classic Huck fashion, he'd left very little to clean up. Carefully, she rinsed each plate before storing it inside the dishwasher, keeping her eyes focused on the back patio. She looked at her watch, her chest tightening with the reality that sunset was just minutes away.

Thanksgiving is about family. One hundred percent. How can you celebrate when half of your family—your most important half—is missing? My first Thanksgiving as a married woman, expecting my first child, and I'm flying solo. What is wrong with this picture?

With chores complete, she joined her father in the living room. Huck had kicked off his boots and lay sprawled out on the sofa, one hand tucked into the waistband of his Wranglers. Sunny sank into a leather armchair, again eyeing her watch.

"I'm really starting to get worried. Where the heck could he have gone?" she said.

"He'll be back," Huck said, his eyes on the television.

"Why is he punishing me again? Didn't he get enough of that this morning?"

"He's not punishing you. He's punishing himself."

She looked at her father with confusion. "And just how do you figure that?"

"If Mathew could be anywhere in the world right now, where do you think he'd be?"

"With me?" she asked.

"Bingo. By staying away from the person he longs to be with most, he punishes himself. Trust me, I know what I'm talking about. It's the exact opposite reason that you left today."

"What's that supposed to mean?"

"You didn't leave to punish yourself. You left to punish him. If you wanted to punish yourself, you'd have stayed right here in the thick of it."

Sunny had to smile, thankful for her father and all his wisdom.

"You know, it makes me look bad when I have to admit you know what you're talking about." She bit back a grin.

Huck laughed. "I won't tell if you won't."

"But it's dark, and he doesn't have a flashlight or anything."

"Sunny, he's fine. He'll come home when he's good and ready. You did, didn't you?"

"Yes…" She sighed heavily.

Huck clapped his hands together. "Now, according to my watch, I believe it's time we set up for our yearly Gin Rummy face-off. That is, if you still feel like playing?"

Of course I don't feel like playing cards. I just want to go upstairs, pull the covers over my head, and forget this day ever happened.

"Sure." Sunny nodded with slight reluctance.

"That's my girl. I'll be right back" He touched her

cheek lightly before exiting the living room.

Kneeling beside the coffee table, Sunny cleared away a stack of magazines and literature. From the time she was just a small girl, she and her father enjoyed their favorite board games and hands of Gin each Thanksgiving. With his help, she'd become a whiz and could beat just about anyone.

Huck returned with a deck of cards in one hand and a fresh drink in the other.

"Do you want anything before we start? Some water or fruit juice?"

"No, I'm fine. I'll get something in a little bit." She took the cards and began shuffling, as skilled as a Vegas dealer. Huck settled in on the sofa and pulled his glasses from his shirt pocket.

"Would you slide my cards this way?" he asked.

"Here you go…" She pushed a stack of eleven cards across the table to her father.

"Now, I've forgotten since the last time we played. Who's up?"

"I'm not sure."

"Well, it doesn't matter because I'll be carving my win in the annals of history this year." He fanned his cards out with a competitive grin.

Sunny paused, her chest suddenly tight. *Carving? The knife! My knife. I must have dropped it somewhere on my way back.*

"Crap! I think I may have lost my knife."

"What knife?"

"My knife. The Swiss Army knife you gave me."

"What on earth were you doing with it?"

"I was going to carve our initials on my tree this morning."

"Are you sure you took it with you? Maybe you left it here."

"No, I definitely had it with me this morning."

"It's right here…"

Sunny turned her head sharply at the sound of Mathew's voice. He stood in the doorway. His cheeks were bright red and the wind had done a number on his hair. By the expression on his face, Sunny recognized her father's dead-on assessment. The signs of punishment were plain. She watched as Mathew fished inside one pocket of his jeans for a moment, then pulled the bright silver knife out into view. His gaze met hers, and now Sunny was caught—trapped in his stare. His once playful eyes now conveyed only sorrow and regret. Everything around them seemed to stop as she looked up at him in silence from the living room floor. She looked away, feeling her heart pulled in opposing directions.

"Mystery solved," Huck commented, taking his drink and quietly slipping out of the room.

Sunny watched her father exit then pushed herself up with the aid of the coffee table, eager to follow suit.

"Sunny, wait—" Mathew reached out for her hand.

"Wait? Wait for what? So you can tell me how sorry you are? How wrong you were? How you can't believe what you did, and that you swear it'll never happen again?"

"Could we please take this conversation somewhere else? Please?" he asked, trying his best to stay collected.

"Oh, so now suddenly you've found some manners, is that it? Asking please and playing nice? Wrong. Try again."

Mathew remained silent.

"Hurts, doesn't it?" Her voice cracked as she folded her arms across her chest.

Mathew lowered his head, looking down at the floor. A full minute passed before he glanced up.

"It certainly does," he said, barely a whisper.

They stood staring at one another, waiting. Sunny's heart continued beating rapidly, and she fought to hold back the tears.

Mathew took a step toward her, lightly touching her shoulder. "I want to make this right. No matter how long it takes. And I want to do it on your terms." He looked into her eyes without blinking.

The truth in his expression caused the knot in Sunny's throat to expand. His eyes didn't lie. Releasing a heavy sigh, she nodded, then turned and walked toward the dining room. Mathew followed with hands tucked inside his pockets. For a brief moment, Sunny caught her reflection in the large mirror for the second time that day. Unlike Mathew's, her eyes told another story.

She opened the doors leading to the patio and stepped outside. A bitter wind met her face, and she could see her breath in the chilly November air. With a shiver, she pulled her thin cardigan around her. A heartbeat later, Sunny felt Mathew's hands and the warmth of his jacket against her. His hands rested on her shoulders for several moments, giving her a loving squeeze. She turned to face him. In the pale light that fell on the patio from inside the house, she again noted that same honest look on his face.

"Mathew, let me go back inside and get my coat." She started to pull his jacket off.

"I'll be okay." His hands hid back inside his pockets.

"It's forty degrees."

"I'm fine."

"Well, you can't stand out here like that. You'll freeze." She turned away from him and eyed the workshop in the distance. Without a word, she silently led the way to the vast metal building. The wind encircled them, blowing Sunny's hair into her eyes and mouth. She had no idea what she was going to say once they were safely out of earshot from her father, but she wasn't planning to hold back.

The shop was pitch black. Sunny felt along the wall for the light switch with one hand while brushing unruly strands of hair out of her face with the other.

"You know..." He stepped in behind her and closed the door. "I'm not quite sure what the protocol is for this."

"For what?"

"For this..." He pointed back and forth between the two of them. "This is a milestone in our marriage, you know. Our first real fight. I'm pretty sure I screwed up the fight part, so I want to make sure I get the apology right." He spoke slowly, and she detected no cynicism in his voice.

"Not exactly a milestone I care to remember." Sunny folded her arms across her chest.

"I talked to Russell."

"I see."

"He told me everything."

"Did he?"

"Yes. He told me he drove you down to your secret spot. He found your knife in the truck and was bringing it back to you when he found me alone instead."

Sunny paused, unsure what to say. "Where have you been since two o'clock?"

He pointed over her shoulder. "Right there. I sat in your father's office all day, watching football and trying to find the right words. Sorry just won't cover it."

"Oh, Mathew…" She reached out for his hand.

"Do you remember the conversation we had at the ranch? The conversation about living a charmed life?"

She nodded.

"You asked me if I ever worry that my life is too good, remember?"

"Yes."

"Do you remember what I said?"

"You said you felt blessed and that you didn't want to live your life waiting for the other shoe to fall."

"Well, I lied. Not about being blessed, because I am blessed more than a man has a right to be. But about that other shoe. I lied about the shoe."

"I don't understand." Her brows drew together, head shaking.

"There's a card that trumps the Trust Card every time. It's the Fear Card. And today, I played it. I not only played it, I let it play me. When I read your note this morning and saw the map, all reasonable thoughts left my mind. I was so afraid of something happening to you that I couldn't think straight. I had these pictures in my mind—awful pictures of finding you out there…" His voice trailed off as his eyes connected with hers. "I've never needed anything or anyone the way I need you. And as beautiful as that is, it has also created one of the greatest obstacles in my life." He studied her eyes, continuing to hold her hand.

"I don't understand what you mean." She searched his face for the true meaning behind his words.

"I don't know how to let you run, giving you the freedoms you need and deserve, when all I want to do is pull back on the reins."

Sunny watched his thumb draw tiny circles on her hand. She took a much-needed breath, suddenly aware that she'd barely breathed as he spoke.

"I want you to understand something. I mean, really understand and hear what I'm saying." He now held both of her hands in his. "I trust you. I know without a doubt that you love me and would never do anything to hurt me. Or our baby. The trust issue is not about you, Sunny. It's about me. I have to learn to trust myself. To not give over to a very real fear I have. Losing you scares me more than anything in this world. Without you, there'd be no me. I was by myself for so long, Sunny, without a soul to cling to. And now that I finally have a real family, I..."

The emotion of his words wrapped warmly around her. Tears returned and rolled down her cheeks in silent streaks. He softly brushed them away. She'd never seen him look more vulnerable. This was the first time that Mathew had ever expressed fear. Mathew—a man who seemed to fear nothing—was afraid. It wasn't an excuse or an easy out.

He continued. "I don't know what else to say, other than I have never been more ashamed of myself. I am truly, truly sorry. I ruined everything. Not just our first holiday, but your father's too. And after he worked so hard to make this day special for all of us. I was completely out of line this morning. The things I said to you…well, I can't even begin to imagine how that must have made you feel. If it hurts this much to be the one to say those things, then I can't even fathom how you felt being on the receiving end."

Sunny gazed at him, and another minute of silence passed between them.

"I'm sorry I ran away. I don't know why I do it, but it's what I do. It's what I've always done. You waited for me on the patio and I was more concerned with hurting you than making this right. You waited, and I just left you there. I was wrong. That's not the way I want our marriage to be." She took another deep breath. "I don't want it to be that way with us. I don't ever want it to be like that."

"You ran because I left you no other choice. It's not like I was prepared to listen to reason. I tried to force your hand, and you folded. You have no blame for this. No blame whatsoever."

"No, that's not right. There are two people in this union. Two people."

"You mean three." He placed his hand on her belly again with a sweet smile.

She placed her hand on top of his as her mind traveled back to the Spartan parking lot. "I felt it. Him. I felt him. For the first time."

"You did?" Mathew's eyes widened with excitement.

"I wanted you to be with me when it happened. If I hadn't left…"

"Sunny, now there's no guarantee that we would have been together when it happened. You have to know that." He gave her a look.

"I know, but I just hoped." She paused.

"Well, what did it feel like? Tell me everything."

"It was exactly like I thought it would be, and at the same time, completely different."

"In what way?"

"Well, I did feel this fluttering, just like we've read about in our books. But the way it made me feel…well, that just can't be put into a book." She looked down at her pregnant form.

"I promise I will make this day up to you."

"Oh, I know you will. I made a list." She poked his midsection.

"A short list or a long one?" He flashed a grin.

"Short. Just one item. But it could take you all night."

"You can't be letting me off this easy."

"Yes, I can." She leaned forward and kissed him lightly. "And I think you've punished yourself enough. I know that you were upset because you were afraid. And I understand that. So it didn't come out exactly as 'loving concern.' I have said some pretty nasty things to you and you always come back with an olive branch in one hand and your heart in the other. We're not perfect. We are blessed to have something as close to perfect as two people can share. I wake up next to you day after day smiling—completely in awe of how happy I am. But we're gonna have those days when we don't like each other very much. And that's okay. As long as we're back to loving each other when our heads hit the pillow."

"I'm crazy about you, you know that?" His fingers found their favorite hiding place in the silky layers of her hair.

"I've had my suspicions for a while now." She

couldn't help but smile, now back to that place of safest love.

****

Dad's Advice: Face Your Fears.

There are going to be times in your life when you make mistakes. Some will be insignificant. Others will be monumental. Whether big or small, major or minor, if you are at fault, step up and take your licks. It's not enough to just say you're sorry. Over time, the word loses its meaning. Anyone can apologize. But it takes maturity to admit the nature of your wrongdoings—to look inside and find the motivation behind your errors. Were you guided by greed, lust, envy, pride, or any of the other deadly sins? From my experience, I've found that all of the deadly sins can be traced back to one thing: fear. Think about it. Greed is the fear of never having enough. Lust is the fear of going without. Envy is the fear of others having more. Pride is the fear of admitting your shortcomings. Gluttony is the fear of hunger. Wrath is the fear of not being in total control. Sloth is the fear of hard work. Fear can eat you up and consume your soul. Fear can make you do things that you know in your heart are wrong. Fear can make you hurt the ones that matter the most. Can you exist in life without fear? Of course not. But you can learn to recognize it and work to control it instead of letting it control you. And when it's time to apologize, let the words come from your heart, not your head. From the most private place inside you.

We're home, but Leo is still in Seattle with Nora and Jake and won't be back for a few days. Your mother is asleep, all curled up under her favorite plaid blanket. I've been sitting here trying to finish another of

Zane Grey's best, but I can't keep my eyes off her. She is so beautiful when she sleeps. I have a feeling that when I watch you sleep, it will be the same way.

With the exception of one incident, this was the best holiday I've ever had. Being with your mom and your grandfather was wonderful. I love watching them together. They remind me of an old Vaudeville comedy team at times. Their quips back and forth are priceless. Your grandfather, as I've told you many times before, is quite a character. I am very blessed to have him as my father-in-law. He knows just when to give advice, and when to hold his tongue. He's also a very shrewd Monopoly player, so watch out for that. I know how much it means to your mom to spend time with him. They are very close. We invited him to spend Christmas with us and he accepted. So, we'll all be together (Leo and Ivy too) next month. This will be our first family Christmas. And I've already sent word to Santa about what a good boy you are. So maybe we'll find a few things under the tree for you this year!

Well, I'm busted. Your mom just opened her eyes and caught me looking. It's like she has radar or something. I tried to throw her off with my best innocent look, but she knows better. Now that she's awake, I better close.

I'm so thankful to be your father!

Love,

Daddy

Chapter Eighteen

Society functions, even for a good cause, were not Sunny's cup of tea. Dressing up and stepping out with her gorgeous husband—yes. But listening to the same staid conversations again and again—no. She'd planned out the entire evening, and hopefully, everything would go accordingly. Pregnant women tire easily, and she intended to put this excuse to the test early on. *Shake a few hands, take a few turns around the dance floor, slip out the side door, and we're back home before the late news.*

The valet line was long, as most of the A-listers of the Houston society scene waited to enter one of the biggest charity balls of the year. The front columns of The Four Seasons Hotel were alive and sparkling with tiny white lights. Everything looked fresh and festive, though the weather was more reminiscent of a late-season beach vacation and not the Christmas holiday.

They inched slowly along until they finally reached the main doors of the hotel. Mathew opened his wife's door and guided her through the cluster of the city's elite. It seemed like forever before they made it to the entrance of the ballroom. Well-wishers swirled around them—all wanting to catch a glimpse of Mathew Ellis's bride and the baby on board. Sunny smiled and nodded with each step, secretly cursing her choice of footwear for the evening. *I should've listened to Leo.* She shifted her weight from one foot to the other. *It's gonna be a long night.*

Inside the doors of the ballroom, they stopped and scanned in search of an open table. Mathew motioned and led the way through the elegantly clad crowd with his fingers laced securely in hers. Sunny kept her eyes focused on the back of her husband's head, but hyper-aware of the ripple that traveled among the masses, as every head turned and watched them. Mathew pulled out a chair at an unoccupied table and waited for her to get settled.

"All right?" he asked.

"Fine."

"Something to drink?"

"I'll have an extra dry martini. Make it a double."

"That bad?"

"I'm afraid so—between these shoes and the fact that everyone here is staring." She flashed a fake grin his way.

"Will you be all right without me for two minutes?"

"I was a Girl Scout. I'm prepared for anything." She gave him a confident salute.

"Send up a smoke signal if you need me." He patted her arm before turning toward the nearest bar.

Sunny watched as the most handsome man in the room walked away from her, stopping every few steps to shake more hands. *That's it! I guess I'm being a little vain. It's not me they're looking at. It's Mathew.* She watched until his body disappeared, swallowed up in a black hole of tuxedoed gentlemen. Though she'd attended several events with Mathew and a few NASA events on her own, she still felt somewhat out of her element–and more so now, with her growing belly. Her gaze traveled around the room, and she counted no less than thirteen couples she could swear were exact replicas of Barbie and Ken. *So, these are the beautiful people. I bet their plastic surgeons are laughing all the way to the bank.* She jumped slightly when she felt a hand on her bare shoulder.

"Sunny?"

"Maggie!" She stood and greeted the wife of Mathew's business associate and dear friend, Archer Martin, with a hug.

"I thought that was you. You look fabulous, my dear. Absolutely radiant."

"Well, thank you very much. And you look stunning."

"Did you lose Mathew to the bar?"

"I did. But he assured me it would just be momentarily. I assume that Archer is doing the same?"

"Indeed, he is."

Sunny motioned toward the table. "Join us?

"We'd love to join you. Thank you."

Sunny retook her seat, smiling warmly at Maggie. Though they'd been together only a couple of times— and both very brief—she'd instantly felt a connection with her. She was a very attractive woman in her late sixties. Smart. Funny. No façade. She was the type of woman that when in her company, it was as if you were visiting with your own mother—attentive and caring and, above all, genuine.

"How are your granddaughter's wedding plans coming along?" Sunny inquired.

"I think most of the heavy lifting is done."

"They're getting married around Valentine's Day,

if I remember correctly?"

"You have an excellent memory."

"What could be more romantic than that?"

"Well, Mathew and Archer smuggling us out of here and taking us dancing somewhere dark and quiet, for starters."

"I take it you're not a fan of these events?"

"I adore the cause but despise the event. I'm all for setting up a drive-thru for these little shindigs. Just pull up, stick your check out the window, and move on. But then, how would most of these poor souls have a chance to show off their body work?"

"Excuse me, ladies, but are these seats taken?" Archer Martin spoke from behind Maggie before placing a glass of champagne on the table in front of his wife.

"Thank you, dear," Maggie said.

"Sunny! My goodness! You get more beautiful every time I see you." Archer extended his hand.

"Thank you. It's so good to see you." Sunny shook hands with him.

"Mathew's on the way with our drinks. I was ahead of him in line at the bar, so I thought I'd take care of you ladies first." He placed a martini glass full of fruit juice in front of Sunny before settling in beside his wife.

"That was very thoughtful, thank you." Sunny nodded at him as she raised her glass.

Archer's gaze swept the room. "This is quite a turnout this year. Every year, more and more."

"The plastic surgeons in this town are bound to run out of silicone, eventually." Maggie tapped her glass against Sunny's.

"Maggie Martin! Behave yourself," Archer scolded with a grin.

"Dear, it's okay. Sunny's on my team."

"So, you're ready for the check too?" Archer asked.

"I'm fine for the moment, but my feet are already crying foul," Sunny whispered, pointing toward the floor.

"I hope you'll save at least one dance for me before you go. I must dance with the most beautiful woman—under sixty—in the room." He gave his wife a sly look and a peck on the cheek.

"Your drink, Guv'ner." Mathew made it back to the table, holding out a highball glass to Archer.

"Thank you, kind sir."

"I see it didn't take you ladies long to find each other." Mathew bent down and kissed Maggie's cheek. "You look lovely this evening, Mrs. Martin."

"Thank you very much, Mr. Ellis. And you're as handsome as ever."

"Eh, I clean up okay." He winked at Sunny.

The two couples spent the next hour sharing the happy news of approaching nuptials and newborn babies. Sunny watched the shine in her husband's eyes grow as he described every movement of Baby Boy Ellis to date. He'd always dazzled her with his ability to tell great stories, but there was something different when he talked about their baby. His eyes and voice had a softness about them. And his hands—the expression in them was gentle and loving. She could still see the way he held the ultrasound pictures when they'd stopped for lunch on the way to the ranch. And the more he spoke, sharing the details of the most special part of their lives, the more she could feel herself slipping away.

The lights in the ballroom dimmed, and the band started to play. And that's when she found herself unable to concentrate on the lively conversation around her. Quietly, she moved her chair closer to his, sliding her hand underneath the table and resting it comfortably on his thigh. Mathew locked eyes with her for a moment, then smiled, reading her thoughts with just a touch and a look.

"Would you two excuse us?" Mathew pulled Sunny's chair out and took her hand. Silently, they made their way to the crowded dance floor. He slipped his arm around her waist and pulled her close. Sunny closed her eyes, allowing her body to relax against his. It only took a moment in his arms and everything—the uncomfortable shoes, the sea of staring eyes—just disappeared. His arms could make it all go away, leaving nothing but the two of them alone. He rubbed her back with a tender touch, and she gripped his hand even tighter. Her head rested on his shoulder, and she softly hummed along as the band played an old Hoagy Carmichael song. In classic Mathew fashion, he tickled her ear with his own version of the lyrics, laced with innuendo and double entendre. She couldn't stop laughing, which caused her to lose count and step on his foot. They stopped dancing and their eyes connected.

He turned with a naughty smirk and led her off the dance floor. They made the obligatory stops en route back to the table. More introductions. More smiles and handshakes. Sunny was beginning to enjoy herself somewhat when Mathew stopped and turned around.

"Are you feeling all right?" he asked.

"I'm fine."

"Now don't be brave for my sake. You're not feeling well...*right*?" He gave her a wink.

"Oh! Yes! You're right. I'm not feeling very well. I think you should take your pregnant wife home."

"That's my girl." He squeezed her hand and they continued toward their table to say goodnight to Archer and Maggie.

"I need to make a detour to the ladies' room first. I'll meet you back at the table, we'll say our goodbyes, and then be on our way. Okay?"

"All right. But hurry." He kissed her hand before letting go of it.

She was somewhat surprised to find the ladies' restroom deserted. Sunny walked quickly to the last stall, unsure if she would make it in time. *Pregnant women live on the toilet.* She struggled a bit with her dress. The speaker above her head piped in serene Christmas music and she mentally went over her Santa To-Do list. She lost her train of thought when she heard loud, laughing voices enter the lounge area. Obviously, they'd just heard a great joke, or they'd had too much to drink. Or both.

"Is anyone in there?" a woman asked.

"No, I don't think so," another woman replied.

Sunny was just about to announce her presence when she heard her husband's name mentioned in their colorful conversation.

"Well, what did I tell you? Mathew Ellis goes down like the rest of them."

"I think this might be the real deal, though. Did you see the way they were dancing? The way he's been looking at her all night. I heard she's an engineer."

"No, honey, she's a scientist at NASA."

"A scientist? Are you sure? She doesn't exactly look the type."

Sunny bit down hard on her lip to suppress a giggle. She knew it was wrong to eavesdrop, but they weren't exactly trying to be quiet. And how often did one get to be the proverbial fly on the wall?

"She probably has something on him. Insider trading maybe? Tax evasion? I mean, it wouldn't be hard, in his line of work."

"Well, from what I can tell, it looks like an old-fashioned love story."

"And from what I can tell, it looks like old-fashioned entrapment."

"No, I don't think so."

"Do the math. They just got married and already she's as big as a house."

"She is not as big as a house, and you know it. She's a beautiful woman. You've got to admit they look incredible together."

"Yes, well, had I known that all it took was a uterus, I'd have gotten a dye job and hit the maternity boutiques years ago."

"Cassandra Christos had a uterus and he sure didn't run down the aisle for her, did he?"

"Good point. He certainly didn't."

"But when you have Mathew Ellis's money, I guess you can allow your bastard child to run around all over Europe without guilt."

"Just a monthly check to the finest Swiss boarding schools…"

The woman's voice trailed off and Sunny heard the

outer door close. She cautiously opened the stall door and peeked out. Slowly, she moved to the sink to wash her hands. Staring up at her reflection in the mirror, she shook her head in denial. Her heart was beating wildly, and she began to feel lightheaded. Carefully, she walked on shaky legs to the chaise in the lounge area. The pain in her heart shot like a rocket to her head, as the words repeatedly pounded inside her brain.

Cassandra Christos. Bastard child.

Chapter Nineteen

Mathew eyed his watch for the third time. *Where is she? Surely the line isn't that long. There are restrooms all over this hotel.*

"Listen, Maggie, could I trouble you for one minute?"

"You want me to go check on her?"

"Would you?" Mathew asked.

"Of course! I'll be right back."

Maggie stood and made her way across the ballroom to the outer alcove. She found Sunny lying down on the chaise just inside the ladies' room, her face pale and beads of sweat clinging to her forehead.

"Sunny? Are you okay?" She bent down, placing her hand lightly on Sunny's shoulder.

"Just give me a minute…I'll be okay."

"You stay right here. I'm going to get Mathew."

"No! Please—don't." She reached out for Maggie's hand.

"Let me get you some water then. You're probably dehydrated. I'll be right back." Maggie quickly walked back to the ballroom, running into Mathew just as she stepped inside the main doors.

"Did you find her?" he asked with concern.

"Oh, Mathew, I'm afraid she's sick. She's lying down in the lounge just inside the ladies' room. You go on. I'm going to get her something to drink." She touched his elbow and then continued toward the bar.

Mathew rushed to the ladies' room, not bothering to knock before he entered.

"Sunny?" He kneeled beside her. "Please tell me this is all part of your act."

"I'll be okay. I just felt faint."

"Let me call Dr. Sumner." He started to stand, but she grabbed his hand, pulling him back down beside her.

"Don't bother Dr. Sumner. I'll be fine. Just take me home."

In a short while, Maggie opened the car door as Archer and Mathew helped Sunny into the passenger seat. Mathew reclined the seat slightly, secured her seat belt around her, then gently closed the door.

"I can't thank you two enough." He turned back toward the Martins. "I'm sorry we have to cut our evening short."

"We're just sorry that Sunny's not feeling well. Please let us know if we can do anything for you. Anything at all." Maggie patted Mathew's hand.

"We really did enjoy our time with you. Let's get together real soon. Right after the holidays? That is, if you're not too deep in the wedding."

"We'll make time. I'll give you a call." Archer extended his hand, and the two men shook firmly.

"Good night." Mathew nodded as he opened his car door.

Once inside, he turned the radio to her favorite soft rock station before pulling away from the valet stand. Sunny remained silent with eyes closed, her body tense. *Careful what you wish for.* He reached for her hand and held it snugly in his.

"I'm so sorry this happened. I guess our little plan backfired."

"I'll be okay," she whispered.

"Are you hungry? I bet you're hungry. You only ate two bites."

"I'm a little hungry, I guess."

"What sounds good? You name the place. I'll take you anywhere you want to go."

"You know what sounds really good?"

"What?"

"Chez Ellis."

"Chez Ellis it is." He brought her hand up to his lips, kissing it tenderly.

They drove home in silence. Mathew switched the radio off for fear of compounding her headache. His mind searched for a viable reason to explain her near fainting spell. Ignoring her request, he called Dr. Sumner anyway, and was told it could be one or a combination of things. The call was short and reassuring, as the doctor stressed that such episodes rarely have ill effects on the mother or fetus. And since Sunny had only become lightheaded, an order for fluids and rest was given, along with Dr. Sumner's home number just in case they suffered a rough night.

The house was dark when they arrived, with Barbara and Leo braving the stores to complete the last of their holiday shopping. Carefully, Mathew helped Sunny upstairs to their bedroom, with Ivy following close behind. She kicked her shoes off as he unzipped her dress, holding her steady as she stepped out of it. He quickly retrieved her favorite maternity pajamas. With loving care, he secured each button.

"Well, this is a first. I'm buttoning you up inside

these. Isn't it usually the other way around?"

"The other way is better." She tried to smile.

"You get in bed and I'll bring up a tray for you." He tossed his tuxedo jacket on the chaise. "C'mon, Ivy. Come help me downstairs. Mommy is sick. Let's get something to make her feel better."

****

Sunny pulled the sheets back and crawled into bed, adjusting the mountain of pillows around her. Her head was still throbbing, but she'd refused Dr. Sumner's offer of any pain medication. Deep down, she knew her pain couldn't be cured with a pill. She needed one thing: the truth. Calm. Rational. Truth. No yelling. No accusations. No ghost of Thanksgiving past. She rested her head on her pillow and waited. *What do I say? Oh, babe, I had the tires rotated on the Suburban, and by the way, I meant to ask you. Did you have a child with another woman?* She pulled the sheets up over her shoulder, as the echoes of the ladies' room conversation filled her with an icy feeling until she drifted off.

Mathew returned with a tray full of her most recent cravings in hand. Sunny opened her eyes when she felt him sit down on the edge of their bed.

"Here, let me help you." He reached out and pulled her into an upright position, readjusting her pillows with loving care. "How's that? Okay?"

"Mathew, there's something I need to talk to you about."

"You need to eat first. Eat, then lights out. We can talk in the morning."

"This can't wait 'til the morning," she said in a firm tone.

"All right." He nodded warily.

Sunny took a deep breath, quietly reminding herself to remain composed. "I'm not exactly sure how to start."

"Just say it. Whatever it is, it will be okay. I promise."

"Two women came into the restroom while I was in there. They were very loud, very tipsy, and very animated in their conversation."

"Was this before or after you felt faint?"

"Before."

"Let me guess…they didn't know you were in there, right?"

"Right."

"And they were talking about us, right?"

"Yes. How did you know?"

"Because our names were on everyone's lips tonight. Surely you heard it too?"

"I tried to tune it out."

"So, what exactly did you overhear?"

"Well, they suspect that I used my uterus to trap you."

Mathew released a frustrated sigh. "Sunny, you and I both know that's not true. I don't know why, but some of the women in this town can be vicious and nasty. They loathe any sort of competition. Hell, you'd think we live in Dallas by the level of cattiness at these events. But I'd be willing to bet this isn't the first time you've encountered this level of jealousy. We're just gonna have to trade in this soft skin of yours for something a little more tough and resilient." He paused for a moment and offered a smile—one to which she didn't respond.

"Sunny, why are you letting this bother you?" He

shook his head, looking confused.

"That's not the part that bothered me. It's what they said after that." She looked down, twisting her wedding ring around on her finger.

"What did they say?"

A moment of silence passed before she brought her eyes up to meet his.

"They wondered why you didn't marry Cassandra Christos after she got pregnant."

Chapter Twenty

Sunny held her breath, eagerly anticipating his response. The seconds seemed like an eternity. *Why is he just sitting there? Why won't he look at me? Oh, God! No! It can't be true. Don't let it be true!* Thousands of emotions ran through her, and she knew his silence could only mean one thing.

"Mathew? Please say something." Her voice was barely a whisper, and she fought to control the flood of tears behind her eyes.

"Oh, Sunny…" He hugged her close, running his fingers through her hair.

"Please tell me it's not true." The first tears began their quiet descent down her cheeks.

"Of course, it's not true. It's not true." Gently, he rocked her in his arms, whispering these words over and over again. Relief washed over Sunny, and her body melted against his.

"But why would they say those things? I don't understand."

It was Mathew's turn to draw a deep breath. Slowly he exhaled and collected his thoughts. "Well, because when Cass and I finally called it quits, she was pregnant." He paused and looked straight into her eyes. "With someone else's baby. Not mine."

Sunny focused on the truth in his eyes, mixed with a tiny amount of pain. And with that pain came a new wave of fear and unanswered questions. Had he wanted a child with Cass? How deeply had she hurt him? She wanted to know everything, but only if he was ready. He'd shared some intimate details of past relationships with her, but very little about Cassandra Christos. *Some rooms remain dark for a reason.*

"I should have told you. But honestly, I didn't think it was that important." He looked down at his hands. "I'm sorry you had to find out the way you did."

"What happened?"

"It's a long story. Why don't you eat and then I'll tell you all about it in the morning, okay?"

"A long story…or a painful one?" she asked, one eyebrow cocked.

"Long and painful, but not for the reasons you might think. Now, enough talk of Cass. I want you to eat."

"Listen, Mathew, I'm so sorry."

"Why are you sorry?"

"A part of me doubted you." Her voice cracked.

"Hey." He smoothed her hair back away from her face. "It's okay."

"No, it's not okay."

"I'm the one who should be apologizing. I should have told you. It's not that I was trying to keep it from you, because I certainly have nothing to hide. Cass got pregnant by someone else. That was it." He spoke matter-of-factly, but Sunny guessed that somewhere inside him, there was still a place that ached. Her head told her to let it go until morning, but her heart…

"You must have been really hurt, huh?"

"The truth? I was relieved it wasn't mine." He stood, pulling his bow tie from around his neck.

"Relieved? You mean you didn't want a child with her?"

"I didn't want a child with anyone. Until now."

"But you must have been so upset that she was sleeping with someone else."

"Not really. We'd already called it quits by then."

"What?" Sunny was surprised. "Why?"

"We'd been unhappy for a while. We knew we didn't really love each other and agreed that it was time to move on. She'd been secretly seeing someone by that time, anyway. Only, it wasn't a secret to me. She'd been in love with one of her father's closest business associates for years. But he was twice her age, and her father would have never given his blessing. And having her father's blessing was everything. Cass wouldn't disappoint her father. Well, they'd only been going out for a short time when she got pregnant. And then her father got sick. Very sick. She didn't have the heart to tell him because she knew he'd be devastated. See, we were still operating in public as a couple at this point. We talked about it and decided that in time, we'd tell him the truth. But he continued to deteriorate. And to complicate matters, her man walked out on her when he found out about the baby. Said he had no intention of raising another family at his age. Said his kids were grown and he wasn't starting over."

"How awful." She shook her head disapprovingly.

"He denied the baby was even his. Said that I'd gotten her pregnant. It got pretty ugly."

"Oh, Mathew…" Sunny could not hide the shock in her voice. "Why didn't you just tell her father the truth? Surely, he would have understood?"

"He would have gone mushroom cloud to find out

that his business partner—a man he had a great amount of respect for—and his baby girl were slipping around behind his back. Not only that, he was overjoyed. It was the only slight improvement we saw in his health there at the end. He was so happy, believing that Cass and I were going to have a baby." Mathew looked away, and Sunny noticed his sadness. She allowed him a much-needed moment of silence before responding.

"So, let me make sure I understand. You let an old man die in peace?"

"Yes."

"Knowing that rumors would run rampant?"

"Yes."

"And you stood beside a woman, pretending that the child she carried was yours, all in the name of someone else's happiness?"

"That's pretty much it." He turned his honest eyes up to meet hers.

Sunny reached for his hands and held them tightly. Her eyes connected with his in a way they never had before. She thought she knew every part of him—every level of Mathew's inner being. And what had he done? Surprised her again with his selfless humanity and compassion.

"I have never been prouder of you than I am at this moment."

****

My Little Prince,

Has it really been a week since I've had a chance to sit down and write? The Christmas season is in full swing, and we've been so busy getting ready for the holiday. The last two weeks have been spent on the town–parties, parties, and more parties. We've enjoyed ourselves, but I'm ready for a break. Your grandfather will be driving down in a few days, and there's still so much to do. I've got a couple of gifts to wrap, and your father's up to his ears in end-of-year meetings. I feel like we've hardly seen each other lately, but once he gets home tonight, he's all mine. I finally came up with what I think will be the perfect gift for him. Leo begged me to tell him, but I'm keeping this one a secret. I just hope Daddy's business affairs are squared away until the New Year!

Looking at my daily planner, I can hardly believe that we've made it to the twenty-four-week mark. You are really growing. You've gained about half a pound this week. You're starting to fill out and look more like a newborn now. You weigh about a pound and a half, and if you were to make a surprise holiday appearance right now, you'd have an excellent chance of making it. But don't get any ideas. We're happy having you simmer the winter away in cozy darkness in there! Just think of Mommy as your own personal stocking. You're about as long as a ruler, and I know from your recent bout of tumbling that you enjoy stretching your little legs. Daddy has always had a hard time keeping his hands off my belly, but now it's nearly impossible. He's so anxious to feel you moving around in there. I've never seen him so excited or so happy. And seeing the happiness in his eyes is the greatest gift I could ever receive. I really don't need anything under the tree. Every day I spend with him is like Christmas!

I know I've said it before, but your father is truly an amazing man. I've never known anyone to be so attentive, so generous, and so caring. We were at a charity function recently, and I learned something new about him. Something that surprised me, but yet didn't surprise me. The strength of that man's character is immeasurable. I know that if everyone had a friend like your daddy—one true friend—the world would be a much better place. A world where the well-being and happiness of others comes first. The story of your father's loving kindness and acceptance of a dear friend renews the spirit of Christmas in me, reminding me of the very reason for the season: a tiny baby...a blessing to the world...given to everyone...to be that one true friend.

Merry Christmas, my angel,
Mommy

Chapter Twenty-One

As he approached the top of the stairs, Mathew glanced toward his favorite room, feeling a warm smile on his lips. *One more peek?* Even though he and Sunny had taken a quick look earlier that day, the impulse hit. He paused at their bedroom door for a moment before continuing down the hall to what would soon be his son's bedroom. The door was slightly ajar, but the room was dark. Slowly, he pushed the door open and hit the light switch. With a click, a soft white light filled what would surely become the happiest room in their home.

The walls were alive with a host of soothing colors—rich cream, buttery yellow, watery blues, and muted greens. Images of stars surrounded him, suspended in a cheerful sky. And a Little Prince, perched proudly atop a distant planet, looked down upon him with quiet confidence. He'd stepped inside the pages of a children's book, as the drawings of St. Exupery's famed work was brought to life, dancing playfully around the perimeter of their baby boy's room. The floor was littered with paint cans and brushes, all shapes and sizes, resting atop a splattered drop cloth. The artist he'd commissioned to create this magical world for his son had far exceeded his expectations. Every stroke was perfect, every detail precise. His gaze traveled around the room. Each wall held a different yet cherished quote from the celebrated story. The words of a young hero. The wisdom of an aged soul. In the far corner of the room, he eyed the new crib. His laughter couldn't be contained as he recalled the comedy of errors that occurred the night he and Leo assembled it...

"It won't fit, Matty." Leo shook his head.

"It's gotta fit. Let's try turning it this way..." Mathew motioned with his hands.

"I'm telling you this won't work. We've turned it every which but loose."

"Damn!" Mathew wiped the sweat from his brow. "How is it that you can slide a king-size bed through any door, but a baby crib won't fit?"

"Well, I guess we've learned a very valuable bit of information."

"Yeah? What's that?" He gave Leo an exasperated look.

"Read the directions first." Leo held out the assembly manual, pointing to a specific page. Mathew took the booklet from him and read the line aloud.

"Note: Assemble crib in room where crib will remain. Crib dimensions are greater than standard door widths." Mathew looked up at Leo, dumbfounded.

"Back to work." Leo rolled his eyes and handed Mathew a screwdriver.

Carefully, Mathew navigated around the collection of the artist's tools to the crib. It was the only piece of furniture they'd purchased. The only piece Sunny knew about, anyway. Santa would be delivering the remaining goodies for them soon. His goal was to have the nursery finished in time for Huck's arrival—and as an extra holiday surprise for his wife. Looking down into the crib, he imagined the tiny body that would rest peacefully inside. Leaning over, he gently rubbed his hand back and forth across the soft white sheet, his heart thumping with anticipation. The feelings inside him were unlike anything he'd experienced. He'd never wanted a child—never thought of raising a child. He remembered the night Cass had informed him of her pregnancy—and the ice-cold chill that ran through him. The words 'I'm pregnant' had barely left her mouth, and already he'd felt like running. Of course, he would never allow his own flesh and blood to grow up fatherless, as he had. But Cass...Cass was a different story. She was everything that a man could want— beautiful, kind, smart, and funny. And no matter how hard he'd tried, he just didn't love her. They'd been the closest of friends and shared quiet times in each other's beds. But it hadn't been enough. The thought of being forever bound to a woman who was anything less than his soulmate scared him. He didn't want to play house.

Now, looking around his son's room, he couldn't imagine being anywhere than exactly where he stood. And it was all because of one person. *If you love a flower that lives on a star, it is sweet to look up at the night sky.* He read the words above his head. One amazing woman had changed everything—changed him. It was as if he was The Little Prince and Sunny, his precious flower. His rose. And he was still learning to hold on loosely without letting go. Taking care not to crush her velvety petals. Close enough to linger in her intoxicating fragrance, but with enough distance to allow the world to admire her grace and beauty. The last words Cass's father had spoken to him crept quietly back into his thoughts. *"My family is my greatest accomplishment, Mathew. Not my business. Not my wealth."*

Sunny. Leo. Huck. Even Ivy. He was already enjoying the blessing of a perfect family. And now, in just a few short months, a baby. He returned to the door, turning back for one last look. A smile crossed his lips, and he pulled the door closed.

Chapter Twenty-Two

Mathew poured a glass of chocolate-flavored vodka over a square ice cube. For his wife, a glass of cranberry juice in a tall Collins glass, complete with an orange wedge. The living room was aglow with sparkling lights and fresh garland. It looked and smelled like Christmas, but the conditions of humid Houston were not cooperating. The weather outside was not frightful. And to build a fire, no matter how delightful, would seem ludicrous. Mathew didn't care. He adjusted the thermostat to a temperature that Jack Frost would find seasonably acceptable and went to work building a small fire.

"A fire? Really?" Sunny commented upon entering the living room.

"What can I say? Santa is a hopeless romantic."

"Is Leo still here?"

"Nope. He and Barbara left about five minutes ago. He's been looking forward to this party all day. You should've seen how his eyes lit up when he answered the door. I think they're close to moving beyond the friend zone."

Mathew continued his chore, while Sunny adjusted a few of the ornaments on the tree. Since their return from Austin at Thanksgiving, he'd come home every day with a new ornament for their tree. *"Twelve days of Christmas just isn't enough,"* he'd told her with a grin as he presented her with yet another ornament. And though there was an immense love for Leo, he couldn't wait to be alone with Sunny, with just the glow of the fire and the Christmas lights around them. They'd planned this evening weeks in advance: dinner, a classic holiday DVD, and their own private gift exchange. The perfect holiday party for two. Two and a half.

Fire now going, Mathew stood and dusted off his hands. He turned and looked at Sunny. They'd both anticipated this moment for days. Mathew crossed the room and flipped the light switch, extinguishing the recessed lights above their heads. A second later, he was beside her, burying his head in her hair. He could taste the sweetness of her skin as he nuzzled a specific spot behind her ear. The house was dark, with only the lights from the fireplace and the Christmas tree around them.

"It's the eve of Christmas Eve." He looked into her eyes.

"Yes, it is." Her arms curled around his waist.

"You know what that means, don't you?" His voice was seductive.

"What?"

"Pizza," he whispered softly in her ear.

Sunny laughed. "Do you want to call it in, or shall I?"

"It's all been taken care of."

"Then why don't I go upstairs and slip into something more comfortable."

"That…" He kissed her once more. "…sounds like a fabulous idea."

"I'll be down in five minutes."

"I'll be up in four." He winked.

As soon as Sunny was out of sight, he made a beeline for the tree. Shifting the mountain of brightly wrapped packages, he searched until he located a slender box. They'd agreed to exchange one gift on the twenty-third, knowing they'd be alone for the first time since Thanksgiving. No parties. No guests. No interruptions. The start of a new tradition. Their intimate gift exchange had one stipulation. It had to be handmade—Sunny's idea. Mathew smiled at the gift in his hand, then placed it on the hearth. From the moment she'd suggested it, he'd known exactly what he'd give her. A call to Huck had confirmed the particulars, and he'd been preparing tirelessly for weeks.

He'd just settled in on the sofa when Sunny came back into the living room. She snuggled in beside him and together they watched the fire in silence.

"I don't need anything except you. This is what Christmas is all about." He kissed the top of her head.

"I've been dreaming of this moment all day."

"Did you decide on the movie?" he asked.

"Yes."

"So, what's it gonna be? *White Christmas* or *It's a Wonderful Life*?"

"Neither. How 'bout *Miracle on 34th Street*?"

"How 'bout *Miracle on Our Couch*?" His hands found their way underneath her pajama top.

"Mathew, your hands are freezing."

"You know what they say."

"Cold hands, warm heart?"

"I've got something warm for you but it's not my heart. Think a little *lower*."

"Mathew! Santa is watching." She warned.

"I'm a lost cause." He ran his hands gently across her breasts. "I've been on the naughty list for years."

Sunny laughed out loud, nodding in agreement. She turned her smiling face up to his, kissing his chin lightly. The doorbell chimed, forcing Mathew to retreat.

"I think an angel just got his wings," Mathew said.

Mathew paid for the pizza. Sunny tossed some pillows from the couch onto the floor beside the coffee table. They ate in front of the fire, straight out of the box, and discussed the game plan for the following day: getting the guest casita ready for Huck's visit, drinks with the Martins, the family gift exchange, and, if she had the energy, a midnight service. They both agreed on a very traditional yet very relaxed holiday. No rushing. No stress. They would savor every moment of it, knowing that the dynamic would be different with each passing year, with the footsteps of a little boy to guide their way.

Mathew stoked the dwindling fire and added another log. Sunny searched through the mass of presents beneath the tree, then smiled as she removed a tiny box. It was wrapped in plain brown parcel paper and tied with a tasteful green silk ribbon. Mathew turned around and caught her eye. He couldn't restrain his grin. He returned the poker to its stand and grabbed his gift from the hearth. They flopped down on the couch side by side. He eyed the tiny box in her hand.

"Did you wrap that all by yourself?" he asked.

"I certainly did. Did you wrap yours?"

"I certainly did. But you can't open it yet."

"Why not?" she asked.

"Well, it wouldn't be fair. I get to open my gift first. I'm the oldest. Age before beauty, right?"

"If you say so." She sighed and placed the box in his hands.

"It's kinda small." Mathew inspected it.

"It's not the size that counts."

"That's not what you told me last night."

"Mathew!" She playfully slapped his arm.

He carefully removed the ribbon and paper. Inside, he found a plain white box—no crest or jeweler's mark. Inside that, a black velvet box. He looked at her with curious eyes.

"Seriously, you did keep our promise, right? Only something handmade?" He held the box up to his ear, giving it a gentle shake.

"Absolutely." She nodded firmly.

He lifted the lid and peeked inside, totally surprised. A sterling silver heart rested on a blanket of black velvet. It was no bigger than a quarter, but the design was exquisite and unlike anything he'd ever seen. The outer edges were lightly hammered, with a second heart carved neatly in the middle. A heart inside a heart.

"Sunny, this is amazing." He carefully picked it up, examining it on all sides.

"Do you like it?" She gave him half a smile. "I designed it myself."

"You did this?"

"I drew up the design, and a local artist I found on Etsy brought it to life."

"It's gorgeous. Really. I love the design."

"Well, I get to carry around a tiny expression of love every day. I thought you should have one too."

"A tiny heart? To carry in my pocket?"

"Uh-huh."

He shook his head again in loving disbelief. "You're something else, you know that?"

"It's been rumored. You know how this town loves to talk."

"Your turn." He handed her his gift.

Smiling, she didn't waste any time. Beneath the paper and ribbon, she found a plain white rectangular box. Carefully removing the lid, she peeled back several layers of paper and found a scroll, tied with a candy cane striped ribbon.

"This looks interesting." She pulled the scroll from the box.

With one tug, the ribbon fell away, and Sunny unrolled the paper. Again, she smiled as her eyes traveled across the sheet.

"Sheet music?" She turned the paper toward him, feeling confused.

"For the piano." He returned her smile with a nod.

"But we don't play the piano."

"Speak for yourself." He winked.

Taking the sheet music in one hand and her hand in the other, he led her over to their piano. He'd insisted they buy one—never mind that neither of them played. Sunny could read dozens of scientific maps, charts, and stacks of data, but not a note of music. Mathew played trumpet in the sixth-grade band, but never tackled any other instruments. Leo could bang out "Heart and Soul," but that was all. It was the first purchase they'd made for their new home after much debate and Sunny's eventual concession. She could appreciate the beauty of it, but hated that it sat quietly in the room, with little more than dust touching it on a regular basis.

Side by side, they sat on the bench. Mathew

smoothed the paper out with his hands before clipping it neatly on the music stand. He placed his hands lightly on the keys and looked up at her.

"You're kidding, right?" Sunny shook her head, ready to call his bluff.

Mathew's fingers went to work, filling the silence around them with the jazzy side of Christmas. Sunny watched as Mathew played her favorite Christmas song–Vince Guaraldi's most recognizable tune of the season. When he finished, he turned to her, a playful expression in his eyes.

"They were wrong. Turns out you can teach an old dog new tricks."

"Mathew Ellis? But how?"

"Our firm's fiscal year ends in October, remember?"

"So, all those late-night, end-of-year meetings you couldn't get out of?"

"Were spent practicing my scales."

"But how did you know? I mean, that's my favorite holiday song."

"I'm in tight with the elves." He slipped his arms around her, resting his forehead against hers.

"You're something else, you know that?" The lights of the tree sparkled in her eyes.

"It's been rumored," he said with a grin.

Chapter Twenty-Three

"Mathew…Mathew, wake up…" Sunny gently nudged his shoulder.

Wrestling between reality and sleep, Mathew mumbled a few unintelligible words before finally opening his eyes. He lay still for a few moments, processing the disturbing scene that had just played out in his subconscious mind.

"Are you okay?" she asked.

"Yeah."

"What happened?"

Mathew hesitated, suddenly feeling trapped. He'd always pressed Sunny for the details of her bizarre dreams. But now, he didn't care to return the favor.

"Can we talk about it later?"

"It was something about me, wasn't it? Something bad?"

"It was about you. More Halloween than Christmas. We're talking Jacob Marley level weird."

"It was just a dream. You can tell me. I always tell you, don't I?"

Mathew exhaled. "I was in a cemetery, surrounded by enormous headstones–like, they were ten feet tall. It was dark and I was looking for you."

"Did you find me?"

"Oh, I found you. That was the scary part. You were a statue…dressed like an angel and holding a baby. Just a big, cold hunk of gray stone."

"Oh, God, Mathew, that's awful. But as you can see, I'm fully alive...and this big hunk is quite warm." She grabbed his hand and pressed it to her belly.

****

Mathew and Sunny sat on the couch waiting for Huck. Mathew watched her eyes, tiny slits that might fall closed at any moment. He'd worn her out on purpose–running around town on a number of ridiculous errands, all in an effort to get her out of the house so his Christmas surprise could be completed. His plan was simple: keep his wife away as long as possible and make sure she stayed clear of the baby's room until later that night. He and his father-in-law had worked out a little scheme, and his confidence level was high. Leo would run interference when necessary, and hopefully, with the arrival of Archer and Maggie soon, Sunny would be too busy to venture upstairs.

The doorbell chimed, and Sunny jumped.

"That must be Father Christmas," Mathew said, standing with a stretch.

Mathew swung open their front door. There stood his father-in-law, wearing a red plaid shirt and jeans. He and Mathew shook hands, then he stepped into the waiting arms of his daughter. Sunny's smile quickly took an unexpected turn upside down when she noticed the cane in her father's hand and the limp that made it necessary.

"Pop!" She hugged him tightly. "What happened?"

"A minor accident."

"Are you all right?" Mathew asked.

"I'm fine. Hit some gravel near a cattle guard and turned a bike over on my leg. It's sore but not fatal."

178

"Do you need to see a doctor?" she asked.

"On Christmas Eve? Hell no. I'm fine. Besides, I'm sure your husband has just what I need.

"A cold beer?"

"Is there a better way to self-medicate? Well, I mean, there is, but I promised Sunny the only thing I'd smoke on this trip is your turkey."

"And you'll find everything you need right there." Mathew motioned across the living room to the bar cart on the wall opposite the fireplace.

Everything was on course. Huck had arrived without incident, they'd had time to rest and prepare for an informal get-together with Archer and Maggie, and the door to the nursery had remained closed all day. Mathew smiled, took Sunny's hand, and led her into the kitchen. Alone, he pulled his wife's body to his and held her close. They stood together for a second or two, without words.

"I love you," he whispered.

"I love you, too."

"Are you okay?" He pulled away and searched her eyes.

"Yes. Why?"

"I just want to make sure this is not stressing you two out."

"Spending Christmas Eve with my most favorite people in the world? How could that be stressful?"

"I'm just checking on you, that's all. Making sure."

"Well, I'm fine. We're fine. I promise."

"If you start to feel tired, just say the word. We'll call it a night."

"I'm all right. Now stop worrying."

They stood still, lost in the moment. The night

before had been a time of restful reconnection. Their first official Christmas memories had been written on the pages of their lives. They'd fallen asleep in each other's arms as the light of the tree and the fire flickered around them. Now, as he kissed her, Mathew longed to whisk his wife upstairs and hide from the rest of the world. Again, his thoughts were interrupted by the doorbell, announcing their visitors. He sighed and pulled grudgingly away.

"Hold that thought," he whispered.

"For how long?"

"For as long as it takes me to get rid of all these people."

"Mathew!" She laughed.

"I'm kidding. But maybe Archer and Maggie would like their cocktails to go?"

"Would you get the door?" she urged.

"One drink, one canape, one Christmas carol, and then everyone's outta here." He motioned definitively with his hand.

"What happened to sharing the Christmas spirit?"

"I have something very spirited to share…but only with you." He flashed a wicked smile as he picked up a serving platter.

****

They watched as Archer and Maggie closed their car doors and exited the driveway behind Barbara. Both continued to wave until the red taillights were gone from sight. Turning to each other, they stole another quiet moment, sharing a sweet kiss.

"You taste like peppermint," Mathew informed her.

"That's because I'm sugar and spice and

everything nice."

"Well, go easy on the sugar. Heavy on the spice." He nuzzled her neck.

"Stop that!" Huck hollered from the living room. "You two have been under the mistletoe enough tonight."

"I say we trade mistletoe for sheets," Sunny said.

"What time is it?" Leo asked.

"It's time for my pregnant wife to get to bed."

"I'm doing the same. Good night, one and all."

Leo hugged all present company before shuffling off to his bedroom. Sunny gathered discarded glasses and dishes while Mathew took Ivy out for a short walk. Huck stayed put on the sofa, true to the plan he'd hatched with his son-in-law. A few minutes later, when all three were together again, Huck gave Mathew a knowing look.

"Well, Mrs. Ellis, I must say that your first Christmas get-together as a wife and mother-to-be was a complete success," Huck said proudly.

"Thank you, Pop. It was a fun night."

"But all good things must come to an end, and this is where I take my leave." He pulled himself up off the sofa with the help of his cane.

"I'll walk you out to the casita." Sunny offered her father her arm for extra support.

"Huck, is there anything I can get you before you head out?" Mathew asked.

"No, I think I'm fine."

"Well, call us if you need anything. I can be out there in two seconds." Mathew lightly kissed his wife's cheek, then touched his father-in-law's shoulder warmly.

"Thank you." Huck nodded quietly.

Sunny and Huck slowly made their way out to the casita–a guest suite they had built on the back side of the garage—retelling the best stories of the night. They both agreed that despite the absence of snow and sleigh bells, it was turning out to be one of the better holidays they'd shared in recent memory. Christmas had always been a difficult time for both of them with Daphne's birthday being the day after. And though Sunny had always found an insane number of gifts on Christmas morning, there was always a sadness that accompanied the season, hanging like a tarnished ornament on her childhood Christmas tree. Throughout her teen years, Huck had made a point of taking his daughter on fabulous winter vacations, and thus began her education in the world of travel. Huck had arranged all sorts of amazing adventures for them. They'd happily traveled the globe together, or so she thought at the time. Looking back, she knew it was her father's way of running away—away from the home he'd built with her mother and memories made too painful by twinkling holiday lights.

Inside the casita, Sunny made a once-through sweep to assure that everything was comfortably in order.

"This is nicer than most hotels I stay in. I'm sure I'll sleep like a baby."

"You heard Mathew. Call us if you need anything."

"Is it too early to place an order for a breakfast Bloody Mary?" He regrettably brought his hand up to his forehead, rubbing it firmly.

"I'll bring you one first thing." She reassured him.

"Listen, baby girl, before you go…" He ambled

over to his suitcase and pulled out a small, wrapped package. "I know we said that we'd wait to open gifts in the morning, but I'd like you to have this now." He handed the small present to her.

"What have you done?" She took the box from his hand, shaking her head.

"It's just a little something I thought you might like to have. Go on, open it."

She removed the gold wrapping and bow, her expression full of curiosity. Inside, she found a stack of brightly colored construction paper cards, held together with a piece of twine. Though her eyes had not seen them for years, she recognized them instantly.

"Do you remember those?" Huck asked.

"Oh, Pop..." Carefully, she pulled the stack of cards from the box. She backed up several feet, blindly finding the bed and sitting down, never taking her eyes off the forgotten treasure she held in her hands. "I had no idea you had these."

"Neither did I. Found them when I pulled out the holiday decorations. They were inside a box that I thought contained ornaments. I didn't know your mother saved them, but I'm not surprised. If you made it, she saved it."

"I can't believe it." Sunny studied the drawings and read the words she'd written to Santa throughout her happiest childhood years.

Huck sat beside his daughter. "Look at your drawings! Just look at that Christmas tree. That's fantastic. Such detail. And you were only four when you drew that. What an artist you were. And I'm not just saying that because I'm your father. You had real talent."

"I wrote the "C" backward." She pointed to the first letter in *Christmas* on the front of the card.

"This was one of your mother's most cherished holiday traditions. She loved sitting down with you on Christmas Eve, watching you make special cards for Santa. Look at this one…" He reached for a yellow card, filled with bright blue scribbles on the front. Smiling, he flipped it over and noted the date on the back. "This was the first card you ever made. You were two. Note your use of bold color in this abstract design. What a genius!" He winked at his daughter.

Sunny laughed. "Yeah, I was a regular Kandinsky."

"You certainly were. At least, you were to us." He paused for a moment, resting a hand on Sunny's thigh. "And you'll think your little boy is the same way. Every scribble, every drawing, every handmade gift will touch you in a way that you can't imagine."

She looked into her father's eyes, noting a shine of fresh tears. A quick blink caused several of her own to fall.

"You amaze me. You constantly amaze me, but I think you should keep these." She held the stack of cards out to him.

"Nope, your mother would want you to have them. *I* want you to have them. And I also want you to have this…" He reached inside his pocket and pulled out a tiny box.

"Now c'mon!" Sunny put a hand up in protest. "You are cheating big time here."

"Just open it." He slipped the box into her hand.

"But what about tomorrow? I thought we were waiting."

His eyes insisted she obey. Shaking her head again, she quietly flipped open the top of the black velvet box. Inside, she found a ring that belonged to her mother. One that she always loved to look at as a child but didn't remember seeing since her mother's passing.

"I bought that ring for your mother right before she had you. Her hands swelled so during the end of her pregnancy, and she couldn't wear her wedding ring. So, I found this one, and she wore it instead. It was larger than her real one. She fell in love with it. And after you were born and her hands returned to their normal size, she continued to wear it."

"I remember. She wore it on her middle finger…"

"Because it was too big for her ring finger, yes, that's right."

"I thought Mom was buried with this ring."

"I kept it in the hopes that I'd give it to you one day, if you decided to become a mother."

"It's beautiful." She slipped it over her middle finger, seeing her mother's hand in her own.

"Your hands. They're so much like your mother's. At dinner, I couldn't stop watching them. The way you hold your fork and the animated way you gesture when you tell a story…" His voice trailed off, signaling the return of his tears.

Sunny moved closer to him, embracing her father tightly. Her tears tumbled once more, and they held each other in silence. Years of hiding their deepest holiday sorrows in foreign hotels and distant airports melted away, and together they released their Ghosts of Christmas Past, making way for the merriest of future traditions.

"Another year without her. I don't know how we

do it." Sunny pulled away, whispering through her tears.

"I do it because I find my strength in you, baby girl." He reached and brushed a tear off her cheek.

****

Dad's Advice: Get in tight with the elves

I only have a few minutes, so I may have to cut this short. It's Christmas Eve, and for the first time today, our house is quiet. Our guests have gone. Uncle Leo has retired to his room. And your mother is out in the casita tucking Grandpa Huck in for the night. We've had a beautiful evening. Lots of good food, good friends, and good stories. Just the way the holidays are supposed to be.

Your grandpa Huck rolled in today with his unique brand of holiday cheer. He limped through the front door, cane in hand. Your mother hates seeing him in pain and showing his age, but in the morning, she'll be relieved to know that it was all an act. I had an entire team of design professionals here today, finishing up your room as a surprise Christmas gift for your mom. All week, she's been so excited to show your grandfather the progress on the nursery. Well, we had to come up with a way to keep her out of there until my big surprise reveal. So, Grandpa faked an injury to avoid the stairs. And she was so busy with our guests that the thought of the nursery never entered her mind. I was afraid that she might want to show it off tonight to our friend, Maggie, but fortunately, Maggie was able to steer the conversation away from all things baby. The secret to my secret-keeping success is surrounding myself with people who know how to keep secrets. I'm getting better at it. I can't wait to see her face. I left a light on up there and will ask her to turn it out on our way up to bed. I only had time to peek at it myself. It's even better than I imagined. You're our Little Prince, so the room must be as unique and special as you are.

I'm starting to get worried about your mother. She's been out with Grandpa for a while now. I know that this is a difficult time of the year for them. Your grandmother would have been celebrating her birthday the day after tomorrow. Your mom tries to put on a strong face and act like it doesn't bother her. But it does. I know this because I do the very same thing and your mom knows it too. When I was a little boy, I used to pray that Santa would bring my parents back to me. I had this story worked out in my head that maybe they'd gone on a trip far away and just couldn't get back to me. And that wherever they were in the world, they were missing me as much as I was missing them. They say it's better to have loved and lost than to never have loved at all. I'm not sure that's entirely true. I never knew my parents. And I hurt every day, but I've learned to separate the pain from the blessings I'm living now. I think it's more regret now than anything. Regret that my mother and father will never get a chance to know you and your mother. The two of you are my greatest treasure.

Loss—of any kind—is never easy. But I am blessed to share this life with your mother, and we'll hold each other up when the memories of our losses weigh us down.

Well, I just heard your mom come in, so I better close. It's time for my Christmas Eve surprise.

Merry Christmas!

Daddy

Chapter Twenty-Four

Mathew looked up from his desk in the study and locked eyes with his wife. The carefree expression Sunny wore all evening had morphed into one heavy with emotion. Her eyes were wet with fresh tears.

"Are you okay?" Mathew asked, quickly shoving the papers in front of him into a drawer.

"Yes." She took a deep breath, then exhaled in relief.

"It's late. Let's head on up."

He slid his arm around her waist and together they walked through the house, clicking lights off as they went. At the bottom of the stairs, he stopped and turned to her.

"He gave you the ring, didn't he?"

She nodded, holding her hand up.

"And the Christmas cards?"

"Yes," she whispered.

"He loves you very much."

"I know he does. And I love him too."

"Your mom is right here with us. They're all here with us. Every person we've ever loved. They never leave. Remember what The Little Prince said? About how sweet the sky is when you love a flower that lives on a star?"

"Mathew, I love you so much." Sunny found her smile. "Thank you."

"No charge." He brushed a tear from her cheek then they continued up the stairs. A light from the direction of the nursery spilled into the hall.

"Hey, did you leave the light on in the nursery?" he asked.

"No, I haven't been in there today."

"Me either. Maybe Leo was up here."

"I'll get it," she offered.

Mathew lingered at the landing for a moment and watched as Sunny approached the slightly cracked door. Pushing it open, she stood frozen at the sight before her. Mathew slipped up behind her and took in the scene. The drop cloths were gone. No sign of paint cans or brushes. The whole room was a fairy tale—one fit for a Little Prince. Every inch of the space was picture-perfect. The furnishings. The fabrics. The artwork. In the light of the wall sconces above the crib, the room looked like an ad for the most upscale baby boutique.

"Santa's pretty amazing. I didn't even know he was up here. He didn't make a peep," Mathew whispered from behind her, his breath tickling her ear.

Sunny spun around to face him. Mathew noted genuine surprise lighting up her eyes. This was the moment he imagined. This was the gift he dreamed of giving her the second she pulled those little white sticks from the pocket of her hotel robe. This was the reason he existed—to fill her life with magical moments. Looking into her face, he was again reminded that he could only define his truest self when in her presence. *It's unquestionably more blessed to give than receive.* His arms wound around her and he kissed her tenderly—further confirming that, because of Sunny, he'd never be the same. And that was just the way he liked it.

"Mathew Ellis." She shook her head.

"What makes you think I had anything to do with this?" he asked, giving her an innocent look.

"It's absolutely magical." She turned her body back around, while Mathew kept his arms snugly around her waist. They stood together, his head on her shoulder, and quietly envisioned the days and nights that waited for them.

"Would you like the fifty-cent tour?"

"Of course." She beamed.

"Follow me." Mathew released her from his grip and stepped into the room.

"Now, over here…this is where our Little Prince will have his royal diaper changed." Mathew pointed to the changing table. "And here…this is where he'll rest his princely head." He ran his hand along the crib railing. "Inside here…" He walked to the closet. "A place to hang his stately wardrobe."

"And what about that?" Sunny pointed to the rocking chair.

"That's where we'll rock His Royal Highness."

He took Sunny's hand and led her to the rocker. "I think we should break it in." Mathew sat down and pulled her down on his lap. He rocked Sunny back and forth until his eyes fell closed and the final moments of Christmas Eve disappeared. Several minutes passed before Sunny spoke.

"Let's go to bed. We're both exhausted," she said.

She stood with a yawn and walked to the door. Together, they turned back and paused for one last look. "It's the most beautiful thing I've ever seen, Mathew."

"It certainly is." He focused his eyes firmly on her.

Hand in hand, they walked to their bedroom, ready for a long winter's nap. Making love to his wife would have to wait another night. Mathew desired more simple pleasures. Draping his arm across her belly. Finding her feet with his own. Feeling her hair against his cheek. Sleeping beside his wife was at the top of his list of favorite things. In truth, his list had only one word. *Sunny.* And in a few months, he'd add another name to that list.

"His room is perfect. I don't know how else to describe it. You've surprised me before, but this time you outdid yourself. When did you do it? It wasn't like that yesterday."

"I was fortunate to find some really energetic and helpful elves."

"It's stunning. It's like a dream."

"That's exactly what I was hoping for."

Once in bed, he spooned in beside her, yawning again. All the running around and nonstop entertaining had finally caught up with him, and he wanted nothing more than to close his eyes.

"Hey. Didn't you promise me a back rub earlier?"

"Now?" He sighed heavily, checking the clock with one eye.

"You promised, remember?"

"How many minutes?"

"Seven. You still owe me from the last time."

"Look, I'll make a deal with you," he said.

"Another one of your famous deals?" Sunny sighed.

"Let's go to sleep and I'll double your pleasure tomorrow."

"Fourteen minutes?" she asked.

"If you turn off that lamp, I'll make it an even twenty."

"Done. Let's shake."

"We don't need to shake. You know I'm good for it."

"I've heard that before." She pulled the sheets back and slipped out of bed.

"Where are you going?" he asked.

"Better make one last pit stop for the night."

"Can you turn the lamp off?" His words were heavy with sleep.

Sunny turned off the lamp. Mathew exhaled, relieved to finally be horizontal in a dark room after a long but fun day. Though he'd celebrated many holidays in his life, none could compare to the one that was just winding down. He was just on the verge of sailing peacefully into the night when Sunny called out his name. Immediately, he was wide awake and rushing into the bathroom—gripped with fright at the urgency and panic in her voice.

"Sunny, what's wrong?" He fumbled in the darkness for the doorknob. Suddenly, light burned his eyes, and he saw his wife standing before him. The fear in her eyes was unmistakable. Something was terribly wrong.

"What is it?" he begged.

"I'm bleeding…"

Chapter Twenty-Five

Sunny hadn't spoken a word since the moment they pulled out of the driveway. Her hands cradled her pregnant belly, and Mathew saw her lips moving in prayer. He allowed her silence to guide them, not wanting to force conversation. From the corner of his eye, he could see the fear on her face. Reaching over, Mathew placed a loving hand atop his wife's as he tried to collect himself. The last few minutes had been a blur. A call to the number on Dr. Sumner's business card solicited nothing more than his answering service. *Of course he's not answering. It's Christmas Eve.* No real need to call an ambulance, since Sunny wasn't experiencing pain. No sense in waking Leo and Huck— there was little they could do. After quickly scanning one of many pregnancy guides, he scrawled a note explaining their absence before quietly loading Sunny into the SUV and heading straight for the ER. It wasn't a lot of blood, but how much is too much? He looked over at her with a reassuring smile and a gentle squeeze of her hand.

"How are you feeling? Any pain?" he asked for the third time.

"Mathew, I feel fine. I was feeling some slight pelvic pressure early, but it wasn't painful."

"You're sure?"

"I told you, I'm not in pain." She paused, leaning

her head against the window. "Scared to death, but not in pain."

"We'll be there soon. Everything's going to be fine. I promise. I'm sure that the bleeding is nothing serious."

"You don't think we're going to have this baby tonight, do you?" Her voice was a soft whisper, but he could hear the alarm in every spoken word.

"I think that whatever happens tonight, I'll be right here with you, and we'll be fine. Okay?" He squeezed her hand once more.

She turned her gaze back to the window and Mathew's heart sank. He had no idea what the hours ahead held for them. Would they be standing in the NICU, looking down at a tiny baby covered in tubes and wires, or would the ER doctors smile reassuringly and send them on their way? The chapter in the pregnancy guide gave him little hope of the latter happening. Bleeding in the second or third trimester was never routine, and usually indicative of potentially dangerous complications. Is this preterm labor? Placenta previa? Placental abruption? Though he'd only scanned the book briefly, he'd committed every terrifying possibility to memory.

The roads to the hospital were deserted, causing his mind to wander into all sorts of dark and forbidden places. The gambler in him tried to weigh the odds, but the stakes were just too high to venture a guess. He knew one thing for sure: this was not the Christmas holiday he'd envisioned. Just hours before they'd gathered at the piano, singing carols and telling stories with nothing but holiday happiness around them. And now he found himself pulled from the warmth of their bed, driving his wife to the hospital with the images of a bad dream creeping steadily back into his head. Sunny and a baby, turned to stone in the icy surroundings of an old cemetery. *Please, God, let them be all right. Just let them be okay.*

The hospital parking lot was alive with several emergency vehicles announcing their arrival with a somber carol of sirens and flashing lights. Sunny sat up, rigid and stiff as a board. Mathew put on his best poker face, ready to tackle whatever truth they found waiting behind the doors of the ER.

He helped her settle into an abandoned wheelchair that sat just inside the entrance of the electric doors. An EMT directed them to the waiting area which, like the parking lot, was completely full—standing room only.

"I guess we should have made a reservation," he whispered in her ear.

"And we thought we were having a lively party tonight."

Mathew surveyed the crowd. Every chair was occupied; every face filled with a mix of urgency and exhaustion. "Let's see what the wait is around here. Maybe I can pull a few strings and get us a good table."

He turned the wheelchair toward the admitting station, finding a line of half a dozen people in front of them. *This is going to be a long night.*

"How're you doing? You okay?" he asked again.

"I'm fine, I promise." She looked up at him, eyes wide and full of anxiety.

"Maybe you could moan a little…for effect, I mean," he teased.

Sunny smirked. "If I thought it would help, I would. I'm pretty sure they know all the tricks here."

A nurse rounded the corner and walked directly over to them. "All LD emergencies bypass the ER and go straight up. I'm heading up there myself. Y'all follow me."

Sunny's face relaxed, and Mathew turned the wheelchair around. In a minute, they were inside an elevator headed up to the third floor. They exchanged holiday pleasantries and gave the nurse a brief summary of what had occurred. When the elevator stopped and the doors opened, the nurse took over driving duties for Mathew.

"Just follow my lead, you two."

She pushed Sunny down to a set of double doors marked The Women's Center. The nurse scanned her ID. The doors opened and within a minute, they were at the nurses' station.

"Listen, this is my sister and her husband. They just came from the ER, but still need to be admitted. She's Level One. Twenty-five weeks. Who's on tonight?" the nurse spoke with an assertive tone as she glanced at the large Dry Erase board on the wall behind them.

"Lerner's here," one nurse responded.

"What about Davis?" she asked.

"No. Davis is off. Navarre's here," another nurse added.

"Great. Get Navarre. And make sure they get the best care, all right?" She turned back to them, placing a hand lovingly on Sunny's shoulder. "Navarre is wonderful. You'll be fine, sis. And I promise I'll check in on you later." She gave them a wink before turning to make her exit.

Another nurse led them to an examination area,

divided into several quadrants by large green curtains. The whole floor was silent, and Mathew was thankful for being out of the noisy chaos of the ER. The nurse gave Sunny a gown, along with a promise to return shortly. After helping her undress, Mathew pulled the light blue hospital gown up around her shoulders, tying a neat bow at her neck. Softly, he kissed the nape of her neck and slipped his arms around her waist, resting his head on her shoulder. He could feel every emotion running through her body—and they mirrored his own.

As promised, the nurse returned, carrying a Doppler stethoscope. Sunny reached for Mathew's arm, and he helped her onto the examination table.

"When was the last time you felt fetal movement?" the nurse asked, shaking a bottle of clear ultrasound jelly.

"I'm not sure. About ten-thirty, I think."

"Have you experienced any other symptoms other than the bleeding?"

"No. Nothing," Sunny answered.

"So, no pain or cramping of any kind?" The nurse placed the Doppler transducer on Sunny's belly, swirling it around in the clear gel.

"I feel fine. Normal." Sunny looked up at Mathew, and again he reached for her hand. Lacing his fingers tightly in hers, he gave her a reassuring nod. "Is that normal?" Sunny asked with uncertainty.

"It's a good sign," the nurse replied, moving the transducer across Sunny's pregnant form. In seconds, the unmistakable sound of their baby's heartbeat filled the air, and together they breathed a huge sigh of relief. Sunny could not contain her emotions as tears slid down her cheeks.

"Nice and strong. One hundred thirty-three beats per minute."

"So, he's okay in there?" Mathew asked.

"A strong heartbeat rules out any major distress. Yes, I think he's completely oblivious to all the worry that's going on out here. Dr. Navarre will want to do an ultrasound and pelvic exam to zero in on the sudden bleeding. She'll be here in a couple of minutes. Just try to relax." Pulling the curtain, the nurse left them alone.

The tears Mathew saw in Sunny's eyes brought a wave of wetness to his own, and for the first time since seeing her fearful face in the bathroom, he allowed himself to release the emotions he'd kept silently in check. So many thoughts ran through his mind. As much as he wanted the doctors and nurses to hurry, standing next to her in blissful ignorance of what might be happening was strangely comforting.

"I know I said it earlier, but I need to say it again. No matter what happens, or what we're told, we will handle it together, okay?"

"I know." She squeezed his hand tightly.

"No one's running away. Not me. Not you. Okay?"

"Okay," she whispered.

"I really do love you." He leaned over, resting his cheek against her head.

"And I really love you."

****

"Just as I thought. Your cervix is opening. It's not much. A little more than a centimeter. That's what's causing your bleeding," Dr. Navarre said.

"Please tell me that I'm not going to have this baby tonight." Alarm returned to Sunny's voice, and Mathew's heart began beating double time.

"No, you're not going to have this baby tonight. But I'd like to talk with Dr. Sumner. I think he'll want to do an emergent cerclage to ensure you make it close to term."

"Emergent cerclage?" Mathew asked.

"Cerclage is a safe procedure where the cervix is sewn shut until about the thirty-eighth week of pregnancy. After that, the stitches are removed without any complication, usually in your doctor's office. They can be removed sooner should your water break or should you start experiencing contractions. You've developed a condition known as cervical incompetence. Your cervix has opened spontaneously, which could possibly lead to preterm labor. While this is not common, it typically occurs between eighteen and twenty-three weeks. But it can occur later, as in your case. You did the right thing by bringing her in right away." Dr. Navarre smiled at Mathew.

"So, I'm not going to deliver tonight?" Sunny asked once more.

"Not on my watch," Dr. Navarre said.

"When will you do the procedure? Now? Are there any risks to Sunny?" Mathew's mind raced with tons of questions.

"I'll call Dr. Sumner and discuss everything with him. He'll probably want to go ahead with the cerclage as soon as possible. In the meantime, we'll get you set up in a room. Your job from this point on is to rest. I will go over all the ins and outs of the surgery with you after I've spoken with Dr. Sumner."

****

"Good morning. Merry Christmas," Dr. Sumner said in a soft tone.

Mathew eyed the clock on the wall, relieved to see that it was still early. Sunny had turned over and lay curled up in a ball with her back to him. As gently as he could, he slipped from the bed and followed Dr. Sumner into the hall.

"Thank you so much for coming." Mathew shook his hand.

"Luckily, I'm married to a very understanding woman. That, and I finished all my official Santa duties about two o'clock this morning."

"I'm so sorry to pull you away from your family on Christmas morning. Dr. Navarre said she would call you, but never mentioned that you would be coming in." Mathew ran a hand through his mussed hair.

"Dr. Navarre is an excellent OB. One of the best I've ever seen. But I would rather take care of the cerclage procedure myself. I'm kinda stingy that way. My patient, my surgery."

"I know Sunny will be thrilled to see you."

"Let her sleep a while. Her cervix was only slightly opened, and since she's resting, I think we can hold off until this afternoon."

"You agree with Dr. Navarre that the cerclage is the way to go?"

"Absolutely. It's a relatively easy procedure that poses little risk. I've done many of them over the years with high success. Most cases make it to thirty-eight weeks or longer without complication. A few even reach the forty-week mark. The fact that Sunny is dilated less than three centimeters is a very good sign."

"How long will she have to stay in the hospital?"

"I think that you'll be able to take her home tomorrow morning."

"Really?" Mathew's eyes widened with surprise. "That soon?"

"I'll put her on antibiotics for a week, just to guard against infection. That, along with something for pain, and she should be fine. But you do understand that she won't be able to travel for a while."

"So, my plan of spending New Year's Eve on the beach in Hawaii is out?"

"You'll have to ring in the New Year from the comfort of your bed, I'm afraid."

Mathew laughed. "There are worse things."

"Some doctors recommend two to three days of bed rest following this type of surgery. But I like to err on the side of caution and go at least a full week."

"I can't thank you enough for being here. And I know Sunny will feel the same way."

"Have your nurse page me as soon as Sunny wakes up. I'll pop in, answer any questions, and then we'll tie up her loose ends, so to speak. I'm going to get her name on the surgery schedule now and talk with the anesthesiologist."

"Thanks again for being here." Mathew said with relief.

****

Sunny opened her eyes and looked around the room with a groggy stare.

"Mathew?" she called out with a weak voice.

"I'm right here." He stood beside her, dropping the magazine he'd been reading on the chair behind him.

"Is it over?"

"It is and you did great." He smiled down at her.

"How's LP?" A worried look crossed her face for a split second.

"LP?"

"Little Prince."

"Little Prince is resting comfortably inside his cozy little hand-sewn sack."

"Is my father still here?"

"No. I sent him and Leo home after Dr. Sumner gave us the good news."

"Is he gonna let me go home tonight?"

"No, not tonight. Tomorrow afternoon. You're a little too punch drunk to be walking outta here tonight."

Sunny looked up at him with hazy eyes. "Some Christmas, huh?"

"Hey now, don't start that."

"We didn't have brunch, or exchange gifts or anything."

"The gifts will be there tomorrow, and we can whip up brunch anytime."

"But Barbara was coming back over and—"

"And Barbara sends her love as well, so stop worrying."

"Me and my incompetent cervix." She sighed heavily.

"Sunny…" he started, in a serious tone.

"It's true. You'll be trading me in for a younger model."

He pointed to her belly. "Now listen, the important thing is that gift is not opened until Easter. Am I right?"

His eyes locked on hers, making a powerful connection that only they shared. Once again, he found himself back in the place he loved best—that place of safest love. He leaned forward and kissed her three times—once for the woman she'd been, once for the woman she'd become, and once for the woman he had yet to discover. Past. Present. Future. Three phases of his life that could only exist when defined by her.

****

The clock on the mantle chimed, bringing Huck's mind back from the painful memory he'd revisited. He glanced at his watch and then looked up, exchanging a nervous look with Leo.

"I wonder what's taking them so long?" Leo asked.

"She said they'd be making a stop to pick up her prescriptions. Maybe they were held up at the pharmacy."

"You're probably right. You want something? A top-off maybe?" He pointed to Huck's half-empty glass.

"I'm fine. But thank you." Huck gave Leo a polite nod, continuing to study the paper in front of him.

"C'mon, Ivy. You haven't been out in a while." Leo snapped his fingers and the dog shuffled toward the front door.

Alone in the living room, Huck reread the lines he'd just written. Two games of Solitaire, one Sudoku Challenge, five hands of gin, and sixteen rounds of Pocket Poker had done little to help pass the time. Leo had been more than accommodating to keep them both entertained, but the house was just too quiet. So, he traded games and puzzles for letter writing, as he tried his best to convey several thoughts on paper to his unborn grandson.

So where was I? Without my other letters here in front of me, I can't remember where I left off. With age comes wisdom and unfortunately a good deal of forgetfulness too. Well, it doesn't matter. There's been enough excitement around here to fill up a new page.

I'm sitting here in the living room of your house. The lights on the Christmas tree are still burning, though Christmas came and went. Your Uncle Leo is outside walking your dog. Your mom and dad are on their way home from the hospital. And thankfully, you are still in utero. Uncle Leo and I woke up to find a very distressing letter on Christmas morning. Not a letter from Santa, mind you, but from your father. Seems your mother had some complications during the night and the two of them spent the early hours of Christmas in the hospital. Fortunately, your mother's condition has been improved with an unexpected surgery and you are doing fine. They are due home any minute, and I can't wait to see them. I spent yesterday afternoon at the hospital with your father, Leo and Barbara. The surgical procedure was a complete success. I haven't seen her since she woke up, but I spoke with her on the phone on two different occasions and she sounded wonderful. She is so relieved that you are okay. We all are. As much as we look forward to your birthday, we are certainly pleased that you decided to stay put for the moment.

Speaking of birthdays—today is a very special day on the calendar. Many years ago, on this very day, a very special person was born—my Daphne. And for reasons unbeknownst to most, this woman fell in love with me. What on earth did she see in me? Even after this many years, I still don't have a clue. She gave me many gifts in our years together, but none as great as your mother, my baby girl, Sunny June Porter.

I still celebrate her special day. Quietly. In my own way. A private party. Over the years, the focus of my celebrations has been less about remembering her birth and more about congratulating myself that I survived another year without her. Yes, I know that's very selfish of me. I know I am blessed to have so many good things in my life. My family. My health. My work. But I would gladly subtract the last decade from my life if I thought I could have more time with her. More time to drink in her laugh. More time to go on long rides together. Time. It surrounds us every day, yet we long for more. There's never enough of it.

Sometimes at night, when the house is dark and quiet, and if I center my thoughts on her, I can still feel the softness of your grandmother's hand in mine. It's a feeling I can't describe. If I rub my thumb and forefinger together lightly, I can almost recall the very texture of her skin. It's a crazy thing to do, I know, but I can't stop. I'm afraid to. Over the last several years, it's become harder and harder to remember. Harder to feel her skin. I know that one day, it will be gone forever. One day, I'll rub my fingers together, and even though I'll rack my brain with incredible intensity, I'll only feel the brittle skin of an old man. That day is coming. It's coming much faster than I care to admit. And when that day finally arrives—the day I can no longer see her eyes, hear her laugh, or feel her skin— that's the day I'll raise my glass, toast my much-blessed life, and ask God to drive me home.

Huck stopped reading, taking a minute to wipe his eyes. He studied the lights on the tree in quiet reflection before putting his pen back to paper.

I guess all this geriatric rambling has finally brought me around to making a point that may be of some value to you one day. My wish for you would be that you savor every moment. The good ones and the ones that break your heart. To live is to feel, as your grandmother would say. Every moment in time is a color, and together all the moments of your life will create a painting that is unique to you. So be bold, young man! Make big, bold, blue scribbles on the canvas of your life just like your mom did on her Christmas card. My canvas is almost full now. All my paints are beginning to fade. But your canvas is clean and white. Nothing but blank space, just waiting for something exciting. There's no such thing as the wrong color. Use them all. Laugh. Cry. Love. Live. Do all of these things, and I know you will create a life nothing short of a masterpiece.

Chapter Twenty-Six

My Precious LP,

Happy New Year, my love! I can hardly believe that another year has come to a close. It truly was the best year of my life. The blessings have been almost too numerous to count. Meeting and marrying your father, getting back on my feet (literally), watching Leo find his way back to himself and us, and then finding out that we were expecting you. I'm speechless but filled with feelings of joy at the good fortune we've experienced. I know that the year ahead will bring forth the most special moments for us all as we gather around you, living every day through the wonder and merriment in your eyes.

I can't imagine what it will be like, seeing the world reveal itself to you. And I can't imagine my heart any fuller than it is at this moment. But with your father, I've learned just how resilient a heart can be. He's shown me the way, like a candle in the dark. There are days when I think to myself, "There's nothing he could do that would make me love him more." And you know what? I'm wrong—every time. My heart has found the ability to expand itself, creating more space. Allowing so much more love inside it. What will my heart do the first time it sees you? How loudly will it beat as I hold you in my arms for the very first time? How will my heart feel when it hears your cries? When it savors your laughter? When it delights in your triumphs and breaks in your disappointments? You're not even here yet, and already my heart breaks for you knowing that I won't be able to protect you from so many things. Knowing that one day, I'll have to do what every mother before me feared. I'll have to turn you over to the world. A world filled with treasure and mystery, but also with pain, loss, and hurt. And it will be that moment when I'll wish I could hide you away— slip you back inside the cozy little nest where you are right now. Sew you up tight inside me with the strongest threads, woven from love, so that nothing will harm you. But that wouldn't be living, now, would it?

A complete life has equal shares of the good and the not-so-good. Your grandmother was a big believer in that. At least, that's what she said. Looking back, I think it was just her way of protecting me and Grandpa. She knew she was leaving us, so she created this idea that we'd be better for the experience. That somehow, her death would make us stronger. She didn't say it in so many words, and even if she had, it would have been lost on me. I was just a baby myself then. How could losing someone better you? How could a young girl become stronger by giving back that which made her strong to begin with? I know one thing for sure: I'll never know the answer to that one.

I'm sitting here in the waiting room at Dr. Sumner's office. Daddy is meeting me for our appointment. He had several meetings today but was able to schedule them and meet me here so we can grab a quick bite afterward. He should have been here by now, but Dr. Sumner is running behind, so he lucked out with a little extra time. We've reached the twenty-

eight-week mark and are now closing out the second trimester. Where has the time gone? It seems like just yesterday I was flashing a tiny white stick, showing your father the evidence of you! This has been the most blessed and life-changing experience for both of us.

Daddy said Leo and Grandpa were really scared when they woke up Christmas morning and found the note he'd left them explaining our need to go to the hospital. But thankfully everything worked out. Because of our little scare, we didn't celebrate Christmas morning the traditional way. Christmas Eve was wonderful with your father, Grandpa, Leo, Barbara, and our friends Archer and Maggie Martin. Lots of stories and laughter. It was a perfect evening. Grandpa surprised me with some cards I'd made for Santa back when I was just a girl. I hadn't thought about those cards in years and had no idea that they'd been saved. He also gave me a very special ring that belonged to your grandmother. I'm wearing it at this very moment.

Oh, that grandfather of yours. He helped Daddy out with a Christmas surprise for me by faking an injury. He hobbled in here with a cane in his hand. His goal was to keep himself and me out of your room by avoiding the stairs. See, that was my big surprise. Your father had a whole team finishing up your room on Christmas Eve while we were out running errands. And so, between your "ailing" grandfather, and preparations for our evening celebration, I stayed out of your room, and Daddy was able to pull off his most special surprise to date. Your room. It's the most magical place in our home. It's a wonderland made just for a Little Prince. Every night before I go to bed, I steal a few moments by myself in there. Daddy bought me this big rocking chair. I like to sit in that chair and imagine you in my arms.

I came home from the hospital the day after Christmas and your father chained me to our bed for a week. He hardly left my side, even though Dr. Sumner assured him that I'd be fine. We decided to wait and exchange our real Christmas gifts on New Year's Eve, giving us something to look forward to. He brought a tiny little tree up to our bedroom on New Year's Eve, along with the packages we were exchanging. Leo joined us, and so did your grandfather (we convinced him to stay on with us, though it didn't take much). The three of them donned fake Santa beards and hats and serenaded me and Ivy with a rousing round of carols. This was long after they'd sampled several glasses of champagne, mind you. It was a unique holiday, to say the least. But very sweet, and one that I will never forget.

Your father and I had our own private gift exchange. We agreed to open our packages at the exact same time, and when we did, we laughed and laughed. Your father bought me the tiniest red bikini known to man. In contrast, I presented him with a pair of Speedos in a very loud print. Unfortunately, our travel plans for Maui are now on the back burner. Hopefully, we will get a green light from Dr. Sumner today and be cleared to make one last trip before your big day–our "babymoon," if you will.

I've resisted doing it for a long time—call it superstition or whatever—but I finally circled the date of your arrival in my day planner. It says "Forty Weeks" in big print. Now that we're beginning the homestretch, I feel I can finally relax a bit. Even after the surprise of having the cerclage, I feel very peaceful about the remainder of our journey. Daddy and Leo have a bet going that you will be the ultimate Easter egg, and that you'll be born on Easter Sunday. What do you think? Will the Easter Bunny bring you then? Whatever you decide, just think about how warm and comfy it is in there. Don't rush it.

I just looked up, and guess who I see leaning against the wall near the entrance of Dr. Sumner's office? With his arms folded smartly across his chest and a very satisfied expression on his face. Yep, it's him.

I love you, my angel.
Mommy

Chapter Twenty-Seven

Eyes closed, Sunny rested her head against his shoulder as they cruised quietly toward the famed island resort. Her body was tired. She hadn't slept well the night before. The anticipation of their last trip as a twosome, coupled with her ever-expanding midsection made finding a comfortable sleeping position difficult. She couldn't wait to slip into a hot shower and into Mathew's arms for the first of many decadent afternoon naps. They'd penned their itinerary with just one word: relaxation. And they mutually agreed that nothing would interfere with their private time—no exceptions.

As he drove up the main drive of the property, Mathew reached over, resting his hand on her thigh.

"Sunny, we're here."

"I'm so sorry." She opened her eyes, sitting up with a small yawn.

"You're not going narcoleptic on me again like you did on the plane, are you?"

"I didn't sleep well last night. I need a nap, then I'm good to go."

"Any excuse to be horizontal with you is okay by me." He squeezed her knee.

"Mathew Ellis, when are you not thinking about sex?"

He didn't answer but continued to move his hand further up her leg.

They pulled up to the entrance of the resort and Mathew helped her from the car. The refreshing breeze blew in her hair, and she instantly felt rejuvenated. Inside the lobby, they were greeted with a stunning array of tropical plants, rich wood tones, and soothing colors. While Mathew registered, Sunny explored the hotel lobby, examining the work of local artists on display.

Within a minute, he was back by her side, smiling slyly and waving a couple of card keys.

"The key to the kingdom?" she asked.

"Better. The key to the elevator—a private elevator to take us directly to our suite. And you know what being in an elevator with you does to me."

Sunny smirked, recalling their first kiss inside a hospital elevator in the Houston Med Center.

"Mathew, you cannot set off the alarm like last time." She shook her head playfully.

"Watch me." He grinned.

Mathew's plan for a repeat makeout session was thwarted, as the elevator stopped on the second floor. The doors opened and Sunny held her breath for a moment.

"Oh my! This is incredible." She walked into their suite, completely stunned.

"What do you think? Can you live here for a week?" he asked, tossing his jacket on the back of the sofa.

"I could live here forever." She made a beeline for the enormous private lanai that framed the spectacular ocean view.

"And I understand their room service is incredible, so we never have to step foot outside if we don't want to." He joined her and draped his arms around her shoulders. She leaned back against him, closing her eyes once more, thankful for their safe arrival.

"Aren't you worried we'll run out of things to do?" She turned toward him, baiting him with a seductive tone.

His cell phone rang with a quiet tone, and they both traded puzzled looks.

"If that's your office…" Sunny frowned.

"There's no way. We've only been here ten minutes." Mathew pulled his cell phone from his pocket and answered the call. It lasted less than thirty seconds, and when he hung up, he turned to Sunny with a smile.

"Who was that?" she asked.

"Room Service." He grabbed his jacket off the back of the sofa, pulling a folded piece of paper from the inner pocket, along with a pen.

"What did they want?"

A knock sounded from behind the elevator door.

"I was thinking…" Mathew rounded the sofa and made his way toward the elevator. "Why settle for twenty minutes when we can have a full sixty?"

"Sixty what?"

He pressed a button and the elevator doors opened. Two women in crisp white shirts and khaki pants entered, carrying what appeared to be massage tables.

"Good afternoon, ladies. You can just set those up out there." Mathew pointed out to the lanai.

The two women nodded and smiled, continuing toward the outdoor space.

"And just what exactly are you up to?" Folding her arms across her chest, Sunny gave him a look.

"I might have made a small list," he confessed.

"I thought we agreed on no itinerary?" Her right eyebrow arched.

"I read an article one time that said the tone of one's vacation is set within the first fifteen minutes of one's arrival. If the accommodations are wrong, or there's a problem of any kind, most people tend to have negative memories of their vacation, regardless of how the remainder of their stay goes. I'm just making sure that we start on the right foot."

"With his and hers massage?"

"The first item on the list." He held the paper up.

"So, what else is on this list?"

"Oh no! It's a secret."

"Not even a hint?"

"Nope, but I promise you will enjoy each and every tantalizing item."

"A thousand and one pleasures?"

"The more the merrier." His eyebrows bounced in a naughty fashion.

****

My Little Prince,

Well, here I am all stretched out on a comfy lounge chair, enjoying the view of a gorgeous pool, and just beyond that, the endless blue waves of the Pacific Ocean. Your daddy and I are here in Maui, enjoying what will be our last vacation before becoming your parents. I must say I was a little skeptical of Hawaii during the winter months. I've always leaned more toward snowy mountains for a winter getaway. But how wrong I was. The weather here is beautiful. Just a couple of scattered rain showers, but otherwise warm and breezy—the perfect place to relax.

We're into day three of our restful retreat but our

first day to make it outside our suite. Your father has showered me with endless attention and five-star pampering from the moment we arrived. Massages, facials, bubble baths, private Yoga sessions. He even surprised me last night with a special dinner for two, cooked by a professional chef inside our suite. The past forty-eight hours have been nothing short of hedonistic, and I've thoroughly enjoyed every minute, but today, I thought we needed some fresh air. So, I stuck a golf club in your father's hand and sent him out to the links. Meanwhile, I am soaking up some sun and sharpening my people-watching skills here at the pool.

I've been sitting out here for a while now, and I cannot keep my eyes off this one little boy. If I had to venture a guess, I would say that he's probably about four years old. Dark hair. Tanned skin. A gorgeous child. He's the only preschooler his age in the pool right now, and it doesn't seem to bother him in the least. He's been keeping himself entertained with a bevy of boats and toys, several of which seem to "accidentally" splash his mother. His mother, however, is armed with a water gun and finds much pleasure in defending herself against him while pretending to hide behind her magazine. He has the most adorable laugh, and squeals with delight. You can just feel the love between the two of them. The way he looks up at her, with the water clinging to his long, dark eyelashes—his eyes are filled with loving devotion. And the way she looks down at him, with eyes full of pride—as if he's the only child in the world. Your grandmother used to look at me that way.

As I sit here watching the two of them, I can't help but wonder what our interactions will be like. Will you look up at me with the same eyes, full of unconditional love? What kind of parent will I be? The playful parent? The stern parent? Overprotective? Probably a combination of all three. I know one thing: your father will play one role really well—that of the playful parent. Oh, he's so crazy about you already! And I don't think I mentioned all the wonderful toys he has waiting for you. Santa certainly did right by you. I'm pretty sure if your father were here with me, he would have quickly befriended this young boy and engaged him in a water fight to rival any. He's just a big kid himself.

Sunny looked up, seeing a flash of something from the corner of her eye. There, just beside her chair, lay an orange Frisbee. Glancing across the pool, she saw the same little boy, shyly hiding behind his mother. The woman smiled apologetically and waved. Sunny reached down for the Frisbee with a grin. She stood, grateful for an excuse to stretch her legs, and walked around the pool toward them. As she approached their chairs, she could hear the woman gently reprimanding her son. She called him Adrien.

"I'm so sorry about that. He's got a great arm, but his aim's a little off."

"Oh, it's no problem. I probably need the practice, anyway." Sunny gave her baby bump a pat.

"Is this your first?" the woman asked.

"Yes."

"Well, you are in for a treat." She turned her eyes back to her son who now sat happily splashing on the steps of the pool.

"He's beautiful," Sunny commented warmly.

"Thank you. He's quite a handful too. All boy. Into

everything. One big mess."

Sunny smiled. "I have one of those myself. Only mine's taller. And pushing fifty. How old is he?"

"Almost five. His birthday is in three weeks. Believe me, if you ask him, he'll tell you all about it."

"He's gorgeous. And such a good little swimmer. He's braver than I am, even with a heated pool."

"Well, he's an Aquarius, so he's just naturally drawn to the water. Except when it's bath time. I can't get him in the tub. Too busy. Then, once he's in, I can't get him out." She rolled her eyes with good humor.

"I have to admit that I've had a hard time concentrating on my book. I just couldn't stop watching the two of you and your water gun showdown."

"I'm so sorry. I hope we weren't being too loud."

"Oh no, it's not that. I was thoroughly enjoying watching the two of you. To be honest, I was making some 'mother-and-son' notes."

"So, you're having a boy?"

"We are. In April—right around Easter."

The little boy joined them again, eyeing Sunny suspiciously before whispering something in his mother's ear.

"I think it's time to call it a day. The potty calls." The woman gave Sunny a grin.

"Well, have a good evening. I enjoyed visiting with you."

"Me too."

The woman stood, collecting and stashing their things in an oversized designer tote bag. She wrapped a large towel around her son, giving him a quick peck on the cheek.

"Maybe we'll see you again. Hopefully next time,

we won't hit you with any flying objects." She stuffed the orange Frisbee into her bag.

A dark, handsome gentleman with a foreign accent and hair the color of Adrien's called out to them from across the pool. The man was dressed casually, but his choice of clothing was very expensive. Sunny studied him, imagining he'd just stepped off the page of an Italian sports car ad. He waved at the woman and the boy, an impatient and frustrated look on his face.

"I guess Daddy's ready for you to call it a day too," Sunny added.

"Oh, that's not his daddy." The woman swung the large tote over her shoulder. "But he sure wishes he was."

****

"You look fabulous." Mathew stood as his wife entered the living area, quickly folding a large roll of cash and hiding it in his pocket. Kissing her lightly on the cheek, he lingered for a second, drinking in her scent.

"What is that?"

"What is what?" he asked innocently.

"All that money? You never carry cash. And when you do, never more than about fifty bucks."

"Oh, that was a little side bet I placed for Leo earlier this afternoon."

"They have horse racing in Maui?" She shook her in disbelief.

"No, not horse racing. On the golf course."

"You were hustling on the golf course?"

"Well, I wouldn't call it hustling exactly. More like proving the old saying that a fool and his money are soon parted."

"Mathew, we have more money than we'll ever be able to spend in this or any other lifetime, and you're *gambling*? On the golf course? During our vacation?"

"What can I say? The guys I was grouped with dared me. And you know me, I don't bluff. Plus, my short game was really on today, so I couldn't miss."

"Mathew?"

"It's not for me. It's for Leo."

"Okay, never mind. You want to have a drink here or at the restaurant?"

"If we don't leave now, I'll never let you out of here." He nibbled her earlobe.

"Then we better go."

"Let me call down for the car." Mathew turned, but Sunny grabbed his arm.

"No, let's walk. It's just around the corner."

"Are you sure? I don't want you to get tired."

"Let's see. Two days holed up in this suite and a day of lounging by the pool. Yep, you're right. I've been going at it entirely too hard. You better go ahead and call for the car." She winked.

The sun was beginning to set as they were seated. The cool night air, they decided, was a bit too chilly, so they opted for an inside table. Though it was early, the restaurant was crowded. Mathew ordered their drinks: a martini for himself and a V-8 for his expectant wife. They immediately fell into a deep conversation and each other's eyes—totally oblivious to the world around them. Their laughter filled the air, drowning out all sounds of the restaurant. Several minutes passed before a waiter appeared, bringing them back to reality. After placing their order, Sunny reached into her bag and removed a box wrapped in silver paper with a black bow. She placed it on the table in front of him with a smile.

"What's this?" he asked.

"Don't question. Just open."

Mathew tore through the wrapping, eager to see his surprise. He laughed as he pulled a bright blue plastic mini water cannon from underneath several layers of tissue paper.

He inspected it on all sides. "Not the sex toy I was expecting, but okay…"

Sunny laughed. "When I was sitting out at the pool today, I couldn't keep my eyes off this precious little boy who was playing in the pool. His mom had all these great pool toys, and they were having the best time splashing and squirting each other. And I thought to myself, *if Mathew were here, he'd be in that pool playing with that little guy and loving every minute of it.*"

"How old was the little boy?" He placed the toy back inside the box.

"Almost five. Adorable. He has this dark curly hair, and these beautiful eyes with the longest eyelashes." Sunny's hand joined the story, as she motioned in the air, sharing all the details of her afternoon encounter. "I wish you could have heard his laugh. It was like a symphony of happiness. And just so natural, too—he was completely focused on his toys and his mom. He was having a ball."

"It sounds like you were having a ball just watching."

"Well, I was. It's silly, I know, but I have this picture of you and LP playing. I can't wait to see the two of you in action."

"It's not silly because I have pictures of the two of you in my head too. Pictures of you rocking him to sleep or falling asleep beside him in our bed." He placed his hand on top of hers, gently rubbing her thumb with his own.

"I talked with the little boy's mother for a few minutes. Beautiful woman. Very friendly. She was asking me questions about my pregnancy, my due date, et cetera, and telling me what a handful her son was. Anyway, just as she was leaving, a man who I thought was her husband called out to her from across the pool. Well, I put my foot in my mouth and said something like *'Oh I guess Daddy's ready to call it a day,'* to which this woman informed me that he was not the father of her child. Then I noticed she wasn't wearing a ring."

"Ouch. Score one for the awkward moment."

"Oh, I don't think my comment bothered her as much as it bothered me. And it's bothered me all day."

"People get divorced, Sunny. It happens. Some children grow up never knowing their parents. And some children lose parents due to tragic circumstances." He gave her a knowing look.

She sighed. "I know. But this little boy is so beautiful. He's a spitfire too. So full of life and mischief. I sat there and I couldn't help but think if this kid's father is alive and well and choosing to miss out on this..."

"Children grow up in all kinds of families. Some traditional, some not. You grew up with two parents for a while, then just your father. I grew up solo. Not exactly a fairy-tale existence. But then I met Leo and look what happened. Now you and I are both happy, well-adjusted adults for the most part. Maybe that little boy you saw today is truly happy, despite whatever his family situation may be."

"You're right. I don't know why I'm letting it bother me. The curse of being a hormonal pregnant woman, I guess. I just wish that Adrien—that's the little boy's name—I wish he was lucky enough to have a father like you. I wish that for all children."

"That's the greatest compliment I've ever been paid. Thank you." He nodded with a soft expression in his eyes.

"I know exactly the kind of father you're going to be. And I know that as long as you have breath in your body, you will not miss out on any of those precious moments. I watched that little boy and I could see you and LP there, laughing and playing. You would have been in Heaven."

"I can promise you, I will be right there in the pool, giving LP hell with one of these." He held up the water cannon with a wink.

****

LP,

We're back in our suite now, and it's very late. Daddy's asleep, but I couldn't find a comfortable position, so here I am. I forgot to pack my favorite pillow and it's making for very long nights. Daddy tries his best to make me more comfortable, but some things are beyond his help. Now don't get me wrong—I'm not complaining. As long as you're comfy in there, that's all that matters to me. And there are some advantages to being up alone. I've always done my best thinking late at night. In college, I was famous for pulling the proverbial all-nighter. There's just something about the

223

night—something mysterious yet calming. The night allows you to run with the thoughts that seem unreasonable in the light of day. And if you're lucky, when you wake in the morning, all those shadowy ideas that danced in darkness will create a kaleidoscope of color to start your day.

Your grandfather is a night owl too. We used to stay up until all hours just talking or playing board games. I used to think it was because he loved conversation and recreation. But now, as the years have formed lines on his face, I can see that it was something else entirely. To climb into the bed that he shared with your grandmother—alone—was a painful task for him. I'm not sure if it's because my mother took her last labored breaths there, or because he can't bear the thought of lying alone in the most sacred place in one's marriage. He's spent more nights asleep on the couch in the living room than in his own bed. I can't even count how many times I've found him that way with his glasses down on the end of his nose and his hands resting quietly atop a racing publication or a parts catalog. His mouth was always turned down with a hint of sadness. It didn't matter if I woke him or not. He rarely made the journey to his room. But there would be days when I would find him there, asleep on his bed. He loved to nap in his room though. If he wasn't out riding on a Sunday afternoon, that's where he'd be. My father loved to curl up with my mother and nap underneath her quilt on the weekends. In my mother's last days, he spent hours beside her. I asked my father about that quilt back at Thanksgiving. His eyes lit up but he never answered. I guess time doesn't heal every wound.

Well, my precious boy, I should try and get some sleep.
Night-night!
Mommy

****

Mathew rolled over, the sound of surf in his head. He reached out for the warm body of his wife but found the spot on her side of the bed empty. Looking across the bedroom of their suite, he could see the silhouette of her pregnant form. She stood at the window, arms folded across her chest, gazing out at the dark waves. The clock beside the bed showed midnight had come and gone. It wasn't the first time he'd awoken to find her somewhere other than in their bed. Sleeping had become a real issue, and she struggled with comfort regularly now. But even in the moonlight, he could tell from her rigid stance that something besides her midsection was keeping her from true rest. Quietly, he joined her at the window.

"I woke you." She spoke apologetically, turning to him and sliding her arms up around his neck.

"Are you all right?" he asked with a voice full of genuine concern.

"I'm fine. I just couldn't sleep. I wrote for a while, but I can't concentrate."

"I worry about you, you know?"

"I know you do. I'll be all right." She nodded and sighed heavily. "I just can't stop thinking about that woman and her little boy at the pool."

"They're still on your mind?"

"Yes. No. It's not really them. I don't know what I'm feeling exactly."

Mathew searched her eyes, looking for a way to

comfort her confused emotions.

"I can't imagine raising a child by myself," she whispered.

"And you're not going to."

"I know. But how do people do it?"

"I don't know." He gently rubbed his hands up and down her back.

"How did my father do it? How did he go on without my mother there?"

"He did it for one reason and one reason only. Love. Your father loves you more than anything or anyone in the world. There's nothing he wouldn't do for you."

"He's a stronger person than I am because I couldn't do it."

"You could do it. You're just as strong. Maybe even stronger. Your father did what he had to do. He didn't have a choice. Sometimes things happen that are beyond our control. But if we've surrounded ourselves with the people who love us most, then we'll always find a way. And I seem to recall albums full of photos and miles of home movie film of a happy girl and her happy father, sharing the blessings of what appeared to be a happy life."

"It wasn't perfect, but it was happy. My father always put my needs ahead of his own."

"And I'm sure that the caring, attentive mother you met at the pool today is doing the very same thing. And we'll do the same for LP—together. That's what families do—no matter what they look like. We're a family, Sunny. You and me. From the moment I kissed you in that elevator, I knew there was no one else I wanted to share my life with."

He took Sunny's hand and led her back to the bed. They stood together for a moment, his arms upon her shoulders, lightly caressing her creamy skin. Though they were well into their vacation, they hadn't made love yet. Instead, they'd savored the quiet moments, connecting in other ways. Gently washing each other's bodies in the outdoor shower. Reading excerpts of their beach novels aloud to one another. Napping together in the warm breeze on the lanai. With Sunny, there were well over a thousand and one pleasures, and he couldn't wait to discover each one.

****

Mommy is in the spa in the hotel adjacent to ours, so I thought I'd steal a few minutes and catch up with you. I can't believe how quickly our time here has flown by. We have been blessed with good weather for the most part, and I think this vacation was just what we needed. Though we've hardly spent a moment away from our suite, I have absolutely no regrets. We sleep late, read, take long showers, and enjoy the ocean from the lanai. It's really given your mother and me a chance to reconnect and refocus with your arrival right around the corner. We're in the final lap now—the last trimester. In no time, I'll be talking to you instead of writing my thoughts down on random scraps of paper. Your mom still has no idea about these letters, though I almost slipped again the other night. I've got to watch that third drink. It really does something to me, and I just can't seem to stop talking.

We'd planned a picnic on the beach for yesterday, but the rain kept us inside. Of course, curling up beside your mom all day is a picnic in itself. We divided our time between crossword puzzles and cable television.

We watched a marathon of movies including one of your mother's favorite musicals: Funny Girl. Now I know why she has a thing for gamblers. She's been smitten with Nicky Arnstein since her youth. We're about three quarters of the way through "the list" and I'm hoping to finish up the few remaining items by tomorrow night.

As the time of your birth grows closer, I can see the emotion growing inside your mother right alongside you. There's more than just a physical representation of the changes that are taking place inside her. There's something more. Something inside her heart and behind those eyes. I've watched her for a couple of weeks now—I could see it and feel it but didn't really know exactly what it was until last night. We stayed up late, talking about children and families and overcoming obstacles and living with tragedy. As each day brings us closer to your arrival, your mother is experiencing some feelings she's never had before...and so am I. We want so much for everything in this life to be perfect for you. We feel so blessed to be living in what we feel is the perfect marriage—the most complete relationship either of us has ever known. And we want to give you all that we have. We want to give you all the love and support that brought us together and helped to create you. Your mother's heart has softened in new ways, making her aware of the depth of her own parents' love and how much they sacrificed. They longed to give her so much yet protect her from so much. It's a fine line. And now, as she thinks about you, she can't help but think about other children too. We both do. Children who will go without. Those that will not feel loving arms around them or will go to bed hungry. Children whose parents will tell them they love them only after inflicting wounds that may never heal. Children whose parents will bless them with every material gift imaginable except their time. It will be these thoughts and many others like them that will cause us to cling tightly to you so that you will never know anything other than sheer joy.

God, you'd never know it by that last paragraph, but I promise I haven't been drinking. These words come from deep inside me, and while they may seem to ramble a bit with little or no cohesion, I assure you they are filled with honesty. You are the most important thing to us and you always will be.

I love you, Little Prince!
Daddy

Chapter Twenty-Eight

"Are you ready?" Sunny hollered.

"Be right there," Mathew called from the bedroom.

She looked around the suite in search of the elevator key. They had reservations for seven, and she didn't want to be late. This would be their last dinner out, as she'd arranged another visit with the private chef for the following evening—their final night before boarding the plane back home.

"You've got the key?" she asked.

He held the plastic card up in confirmation. "I do, but I've been thinking. Wanna order in? A little surf and turf...in bed?"

"Mathew, we've been in bed all afternoon."

"Exactly. If it ain't broke..." He shot her a look.

"You're hopeless." She took his hand and pulled him toward the elevator.

As the elevator doors opened, a larger-than-usual crowd assembled in the lobby surprised them. The afternoon rain had moved on, and teasing rays of sunshine now coaxed many from their suites. They'd only just stepped from the elevator when Mathew's cell phone rang. He shook his head with frustration as he reached into his pocket.

"Hello?" he answered.

"It's me, Matty," Leo said.

"Leo, is everything okay? It's late there. Are you

all right?"

Not only could Sunny hear the alarm in his voice, she could see it on his face. She tried her best to decipher the call, but being privy to only one side of the conversation made it difficult. After a minute, Mathew said his goodbyes and returned the phone to his pocket.

"Is Leo all right?"

"Leo is fine. It's a work thing."

"Is there a crisis of some sort?"

"Apparently." Mathew glanced around, taking a moment to collect his thoughts while checking his pockets.

"What can I do?" she asked.

"I know I swore I wouldn't do this, but I've got to make a quick call. I need to go back up to the suite to get the number from my wallet, which I apparently left on the dresser. I promise I'll have it taken care of in five minutes."

"Mathew, it's fine, I promise. I'll wait right here."

He turned and walked with quick steps back to the elevator, blowing a kiss to her just as the doors closed. Sunny continued toward the main doors. She spoke with the valet, requesting delivery of their rental car. Alone at the entrance of the hotel, she kept a watchful eye turned toward the elevators. She nodded politely at the couples and families going in and out of the hotel. Looking down at her watch, she wondered if their table would still be available. She felt a hand on her arm and turned around.

"Hello again," a woman's voice spoke with a warm tone.

"Oh, hello." Sunny instantly recognized the woman from the pool. "How are you?"

"Fine. On our way out to dinner. It's our last night," she said with a hint of sadness.

"It always goes by too fast, doesn't it?"

"It certainly does." The woman nodded.

"Where's your little swimmer?"

"He's on his way from Children's Hour in the Play Zone. They have the most fantastic children's area here. Very sweet and helpful attendants. Adrien begs to play with them every day. I think they've had more quality time with him than I have."

"Sounds like fun."

"They'll be bringing him to me any minute. Are you on your way in or out?"

"Out. Just waiting for my husband. An unexpected business call. He should be here any minute too."

"Are you staying through the weekend?" she asked.

"No. We're leaving the day after tomorrow."

****

Mathew stepped from the elevator, his face marked with lines of annoyance. The so-called crisis turned out to be a simple misunderstanding that should never have made it all the way up the proverbial chain to him. Thankfully, the sight of Sunny across the lobby instantly calmed him, returning him to his former good mood. Mathew couldn't resist spying on her for a minute, watching her have what appeared to be a very animated conversation with a woman. Sunny's hands were doing the majority of the talking, and she gestured wildly. It was one of the things he loved most about his wife. There were days when it was all about her hair. Or her eyes. Or her smile. But at that moment, it was about her hands, and the way they created a story within a story.

When Sunny's laugh bounced off the tile floors of the lobby, it triggered his own laugh. With a smirk and a shake of his head, Mathew headed toward the main door. Sunny glanced in his direction and smiled. Just steps away from her, she announced his presence.

"I don't believe you've met my husband." Sunny gestured proudly in Mathew's direction.

The woman turned around, locking eyes with him.

"Cass?" The satisfied look vanished from Mathew's face, replaced with one of shock.

Chapter Twenty-Nine

Several seconds of silence lapsed before Cass whispered his name in recognition. Sunny stood dumbfounded, stunned as fate reintroduced them. She watched her husband's eyes as he mentally processed their surprise reunion.

"How are you?" He pulled her in for a welcoming hug.

"Oh, it's so good to see you!" She returned his affections with a light kiss on both cheeks.

"It's been forever," he said.

"Too long," she added.

"You look great! What on earth are you doing here on Maui?" Mathew asked.

"Just needed a vacation. And Adrien loves the ocean, so here we are."

"Adrien?" He looked at Sunny, trying to recall where he'd heard that name.

"My son."

"Right! I heard something about the two of you and a water cannon fight at the pool the other day. Only we had no idea…" He traded a confused look with his wife. "Oh, I'm sorry. Forgive me. Sunny, this is Cass. Cass Christos."

And the plot thickens, Sunny thought before responding.

"Hi, I'm Sunny, your poolside confidant and

official Frisbee retriever." She held out her hand to Cass.

"Well, isn't this something?" Cass shook Sunny's hand warmly. "Walt Disney was right. It is a small world after all."

"Mommy!" A little voice called out and they turned their heads to see the young dark-haired boy tearing through the doors.

"Hello, my angel!" Cass bent down and scooped the boy up in her arms. "Did you have fun?"

He nodded warily, eyeing the strangers beside them.

"Adrien, I want to introduce you to a very old friend of Mommy's. This is Mathew." Cass said.

"How are you, young man?" Mathew extended his hand, but the boy turned away, snuggling against his mother.

"And you remember the beautiful woman we saw at the pool? This is his wife, Sunny."

Adrien shyly regarded Sunny.

"I certainly remember you. You are one amazing swimmer." Sunny shared a sweet smile.

Cass's gaze bounced between the two of them for a moment before she spoke.

"I haven't had a chance to congratulate you, Mathew. You're having a boy, right?"

"Yes, we are. Around Easter." Mathew's face lit up with pride, while Sunny's mind raced back in time to a conversation overheard in a bathroom stall in the Four Seasons Hotel.

"I know you must be thrilled. It truly is a blessing."

"We're very excited," Mathew said with a nod.

"Listen, I know you two are on your way to dinner,

and I don't want to keep you, but I must know. How is Leo?"

"He's fine. He suffered a brain aneurysm last year but has made an amazing recovery. He's actually doing really well, despite all he's been through."

"Oh, I'm so sorry to hear that." She shook her head sympathetically. "Dear, sweet Leo. He's one tough cookie."

"That he is." He nodded in agreement.

"Please give him my love." She paused, focusing firmly on Mathew's eyes. "I think about the two of you a lot."

Mathew nodded again. Sunny held her breath, ready for the grandest of awkward moments to disappear while she searched for a meaningful yet lighthearted response that would wrap up the entire exchange. They stood together, just three smiling faces with nothing to say. *I'm sure we left ex-girlfriends off The List.*

"Sunny, it's so nice to meet you—officially, I mean. I wish you all the best in the birth of your little handful." She offered her hand again, shifting her weight slightly as she held the small boy in her arms. "We've got to get going. I promised this guy some fire dancers before we leave."

"You're not having dinner at The Royal by chance?" Sunny asked.

"Our exact destination, as a matter of fact," Cass confirmed.

"Oh…ours too." She exchanged a knowing look with her husband.

****

Mathew shifted the car forcibly into gear, taking

the corners tightly. Though normally a cautious driver, the scene at the entrance of the hotel caused his mind to race, allowing his foot to grow heavy on the accelerator. They hadn't spoken a word since departing. Would Sunny break the silence? He eyed the black limousine in the rear-view mirror, curious as to what thoughts might be traveling through the mind of his former lover as she followed behind them. A glance in Sunny's direction to gage her feelings provided no clue. No look of distress. No questionable body language.

"Counsel requests permission to speak," he announced.

"Permission granted," she responded with a business-like tone.

"Let the record show that I had absolutely nothing to do with the selection of additional dinner guests."

"Am I to understand you're representing yourself in the case, sir?"

"I am, Your Honor."

"Proceed." She nodded.

"I would like to submit Exhibit A..." He reached inside the inner pocket of his jacket, producing a small scrap of paper.

"Ah, yes. Exhibit A." She took the paper from his hand and studied it with a thoughtful eye.

"If it pleases the court, your Excellency, I would also like to point out that nowhere on The List is there mention of any activities involving former lovers, bed partners, or old flames of any kind."

"Do you have any further submissions or arguments at this time?" she asked.

"Nothing further, Your Honor."

"Well, counselor, in light of this evidence, I feel it

is my duty to render a ruling." She folded the piece of paper and held it out to him. "Not guilty."

"Well, someone in this car is guilty. And if it's not me…" He gave her a look.

"Don't be mad," she pleaded.

"I'm not mad. I'm just surprised."

"Why? Because I asked your ex-girlfriend to join us for dinner?"

"Ya think?"

"I would have invited them whether you had a past with her or not. She's delightful. And Adrien is precious. I would really enjoy getting to know her. I'll be honest. I was jealous for two seconds. Then I remembered our chat at the pool. I'm trying to act like a certified adult here."

Mathew didn't respond but continued to drive aggressively. After a couple of minutes of silence, she reached out, placing her hand on his atop the gearshift.

"I firmly believe everything happens for a reason. You know that. Cass and her father were an important part of your life. You sat together at his deathbed. You stood by her during a very difficult and emotionally draining time. She lost her father and the father of her child. I think the least we can do is take the woman to dinner."

****

It was after seven when they arrived at The Royal. The luau was in full swing. Bursts of applause, toasts, and laughter from many diners around them filled the atmosphere with a carnival-like quality. Mathew watched the wonder in Adrien's eyes. The young boy absorbed their surroundings with a look of awe.

A cheerful hostess escorted them to their table.

Mathew ordered their drinks, while the ladies guided Adrien through the buffet line. Looking around, he considered the odds of the many bets he could have placed that day. A walk on the beach? Three to one. An afternoon nap? Two to one. Being intimate with his wife? A sure thing. Dinner with Cass Christos? No way in hell.

Mathew quickly downed a Scotch and soda, motioning for a refill before the return of his dinner companions. His gaze zeroed in on the two women who'd be sharing his table, talking and gesturing in a friendly manner. Sunny eyes appeared to be bright and engaging—a sign that she truly wasn't bothered in the least. His focus stayed on them, watching as Sunny led Adrien by the hand while Cass balanced two plates in hers, weaving through the crowd. Seeing his pregnant wife and his ex-lover smiling upon approach, only one thought crossed his mind. *How in the hell did I let this happen?*

He stood, pulling out chairs for each of them, then headed out in search of his own dinner. By the time he returned, Sunny and Cass were engrossed in the same type of animated conversation he'd witnessed in the lobby of the hotel.

"I was just telling Sunny about the time the police busted a drug deal when we were staying in that hotel in Madrid. What was the name of it? The old palace in Chamberi?" Cass looked up at Mathew, snapping her fingers several times to jog her memory.

"It wouldn't have been Santo Mauro, would it?" Sunny asked.

"Oh, my God! Yes! Santo Mauro." Cass's eyes shined. "I love that hotel."

"Me too! The history…the architecture! It's phenomenal," Sunny added.

Mathew sat, fork in hand, completely flabbergasted as he watched the two women carry on like the best of friends. Before he could speak, their discussion of the historic boutique hotel turned into a dialogue on French antiques, which then morphed into a debate on the renowned works of European artists. *Is it gonna be like this all through dinner?* He turned his attention to the curly-haired boy, quietly sitting across from him.

"Young man, I'm afraid we're in for a very long night," he said, reaching for his second Scotch and soda.

Stories and laughter continued to flow throughout dinner as they emptied their plates and refilled their glasses. Conversation danced around the table and Mathew couldn't remember when he'd had a more enjoyable evening. Sunny and Cass found delight in discussing everything from childbirth to Greek philosophy, while Mathew entertained Adrien with origami and magic tricks involving cocktail napkins and pocket change. Observing the amusement on the boy's face filled his heart, and he couldn't stop thinking about the tiny life growing inside the woman beside him. *Sunny was right. His laughter is a symphony of happiness.*

Just as the waiter cleared their dishes away, the lights around them dimmed. A drumbeat sounded in a steady, tribal rhythm, and suddenly their faces were illuminated by flaming torches. Watching the young boy's face, Mathew could see the excitement and curiosity building behind his eyes. Shifting in his seat, Adrien tried to gain a better vantage point, unable to see the Hawaiian fire dancers over the crowd. Sunny noticed his distress and looked at her husband. With a nod, she placed her napkin on the table and stood, walking to Adrien's side of the table.

"Why don't we sneak up and get a closer look at those dancers?" She leaned over and whispered, glancing in Cass's direction in search of a permissive nod.

"It's fine with me." Cass raised her glass in approval.

Adrien followed alongside his new friend as they moved closer to the action, leaving Mathew and Cass alone for the first time. He watched as his wife disappeared into the crowd before turning his face back to his old friend.

"You have one special little guy there."

"He's an angel—my saving grace. A reminder of the best of humanity."

"You're a wonderful mother, Cass. I mean it. Really wonderful."

"He makes it easy. I don't know what I'd do without Adrien. He was my light during a very dark time. I only wish my father…" She paused, nervously pushing her straw around the rim of her glass.

"Oh, he's watching. I can promise you that." Mathew's eyes softened, as he recalled the memory of Cass's father.

"Speaking of angels and the best of humanity…" With a grin, she changed the subject.

"It's pretty obvious, isn't it?"

"Obvious?" She laughed out loud. "You're completely transparent. I'm sure you've lost your knack for poker now too."

"Leo says the same thing."

"You know, I used to think that the woman who finally landed you would be the luckiest person in the world. Now, I think I have to change my answer. *You're* the lucky one this time. She's amazing, Mathew. A beautiful person, inside and out."

"Well, you'll get no argument from me."

"I bet it was a ton of bricks moment for you, wasn't it?"

"Ton of bricks?"

"When you met her. It was probably something so unexpected—but it hit you like a ton of bricks. I'm guessing it was some random encounter like in the Pro Shop at the golf course, or maybe you were just waiting in line at the DMV, getting your license renewed…"

"It was an elevator. At the hospital. During Leo's ordeal with the aneurysm."

"Love in an elevator?"

Mathew laughed. "Sounds like a rock song, right?"

"I don't know what it sounds like, but it looks good on you. You're blissful. You're smitten. You're ruined."

"Guilty. Guilty. And guilty."

"Well, you deserve it all." Cass nodded. "Every drop of happiness. The world owes you."

"The world owes me nothing. I've been given everything—*everything*."

"No, you've worked your ass off for everything. I always wondered what true happiness would look like in those eyes of yours." She reached out and held his hand across the table. "It looks damn good, Matty."

"It feels pretty damn good too." He gave her hand a friendly squeeze.

After a moment of unspoken conversation, Cass released his hand. Reaching into her purse, she retrieved a long, thin cigarette, along with an engraved Zippo, just like the one her father carried. Always the gentleman, Mathew took it from her and lit her cigarette.

"You really need to give it up, you know."

"I know, I know. But smoking's the only real vice I've got left."

"I can still see the way your father would flip his lighter open. God, that man must've smoked two packs a day."

"Yep. He loved his Leaders."

"No, he loved Next. Next Red Twenty-Fives," he said with a grin.

"And you would know that because?"

"Because I might've smoked a couple of them with him from time to time."

"Do as I say, not as I do?" She took a long drag.

"Something like that."

Another quiet moment passed, and Mathew decided it was time to put all kidding aside.

"Your father was a good man. I loved him very much, Cass." He returned the lighter to her.

"I know you did. And he loved you too. You were just another one of his boys."

"I only hope that I will be the kind of father to my child that your father was to all of you."

"Oh, Mathew, you will be everything my father was and so much more."

"You know, there are times when something will happen during a meeting that I think to myself, *I wonder what the old man would do.* He always made the right decisions, no matter what. He knew exactly what to do in every situation."

"Not every situation. When he lost my mother, I thought for sure we lost him too. We lost him for a long time after that. But thankfully, with a lot of persistence and prayer, he found his way back to us."

"I know he loved your mother very much. Even though I never had a chance to meet her, I felt like I knew her just by the stories he used to tell of her. Talk about blissful, smitten, and ruined." He smiled again.

"They were crazy in love until the day she died." Cass sighed.

"Their story reminds me a lot of Sunny's mother and father. She lost her mother when she was young, and it's taken her father numerous years and an undisclosed amount of beer and pot to recover."

"Some people drink their way to happiness; some people smoke their way." She casually blew a thin line of smoke over her right shoulder.

"Surely you need more than just a regular tobacco fix."

"Well, having a four-year-old on your heels is a definite reality check."

"You know, I can see why people think Adrien is mine. Those eyes of his…"

"It's crazy, huh?"

"But the hair and skin and the shape of his face. There's no doubt who his father is."

"By genetics only." She took another drag of her cigarette.

"So, Adrien doesn't see his father?"

"He's never seen Nico. And he never will."

"Oh c'mon, Cass. Are you sure that's what you

want?"

"I didn't think so for a long time. But I do now. Adrien has everything he needs. Don't forget all those uncles of his. They dote on him like you can't imagine."

"Where's Nico now? Do you know?"

"Somewhere in Europe, probably doing one of the two things he enjoys most. Mounting some hostile takeover or some young girl. He's quite the gardener too, you know."

"What do you mean?"

"I mean, Adrien's not the only seed he's planted. He has two other children. Twins. Just about eighteen months younger than Adrien."

"And no relationship with them either?"

"None. He doesn't want relationships. He's only interested in one thing. He thought by getting a piece of me, he'd get a piece of my father. But he soon realized that was never going to happen. The Christos Empire will always be controlled by a Christos. I thought initially he'd try to use Adrien as a bargaining chip, but I was wrong." She spoke with a cool and composed tone.

"And what about you? How are you dealing with all this? Being a single mother is never easy, even with The Empire backing you up."

"Honestly? I wish The Empire would back off a little."

"Five boys and only one girl? You know that's never going to happen."

"Little sister is all grown up now. I can carry the ball by myself."

"I know you can. But they love you and want to

protect you, that's all."

"They love me and want to control me."

"Cass, that's not fair, and you know it."

"They even sent a babysitter along. I can't even take my son on vacation alone."

"Sunny mentioned some guy at the pool. Who is he?"

"Some *Security Specialist* that my brothers hired. That's a fancy title for goon. I told him he was not invited on our outing tonight, but I won't be surprised if he shows up here."

"Is it really that bad? Honestly?" His brows furrowed, staring at her.

"Okay, it's not *that* bad. But playing the Heiress-in-Distress is quite becoming, don't you think?" She swept her dark hair back off her shoulder dramatically.

"I've never known you to be truly distressed. And rarely have I seen you play the heiress card."

"That's because I used to run around with a brave knight who fought for my honor on a number of occasions."

"Who are you running with now? Or are you just running?" Mathew asked with a serious tone.

"I've stopped running. I'm happy to walk beside my son and see the world through those beautiful eyes."

"And what will you tell Adrien? About his father, I mean. Because he's going to want to know eventually."

"I've told him all about his father. That brave, handsome knight with the same color eyes who rescued Mommy many, many times."

"And when he wants to know the truth?" He gave her a hard stare.

"He'll never want to know the truth. The fairy tale

is so much more fun." She dropped her cigarette into his glass with a mischievous grin.

****

Sunny followed the limousine back to the hotel. Mathew leaned back against the headrest in the passenger seat. She could tell from his expression that despite the pounding inside his head, he'd had a wonderful evening. As she cruised along the dark, winding roads, she couldn't help but smile. Watching Mathew's interactions with Adrien had been the best part of her night. He'd made pennies disappear and nickels move through the table. He'd created tiny white cranes from cocktail napkins. He'd shared silly stories of Ivy and Leo. It didn't matter what he did, Mathew could captivate an audience regardless of age. And on their way out to the car, he'd carried the young boy up on his shoulders, as their collective laughter filled the air.

"You're something, you know that?" Sunny reached for his hand.

"I'm not about to get a lecture on holding one's liquor, am I?" he asked.

"No, that's not what I mean. I'm talking about you and Adrien."

"He's a great kid."

"And you were great with him tonight. He was fascinated by you."

"All kids love magic tricks."

"But it wasn't just that. He listened to every word you said with complete concentration."

"I've picked up a few storytelling tricks from Leo over the years."

"Mathew, you're going to be a fantastic father."

"As long as you're beside me, I can do anything."

Sunny squeezed his hand. For several miles, silence filled the rental car. There was one question burning her insides with curiosity but asking it might come off as jealous.

You're not a jealous person. Mathew knows this. If you can't ask your husband a simple question…

"Did you and Cass have a good time catching up—when Adrien and I went to check out the fire dancers?"

"It was both wonderful and sad."

"Really? In what way?"

"Wonderful to see her so happy as a mom, but sad to see her so miserable beyond that."

"Even with all her family's money?"

"Like the saying goes, it can't buy happiness."

Sunny pulled up to the entrance of their hotel just as Cass and Adrien emerged from the back of their limo. Mother and child waited at the door while Mathew took care of business with the valet. Just steps inside the lobby, Cass turned and caught his arm.

"I can't tell you what this night has meant to me. And Adrien. I don't know how to thank you both."

"No thanks are necessary. It was a wonderful evening, and we truly enjoyed every minute," Sunny said.

"You have a great little guy there, Mom." Mathew high-fived the boy.

"We're leaving first thing in the morning, so we probably won't see you again." Cass paused, tears forming in her eyes. "Seeing the two of you together—the love and respect you have for each other. It's renewed a dream in me I thought died long ago. And this little man." She placed a gentle hand on Sunny's belly. "What a lucky little boy to have such loving, caring parents." She reached and took each of them by the hand. "I wish you both all the happiness in the world."

Sunny shared a warm embrace with Cass, her own tears now buildings. As she pulled away, Cass stepped back and looked at Mathew.

"This is normally the part where the ex-girlfriend tells you that you let the right woman get away...but not this time." She hugged him tightly, whispering in his ear, "Take good care of them, Matty. They're your greatest treasure, you know."

Chapter Thirty

Dear Kid,

Or maybe I should call you LP. I overheard your mom and dad call you that a few weeks ago. I didn't ask them but I'm guessing it's your initials. They are determined to keep your name a secret from everyone. And far be it from me to ask. But I have spent a few nights going back through my book of names, trying to see if I could figure it out. Are you going to be Landon? I think Sunny had that one on her shortlist at one time. What about Logan? I think your dad liked that name. Well, whatever moniker they've decided on, I'm sure it will be the perfect name for you. I have yet to see your parents fail at anything. If they're still debating, they'll have to get a move on. You've hit the thirty-six-week mark now and it won't be long until you make a public appearance. Just one more month. The home stretch. The final lap. You might surprise us with an early arrival, but I doubt it. From what I've read, most first-time deliveries are later rather than early. I hope for your mom's sake that you'll be early or right on time at least. She's really struggling with sleep these days. Maybe the doctor will have some news for them today. You might be closer to being with us than we think.

They're at Dr. Sumner's office right now. They made an early appointment because your dad has a surprise planned for your mom later. Tonight, your dad is taking your mom out to a fancy dinner. Only it isn't dinner exactly. Your old man reserved the Museum of Fine Art (in exchange for a hefty donation) and is having some famous photographer take photos of your mother and you while you're still in the oven. Sounds a little extravagant, if you ask me. But your father never does anything halfway. It's all or nothing—especially where your mom is concerned. I say some Tex-Mex and a Polaroid or two would suffice, but then I haven't had much worth photographing in a while.

    More later,

    Uncle Leo

    P.S. I don't think I mentioned this in my last letter, but your mom and dad finally received their diplomas in the mail the other day—the ones from the birthing classes they took at the hospital. Remember I told you about that in my last letter? I guess they're officially deemed worthy to be parents. Word is that their instructor is a good friend of Dr. Sumner, and she gave your father a pretty hard time. Whenever she asked for a volunteer, she picked your dad every time, whether he wanted to participate or not. Your mom said he was very funny and everyone's favorite comic throughout the course. On the final night of class, the instructor gave out awards to all the would-be moms and their coaches. Your dad was given the "Class Clown" award while your mom was named "Most Likely To Give Birth While Looking Fabulous." Just three nights with them and that instructor had them pegged. I can't wait to see your father in action with you. He's going to be a great dad!

****

Mathew studied the picture of a fetus at thirty-seven weeks while Sunny secured the light blue hospital gown around her neck. A knock on the door was followed by Dr. Sumner's head peeking inside the examination room.

"Good morning, Ellis family." He greeted them.

"Morning," Mathew said, his tone upbeat.

"And how is everyone on this beautiful Friday morning?"

"Fine. Tired but fine." Sunny responded.

"Sleep issues are the same, I take it?"

"No change." She shook her head.

"Just a little while longer. You think you have sleep issues now," he said with a laugh.

"But we won't mind waking up to our new alarm clock." Mathew smiled lovingly at his wife.

"Well, let's get it over with. Same song, different verse. I'll check the cerclage, ask the standard questions, and then we'll see you back here next week." He opened the cabinet on the wall behind him just as a nurse entered.

"Any chance we could push the delivery up?" Mathew asked.

"Only if I thought there was a problem. But I promise that when the forty-week mark comes and goes, we'll end the suspense." He snapped on a fresh pair of latex gloves before settling himself on the small rolling stool.

"What are the chances of actually making it to forty weeks once the stitches are removed?" he asked, helping Sunny lie back in position.

"It's a fifty-fifty shot. Some make it, others don't. Sunny's cervical opening was small, so her chances are somewhat better—but only slightly. Now breathe deeply for me, Sunny."

Mathew held one of her hands and gently smoothed her hair back with his other. She closed her eyes, eager to hear Dr. Sumner's comforting confirmation that all was well. Though she'd been through this same routine for weeks, she always held her breath. After a minute, he stood with a smile.

"Just like last week. Everything looks great."

The next several minutes were spent locating and recording LP's heartbeat and answering the obligatory questions that all pregnant women answer when entering the last month.

"I double-checked and your paperwork has been processed at the hospital. Your reservation is all set."

"That's good news." She nodded.

"Your bags are packed?"

"Yes," she and Mathew said simultaneously.

"Any other questions you can think of?"

"I think we're just ready to get the show on the road," Mathew answered.

"Next week I'll remove the stitches and then we'll see what happens." He extended his hand.

"Thanks so much, Dr. Sumner. We appreciate all you're doing for us." Mathew shook his hand.

"Just keep her comfortable and see that she takes plenty of catnaps following those difficult nights."

Back at the elevator, Mathew reached for Sunny's hand.

"Are you disappointed?" he asked.

"That he didn't whisk me away to the hospital and take this baby out? No, I'm really not. Are you?"

"Not at all. I don't want to rush this. This is such a special time for us."

It was close to two o'clock when they finally got home. Mathew knew she was growing tired and talk of a nap earlier was beginning to sound good to him. They found Leo and Ivy curled up together on the sofa, catching forty winks a piece. Quietly, they climbed the stairs to their bedroom. She quickly changed into one of his t-shirts and a pair of maternity shorts before settling herself in among the pillows. Mathew stripped down to a pair of boxers.

He continued around to his side of the bed and crawled up beside her, giving her pillows a loving fluff as he burrowed in next to her. Of all their travels and adventures, sleeping beside his wife in the middle of the day was his favorite escape.

"Mathew?"

"Hmm?"

"How did you do it?"

"Do what?"

"How did you manage to keep yourself single until I came along?"

"What?" He laughed.

"I'm serious."

"It wasn't that hard."

"But they all wanted you. Every single one. How could they not?"

"You didn't know me back then. I was different."

"In what way?"

"In every way. I didn't love them. I love you. I'm a completely different person with you than I was with every other woman in my past."

"Different how?"

"I don't know. I was more arrogant back then. I was proud. Cocky."

"I don't believe you."

"Ask Leo. He'll tell you. But from the moment I met you, that all changed. Just being around you and discovering new things about you made me want to be a better person. For the first time in my life, I wanted to be vulnerable because you were worth the risk. You gave me the courage to do that."

"I don't want anything to change between us when this baby comes."

"It won't. We'll just have one more thing to smile about."

"Promise me that we'll still make time for this." She wrapped her fingers around his.

He could hear it in her voice—a tone of uncertainty.

"We've always made time for this, and we always will."

She turned over and stared at him, her eyes filled with apprehension.

"Sunny, what's going on? Having doubts here in the bottom of the ninth is not very encouraging."

"I'm not having doubts about LP."

"Then what?" he asked.

"There's a tiny part of me that doesn't want the dynamic to change. Is that bad?"

"Of course, it's not bad. It's normal. I've had the same thought myself—only mine was fueled by something much more selfish."

"What do you mean?"

"I'm not very good at sharing."

"That's not true. You're one of the most generous people I know."

"That's not what I mean. I can be generous with

money, but I don't want to share *you*."

"Oh," she answered quietly.

"I can't wait to hold him and love him and share everything in the world with him, but there's a little place inside of me that feels the same way you do. It's been you and me every day. There will always be a part of me that will long for those days. But the days ahead will be lit with such a bright light that we won't want to look back very often."

"I read an article online yesterday and this woman wrote that she can't remember back before her baby arrived—that her life didn't really start until she became a mom. Now I know she meant it in the sweetest way possible, but it scared me. I don't want to forget us, Mathew. Being us is the truest I've ever been to myself. It's the most vulnerable I've allowed *myself* to be. I don't want to lose us."

Chapter Thirty-One

I can't believe it, but we made it another week! Thirty-nine weeks and three days and you're still resting comfortably inside your mother's beautiful belly. I thought for sure that as soon as Dr. Sumner removed the cerclage last week that we'd be holding you by now. But if you're happy staying put where you are, then that's fine by me. At yesterday's appointment, we got to take a peek at you. Dr. Sumner performed another ultrasound and internal exam, and you are starting to make your way into the birth canal. Your head is down and you're getting into position. It could be anytime now, even though you could technically stay put for another full week. He told us the average interval between cerclage removal and delivery is somewhere around fifteen days. So, you might go beyond the forty-week mark and Easter Sunday, after all. Mommy has gained twenty-nine glorious pounds, and Dr. Sumner predicts that you'll be tipping the scales around the seven-pound mark.

Can it really be true? Are you almost here? I've read the final chapters of our pregnancy guides at least half a dozen times over the last week. Your room is ready, the car seat is secure inside Mommy's SUV, and all your tiny clothes are washed and folded. I wish your mom was feeling better. She's been battling some awful allergies that popped up a few days ago and she just isn't herself. She's been the picture of health throughout her entire pregnancy, and I hate to see her running out of steam just as we get to the finish line. The doctor prescribed a safe antihistamine, but she's afraid to take it. She's been strictly by the book, and I don't think she'll give in to the tree pollen monster with less than a week to go. We've tried every homemade remedy that Leo and I can think of, but nothing seems to work. Maybe the fact that Grandpa Huck is driving in tonight will perk her up a bit. It's nice that he'll be here with us this weekend for Easter. Will you be here for Easter? That's the millionaire dollar question.

We finally decided on a middle name for you. We've been all over the internet, back and forth through our baby name books, and page by page through the book where we found your first name. Actually, your grandpa gave us a hint about your middle name, though he didn't know it at the time. We were talking about names during Christmas and he mentioned something that stood out to your mom and me. We talked about it and agreed it was perfect for several reasons, if you arrive when we think you will. So, I am happy to report that you will enter this world with a first, middle, and last name.

Well, it seems that I'm now late for a meeting. I just had a few minutes to jot these thoughts down, and like always, our time together slips by too fast. If it's going by this fast on paper, I can't imagine how quickly the days will go once you are here. With each line, I wonder if this will be the last letter I write before I'm holding you and looking into your face. I know I've tried in the past to describe how blessed I feel to be sharing this journey with your mother. But the words necessary to convey the intensity of my feelings escape me. Seeing her change and grow has been the most humbling experience. Every day I am inspired by her love and commitment, not only to me but to keeping you safe and healthy. I have had the pleasure of gazing upon some of the most exquisite landscapes in the world. I've stood and studied priceless works of art in museums around the globe. Nothing compares to the beauty that I have witnessed in your mother over these past months. I truly am the luckiest man in the world.

I love you!
Daddy

*****

Dear LP,

Thirty-nine plus weeks and no sign that you're ready to leave the confines of my uterus. It must be really cozy in there because you've all but given up your fetal gymnastics. I guess your baby condo is quickly running out of square footage. I hate to rush you but we're all very eager to meet you and celebrate what will be the happiest day on our calendar—your birthday. Grandpa Huck got here yesterday afternoon, and you know how impatient he is. Let's not keep him waiting too much longer. He settled all his affairs just to be here with you from the moment you take your first breaths. I can hardly believe that we're almost to the forty-week mark. The Easter Bunny arrives tomorrow— will you? Or will Daddy and Uncle Leo lose their bets? From the time Dr. Sumner confirmed your due date, they've been convinced that you would arrive on Easter Sunday. Let's keep them in the black, shall we?

I've spent the majority of today in bed, still battling this allergy. My Three Stooges have done their best to keep me fed and entertained. Barbara stopped by with her famous chicken soup for lunch. Daddy and I watched an old movie together, and your grandfather and I looked through some old photo albums that he brought with him—photos of when I was a baby. The pictures of my mom holding me are how I see myself holding you. God, she was so beautiful. I wish she could be here with us. I know she's keeping your soul close to her heart, just waiting for the perfect moment to send you down to us because that's what angels do.

I wish you could see your father in action. He's been feathering the nest for the last week, making sure that everything's in order. He's packed and repacked his bag for the hospital. Your car seat has been checked and double-checked. He's strategically placed diapers and wipes all over the house to save time. And he's worn the cover off his birthing book. I don't know what I've enjoyed more, watching my belly or watching him. And I don't know what I'm looking forward to more, watching you or watching him watching you. I do know that I plan to take some very good and timely advice: I will enjoy every precious moment because I know they will be tiny drops of time.

I've spent the last few days thinking about the influence your father has had on me. Without a doubt, he's the single most important person in my life. His love molds me into a better person. I don't know why, but for a very long time, I thought I would never experience the blessings that I'm currently enjoying. I've always known that I'm basically a good person on the inside. I'm honest, fair, hard-working, and kind to all animals and most people. But the fairy tale was something I never considered. It's not that I didn't see myself as worthy. I just always pictured myself on another road. And now, your father and I will take each other's hands and step onto a new road. A well-traveled road, but one that our feet have never touched. And though I won't have a map to guide me, I will look to your father to be my compass.

I love you, I love you, I love you,
Mommy

****

"Can I get you anything?" Mathew called from the bathroom.

"An anesthesiologist and some forceps?" Sunny called back.

"Not funny." He walked back into their bedroom. "Would you like a back rub or one of my famous foot massages?" He reached over and rubbed her foot tenderly.

"You know what would really help me relax?"

"What?"

"If you read to us." She rested her hands on her belly.

"One bedtime story coming up." He gently crawled off the bed and slipped quietly out of their bedroom. Within a minute he was back, several books in hand.

"Take your pick. *Goodnight Moon*, *Where the Wild Things Are*, or my personal favorite, *Anatole.*"

"They're all classics, but I love *Anatole*."

"The honorable rodent with a penchant for tasty French fromage? Excellent choice." Bending down, he spoke in a soothing tone, his lips hovering just above Sunny's belly.

"Testing…one, two, three. Can you hear me in there?"

"I think he's ready. At least I hope he is. He's been very still today. Too still." Sunny gave herself a pat.

"Well, what started out as a mansion is now a one-room flat."

"Do you think he's okay?"

"He's fine. Very cramped quarters in there."

"I know you're right, but I worry."

"See? It's easily your favorite pastime too. Now, with or without my best French accent?" he asked, holding up the children's book.

"*Avec, naturellement.*"

Mathew read the story aloud to her, making her laugh with his silly character voices. She was just beginning to relax when she felt an unusual tightening inside. It was completely different from the Braxton-Hicks contractions she'd experienced. It wasn't painful exactly, but it didn't feel normal. She grabbed Mathew's hand, keeping her body totally still.

"What's wrong?" he asked.

"I don't know," she responded in a whisper.

The words had barely left her mouth when she looked down and watched the contortions of her pregnant form. She felt as though every abdominal muscle was being pulled to its limit. Squeezing his hand firmly, she held her breath.

"Are you having a contraction?"

"I don't think so. This is nothing like what I've been having."

"But Dr. Sumner said they'd be more intense." He checked the clock, making a mental note of the time.

"I don't know what just happened, but I don't think it was a contraction."

"Are you in any pain?"

"No, not really. I just feel like my stomach muscles have been pulled in two different directions. Almost like my uterus did a complete flip." She closed her eyes, trying to concentrate on her breathing.

"Well, let's lie very still and see if it happens again." He rubbed his thumb gently across her hand.

They waited in silence for what seemed like an eternity. After ten uneventful minutes, Mathew spoke. "You haven't felt anything?"

"Nothing."

"And you're not in any pain?"

"No."

"I think if you were going into labor, you'd have had another contraction by now."

"I'm telling you, that was *not* a contraction."

"Then what was it?"

"I have no idea, but I certainly hope it doesn't happen again."

"Maybe LP's just moving further down into position."

"Maybe." She didn't sound convinced.

"Do you want to finish reading?"

"Would you mind if we just turned out the lights?"

"Okay." He could see the worry in her eyes.

Mathew moved the stack of books to his bedside table and turned the lamp off.

"Everything's going to be fine. Let's try to get some sleep, okay?" His tone conveyed nothing but love and comfort.

"I'll try." She drew and released a deep breath, feeling everything except relaxed.

****

Sunny looked at the clock again. Sleep had come

easily to her husband. She, on the other hand, had spent the last two hours unable to give herself over to dreams. From the time he'd turned out the light, she'd wrestled with the words of Dr. Sumner over and over in her mind. *If something doesn't feel right, then get yourself to the hospital. The worst thing that will happen is that we send you home.*

She curled up on her left side, cradling her pregnant form. Focusing all her attention on the baby inside her, she spoke to him in a whisper.

"Just give me a sign. Just a tiny little kick and then I'll go right to sleep, I promise."

She lay watching the clock for another five minutes, with no response from LP. With every second that passed, her anxiety grew. It was time to be proactive.

"Mathew?" She turned over and touched his arm.

"Is it time?" he asked in a groggy voice.

"I don't know. But something doesn't feel right."

"Did it happen again? The tightening?" He sat up, turning the lamp back on. The light on her face illuminated fear.

"No, but I just don't feel right." She continued to keep her hands firmly around her stomach.

"Are you in any pain whatsoever?" he asked again.

"No, but—" She struggled to find the right words.

"Sunny, I'm sure it's nothing. You're going to feel worse if you don't stop worrying and try to get some rest."

"I can't rest. I think we should just go."

"To the hospital?"

"Yes." She nodded, clearly distressed.

"All right." He brushed her hair off her forehead

before kissing it softly.

****

The middle-of-the-night ride to the hospital was not unlike the one they'd made once before. Sunny rested her head against the window, staring out into the darkness without a sound. Mathew left her alone with her thoughts for several minutes as he sorted out his own. He'd never known her to be irrational or melodramatic during her pregnancy. Even when they'd made that first late-night journey to the hospital following the bleeding, she'd been surprisingly calm. Before and after the cerclage, she'd remained tranquil and composed. His mind raced back through the final pages of the pregnancy guide—the section on the phases of labor in particular. *Maybe this is it? Maybe she was having a contraction earlier, only didn't know it? How would she know for sure? We have nothing to compare it to. This might be it. In a few hours, we might be holding our Little Prince.*

And with that thought, Mathew relaxed for the first time since Sunny woke him. It was then he realized that fatherhood was probably no more than a few hours away.

"Happy Easter, by the way." He broke the silence, taking her hand in his.

"Well, you called it. You said Easter from the get-go and here we are on our way to the hospital. I really think this is it."

"How are you feeling?"

"I'm fine. Just scared."

"I'll be right with you every step of the way, I promise." He kissed her hand, right near her wedding ring.

265

He offered to drop her at the entrance to the ER, but she insisted on walking with him from the parking area. Again, he'd left a note for Huck and Leo. Birthing babies is an unpredictable business, and they agreed it was best to let them sleep. Mathew made a written promise to call as soon as they had more concrete information. They walked hand in hand straight to the elevators, bypassing the bedlam inside the ER. Unsure of what lay ahead, he decided to leave their bags in the car. He held her hand and smiled reassuringly as they made the short trip up. As the doors opened, his hand found its comforting and protective place on the small of her back as they stepped into the labor and delivery area of the hospital.

The floor was quiet, with only one nurse keeping vigil at the nurses' station. She looked up from her paperwork as they approached the desk.

"Good morning," she said.

"Good morning. The name is Ellis. Sunny Ellis." Mathew leaned against the counter.

The nurse nodded and entered the information into the computer.

"How far apart are your contractions?" she asked Sunny.

"I'm not having contractions—at least, I don't think I am. I had a very unusual tightening—a stretching really—of my stomach muscles. It felt like my uterus did a backflip."

"What time was this?"

"About ten o'clock."

"Any pain or discharge?"

"No. But Dr. Sumner told me that if something didn't feel right to come in. And that certainly didn't feel right."

"Okay. We'll get you into the examination area and get you checked out. I'll page Dr. Sumner and let him know you're here." She glanced at the large dry-erase board on the wall behind her. "He just finished a delivery about twenty minutes ago, so he's not far."

Picking up the phone, she dialed a number and waited for several seconds before entering a code. Replacing the receiver, she smiled up at them once more.

"He should be checking in shortly. Let's head on back."

They followed the nurse into the very same area they'd been placed prior to the cerclage. The nurse excused herself momentarily while Sunny changed into the requisite light blue gown. After a minute or two, the same nurse returned, carrying a handheld Doppler stethoscope along with a file folder.

"You were here not long ago for a cerclage?" she asked.

"Yes, we were," Mathew answered.

"And your stitches have been removed, is that correct?"

"Yes." Sunny nodded.

"Lie back for me." The nurse removed a bottle of ultrasound gel from a warming bin and shook it vigorously. She applied a large amount on Sunny's belly and gently rolled the transducer around in it.

"When was the last time you felt movement?"

"I guess around dinner time."

"Was that six o'clock? Seven?" She continued to move the transducer.

"About six-thirty."

"Why aren't we hearing anything?" Mathew asked nervously.

"I'm not sure." The nurse moved the transducer more slowly.

"Something's wrong, isn't it? Really wrong," Sunny asked, her voice filled with alarm.

"Not necessarily. The baby may have turned in an awkward position, and that would explain the strange stretching sensation you experienced. The heartbeat is not registering with this instrument—which is probably nothing more than technology failure. Believe me, it happens. Let me switch this one out with another one." She offered Sunny a supportive pat on the arm, then excused herself, pulling the curtain behind her.

"Mathew?" Sunny looked up at him with eyes full of panic.

"Let's stay calm. You heard what she said. She'll try another monitor and then we'll know more. Okay?" He tried his best to mask the fear in his voice as he smoothed her hair back off her forehead. At that very moment, he could hear Dr. Sumner's voice behind the curtain, and he breathed deeply in relief.

"Once again, it looks like you'll make good on your bet." Dr. Sumner pulled the curtain as he entered the small examination area.

"Well, we're erring on the side of caution, but if we do deliver today, bragging rights are all mine." Mathew shook his hand.

"Tell me about this stretching sensation, Sunny." He located a pair of latex gloves in a drawer as the nurse returned with a rolling cart of computer instrumentation. Though his words and tone conveyed calm, his body moved with hasty motion. Mathew picked up on it immediately.

"It was about ten o'clock. We were lying in bed reading when I suddenly felt like my stomach muscles were being pulled in two different directions. It didn't hurt, but it didn't feel right either. I don't think it was a contraction."

"And it only happened one time? It hasn't happened again?"

"No." She shook her head.

"We're going to try a more sensitive fetal monitor, along with one to monitor any uterine contractions. Sometimes the handheld Dopplers don't cooperate, but they're worth a shot in terms of convenience. We'll attach these straps around you and the sensors will register and record what's going on inside you. Now I need you to lie back, be completely still, breathe deeply, and concentrate on relaxing."

Sunny complied as the nurse secured the bands around her. Dr. Sumner moved the sensors around for several seconds to locate the heartbeat they were all so desperate to hear. After a minute, Dr. Sumner exchanged a knowing look with the nurse.

"I think your little guy may have turned breech and is experiencing some distress. We need to get you into the OR for a section right now."

"What?" Sunny cried out, looking to Mathew for support.

"You have to go *now*." Dr. Sumner's tone was firm.

He turned back to the nurse, speaking to her in what sounded to Mathew like a foreign language. Their rapid verbal exchange of medical jargon became muffled as a group of nurses entered their area in a matter of seconds. Commands and directives from Dr. Sumner brought a team together in what appeared to be organized chaos. Thousands of questions rang out like shots in his mind, but there was no time to ask them. In the next minute, he found himself jogging alongside the gurney toward the double doors to the OR. One of the nurses quickly entered the admittance code on the keypad, and Dr. Sumner turned to Mathew.

"I'll let you know first thing." He placed his hand on Mathew's shoulder.

"But I'm coming with you."

"I'm sorry, but you must wait here. I promise to take good care of her."

"Mathew, you can't leave me." Sunny held out her hand to him as tears stung her eyes.

"I'll be right here waiting, I promise. You can do this." His own eyes filled with tears, and he squeezed her hand tightly. He bent down and kissed her forehead, then tried his best to smile. Their hands slipped apart as the team rolled the gurney away, and Mathew watched through the small window until he could no longer see her.

He stood alone at the doors for a moment, trying to process the unexpected turn of events. The pictures he'd created in his mind over the past nine months were suddenly blown away like a flower on a beach. He'd never considered being anywhere other than right beside her when their child entered the world. Never thought that their journey would end with an emergency. One word played over and over in his mind, as he marched back and forth outside the doors to the OR. *Distress, distress, distress…*

A nurse approached him, trying to coax him into

the waiting area with an offer of hot coffee. He had no words for her, only responding with a shake of his head. Reaching inside his pocket, his fingers tapped against his cell phone in hesitation. *I should call home, but I don't want to scare Huck and Leo.* A tightness took hold of his chest, preventing him from taking a cleansing breath. Mathew paced, the walls of the hallway closing in on him with each step. Five minutes passed and his phone rang, jarring him back to consciousness.

"Yes," he whispered.

"Is everything okay?" his father-in-law asked with a panicked tone.

"She's in surgery now." Mathew's voice cracked.

****

Mathew leaned against the wall in the waiting area, his arms folded across his chest. His eyes fell closed and he replayed the tender scene they'd shared in their honeymoon suite when he'd learned of the pregnancy. He could still see the sparkle in her eyes, wet with joyful tears—eyes that held real fear when they'd been forced to separate.

He relented to the nurse's request, retreating to the waiting area, but still denying offers of snacks or beverages. The clock on the wall was little comfort. The forty-five minutes she'd been away from him had seemed like hours. Leo and Huck would be rolling up any moment, their familiar and understanding faces would be a welcomed sight. He motioned to the nurse at the main desk but was met with a shrugging of her shoulders. *God, when will they let me know?*

Ten more minutes passed before he was approached by a nurse. "Dr. Sumner will be out to see you shortly."

"Is she okay?" Mathew asked.

"I wasn't given any information, sir. I'm sorry. It should be just a minute or two." She nodded at him with friendly reassurance.

Mathew ran a hand through his hair and walked briskly toward the OR. With every step, he sent up silent prayers. He rounded the corner just as Dr. Sumner passed through the double doors. The man stopped, slowly pulling the colorful surgical cap from his head. Their eyes met, and instantly Mathew knew. A deafening reverberation of loss echoed with ear-splitting clarity throughout the hospital. It could only mean one thing.

The other shoe fell.

Chapter Thirty-Two

"Do you ever get the feeling that you're living a charmed life?"

"Define charmed."

"Do you ever think your life is just too good?"

"You mean waiting for the proverbial shoe to drop?"

"Exactly."

"No."

"Not even a little bit?"

"I prefer to think of my life as blessed, not charmed. Charms can wear off, but a blessing can last forever."

"I guess this whole pregnancy thing has caused my worrying hormones to kick into overdrive. I worry all the time."

"Why have you never told me?"

"Well, I don't know. Mostly because I'm sure that most of my fears are irrational ones."

"Such as?"

"I have this fear of something happening to you or the baby."

"Nothing's going to happen to us, Sunny."

The loss of their son had left him blind to the days ahead, yet he could see with complete clarity what lay behind. Every thought, every word, and every happy moment that preceded Easter Sunday had been filled with hope, laughter, and light. The memory of the conversation they shared at their ranch played on repeat in his mind, as the limousine inched closer to the memorial park.

Sunny sat quietly beside him, hidden behind her large sunglasses. She'd spoken only a handful of words that morning, moving through the rooms of their home with an eerie silence. Ghostlike. Expressionless. Now balancing on the edge of consciousness, a mild sedative inside her body worked to mask the pain. He reached for her hand, lacing his fingers tightly in hers. Squeezing it, he waited for her response to his touch. He got none.

Huck sat on the other side of Sunny, a protective arm around her. Though he grieved for the loss of his grandchild, Mathew recognized the anguish on his weathered face—his powerlessness to shield Sunny from pain.

Huck had stood shoulder to shoulder with Mathew, listening as Dr. Sumner delivered the news no one expected to hear. Both of them, frozen with blank expressions as the doctor quietly ran through a list of medical terms. *Distress. Breech. Nuchal cord. Type A. Accident.* Just a handful of words that meant nothing separately, but when placed together, created his worst nightmare. The light that had illuminated his path for nine beautiful months was cruelly extinguished.

The grounds of the cemetery were immaculately manicured, with everything fresh and green in the first breaths of spring. Statues of angelic cherubs dotted the landscape, keeping vigil over the tiny bodies that slept silently under the earth. The car slowed, and it was then that Mathew spied a statue of a Madonna and child, sharing a tender embrace. His mind raced back to a restless night where he'd rushed frantically to save Sunny and their baby, only to find them frozen in time as a hunk of gray stone. He turned his head slightly to the woman beside him. Hoping to find some minute sense of warmth, he was met only with a despondent stare, as his wife now resembled the statue from his dream more than ever.

Forget living one day at a time. Forget most everything beyond the immediate present. He was now unable to calculate his next move in anything other than minutes. Would he even be able to get out of the limousine? The driver parked behind the hearse and Mathew tried again, giving Sunny's hand another squeeze. With the little strength she had, she gave him a light squeeze in return, along with a slight nod. It was the first positive response he'd seen from her, though to a passing stranger, it would have gone unnoticed. But the days and weeks ahead would be traveled on heavy legs…inch by inch…minute by minute…and he was more than thankful for the tiniest sign of encouragement from her.

Huck exited the car first, stepping onto a stretch of artificial turf that would lead the way to their places beneath the tent. He reached for his daughter's hand and helped her out. Mathew followed right behind her. With his hand firmly on the small of her back, they made the short but difficult journey to the tent, and the tiny silver casket that waited for them. The air was still, but Mathew could feel Sunny shivering beneath his touch. Slipping his arm securely around her shoulder, he pulled her body close to his, resting his other hand inside his pocket. His fingers brushed against the tiny silver heart that he'd carried with him every day since Christmas. Taking it in his thumb and forefinger, he rubbed it repeatedly until they took their seats in the middle of the front row. Huck resumed his place at Sunny's right hand, while Leo and Barbara sat to Mathew's left. With his arm around Mathew's shoulder, Leo shared a loving, supportive pat, unable to hide his tears as the remainder of the funeral party found their seats.

A funeral director stepped forward, wearing a tranquil expression. The absence of sound was deafening, and Mathew grew light-headed. Looking into the eyes of tearful mourners, the man spoke in a soothing, peaceful tone. It was then that Mathew drifted away, disconnecting his heart and mind from the scene playing out before him. His body remained under the tent, but his soul took a little prince by the hand and hid up in the heavens, exploring worlds beyond.

Chapter Thirty-Three

Lying back, Mathew tucked one arm underneath his head and stared up at the ceiling, analyzing every sound that echoed through the quiet house. Two weeks had passed since they'd buried their son, and each morning, like clockwork, he opened his eyes to find that Sunny had slipped out of bed without his knowledge.

The first time it happened, he literally jumped and ran out of the room, gripped with fear that maybe she'd done something desperate. Thankfully, he found her asleep in the rocking chair in Lucien's room. He didn't wake her but leaned quietly against the doorframe and watched her sleep, relieved that she was finally getting some real rest. Since the funeral, he'd come into the nursery only once by himself. Feelings of loss and defeat were just too overwhelming and he couldn't take the torture.

He didn't hurry to get up, knowing Sunny was just down the hall. Well, her body was, anyway. Where her mind was…a totally different question. The number of interactions they had on a given day could be counted on one hand. She'd retreated deep inside herself—not even responding to Huck. Of course, he couldn't rush her through her grief. Pushing her too hard, too soon might only cause more damage. They had grown to love their baby boy and moving on would take time.

How much time? Mathew had no clue.

After ten minutes of internal arguments, he slipped from their bed and tiptoed down the hall. This time he found Sunny curled up in the rocking chair beneath her mother's favorite antique quilt. Immediately, Mathew noticed something around the index finger of her left hand. He crept inside for a closer look, surprised by his discovery—the tiny ID bracelet from the hospital that encircled LP's ankle. Her thumb and pinky were bare, yet the three fingers in the middle created an interesting picture. Her mother's ring on her middle finger, representing Sunny's past. Her wedding ring, representing the present and their life together. And the most precious ring of all, made of nothing but plastic and paper, encircling her index finger. A visual reminder of what was to be their future. A future that would now take a different direction.

Without a sound, he backed out of the nursery and made his way downstairs in search of some coffee. But as he turned from the stairway toward the living room, he could see a hint of light coming from the kitchen, and knew he wasn't the only one awake. *Good ol' Leo.*

He rounded the corner, surprised to find his father-in-law, already dressed and holding a cup of coffee. Huck regarded him with a nod, motioning silently to the coffee maker. Mathew nodded back and took his advice, filling his favorite mug before joining him at the breakfast table.

"How'd you sleep?" Huck asked.

"I'm guessing better than you. It's six-thirty and you're already dressed."

"Only because I never sleep well the night before I travel."

"I know what you mean." Mathew blew small ripples in the hot coffee before taking a sip.

"Sunny's still asleep?"

"Yes." He nodded.

"In your bed?"

"No."

Huck nodded. The look on his face morphed into one of concern. "She's been doing that quite a bit, hasn't she?"

"Almost every night," Mathew answered.

"I'd dismiss it if it only happened a couple of times. But from what I can tell, this has all the makings of a pattern–and not a healthy one."

"I don't know what to do, Huck."

"That makes two of us. I've tried everything to get her to talk to me, but the only thing she's willing to share openly are tears."

"I'm scared to death to push her, but let's be honest here. She can't sleep in that room forever. She can't just stop living." He avoided Huck's eyes, unsure if his comment would be met with acceptance or scorn.

"You're one hundred percent right," Huck agreed.

"I've tried for days to get her to talk to me, but she won't. I guess she's not ready, but I don't know how long I can do this. The silence is killing me. I know it's only been two weeks. The last thing I want to do is push her further away." Mathew's voice cracked, and he continued to stare down into his mug.

"You have been nothing but loving and supportive of her. The magnitude of what the two of you have been through cannot even be put into words." He paused. "Do you think maybe it's time you gave that doctor a call?"

"I don't know." He sighed heavily, feeling the emotion building inside him.

"It's a lonely feeling. I know because I've been there. But those feelings will pass. It won't be today or tomorrow or even next week. But every second that sweeps past the face of your inner clock will help you heal."

"Can I ask you something?" Mathew looked up at him with red, misty eyes.

"Certainly."

"How do you do it? All these years alone without Daphne. How do you do it?"

"Not very well, I'm afraid."

"But you always seem so matter-of-fact about the whole thing. So…*composed*."

"It's all an act. A damn good one."

"You think I should give that doctor a call? The one Dr. Sumner recommended?"

"I think it's a good idea. Not just for Sunny, but for yourself."

"I don't think she'll see anyone yet."

"But it's worth a try. And maybe you have to lead by example." He reached out, resting his hand on Mathew's with fatherly compassion.

Huck returned to the casita to pack. He'd been a symbol of comfort and stability and a much-needed confidant for Mathew, as he struggled to deal with not just his own pain but that of Sunny's. As much as he hated to see him go, he knew it was the next step toward their collective recovery. Huck had been their crutch, and it was time he and Sunny tried walking on their own.

Mathew stood at the sink, giving his mug a rinse

before placing it in the dishwasher. Looking out the window, he could see the images he'd created for months. Splashing in the pool. Playing fetch with Ivy. Building a swing. Chasing butterflies. He'd spent months making memories to be. Now he'd spend years trying to forget.

He located Sunny's favorite mug in the cabinet and poured a cup for her. It has always been part of their routine—waiting with a cup of her favorite blend when she exited the shower. The months of her pregnancy had been difficult, as she'd given up her morning coffee ritual. He could hear her quiet footfalls from above, and knew she was awake. Though she hadn't said a word, there was no doubt this would be another day of mourning for his wife when she watched her father drive away.

Slowly, he climbed the stairs, the sound of running water coming from their bedroom. *I guess she's already in the shower.* It was a good sign, as most days she didn't even make it downstairs until noon. There was so much he wanted to say. *Maybe we just need to be alone...totally alone...away from this house and every reminder of LP. If I could just get her to look at me...really look at me and know that we will find our way through this together...*

He'd taken only a few steps into their bedroom when he heard her. The noise of the shower did little to hide her pain. Just outside the entrance to their bathroom, he listened as her tears fell like rain. He stood frozen for a minute, her steaming mug of coffee still in his hand, and debated. Every muscle in his body tensed with longing—a need to pull her wet body from the shower and wrap her up inside his love. Aside from their time at the hospital, they'd grieved independently, and not by Mathew's choosing. Huck's words still fresh, he made a firm decision. His mind cycled through a mental Rolodex for the name of the psychologist Dr. Sumner had suggested. Dr. McNeff? McNabb? It was Mc-Something, but he couldn't remember.

Mathew opened the bedside table drawer in search of the business card Dr. Sumner had left with them. And that's when he saw them. The letters. *His* letters. Dozens of them. Written on everything from notebook paper to company letterhead...cocktail napkins to discarded junk mail. It had been over two weeks since he'd written a letter to his son, and seeing the stack of his most private thoughts in front of him caused his heart to beat even faster. He stared at them for a moment, then selected one at random. Sitting down on the edge of their bed, he began reading the words that he'd penned months before. He couldn't believe they belonged to him. Of course, he recognized his handwriting. Of course, he remembered writing them. But the words themselves didn't sound like him. These words had been written by someone else. Another man. A man who'd recorded his most intimate thoughts about love and life and commitment. A man who wrote with a tone of purest hope and matchless optimism for embracing all that life had to offer. A man who resigned himself not to be controlled by fear, but to live each moment for what it was: a gift. Mathew knew the man—knew him well. They'd been extremely close at one time, but not anymore. And with each day that'd followed a bright spring morning spent under a green tent, the distance between them had grown so that his old friend was now almost unrecognizable. Quietly, he folded the letter, returning it to the drawer.

Lying back on the bed, his thoughts ebbed and flowed with bits and pieces of conversations he'd shared with the people he cared most about. Sunny. Huck. Leo. Waves of memories, one after another, crashed upon his mind as he tried to make sense of the world around him. Their peaceful journey in the sun had turned into a horrendous storm and still, he sat in the dark. He closed his eyes and saw himself back in Leo's hospital room, sharing an exchange that now seemed to be more chilling prophecy than comforting conversation...

"A wise man once said 'Faith is like electricity. You can't see it, but you can see the light.' That part of my life—the part with my wife—has been dark for a long time. But I had a chance to be in the light—to live in the light for just a little while. And it was bright and shining and made everything around me glow. Would I give back those few days of light? Not on your life."

He was so far away in his thoughts that he didn't hear Sunny enter their bedroom. She stood beside the bed, staring at him with vacant eyes. Drops of water from her hair dripped on the carpet, and a towel wrapped around her damp body. Her face showed all the classic signs of sorrow: redness in her eyes and on her nose. Mathew barely recognized her. She didn't look like his wife. And seeing her standing before him, so pale and delicate, he'd never been more afraid in his life.

"Are you okay?" he asked.

"I need to sit down for a minute. I guess the shower was a little too hot. I feel kind of dizzy." It was the most consecutive words she'd spoken in days, though they conveyed little emotion.

"Here, let me help you…" He took her hand and led her to their bed.

"Thank you," she whispered but avoided eye contact.

"Let me get you some water," he offered.

"I smell coffee."

"I brought you a cup. Do you want it?"

"Yes." She nodded weakly.

Mathew reclaimed the mug and held it out to her. He shared a smile, hoping for further interaction. Sunny avoided his eyes, shivering as the water from her hair continued to drip onto her shoulders and down her back. He quickly retrieved a fresh towel from the bathroom and returned to her. As he squeezed the ends of her hair, she turned her face to his. Their eyes connected, and for a moment, Mathew saw a spark. It lasted only a split second, but the woman he fell in love with was in there. The woman who brought out the best in him. The only person to truly heal his heart. And then, as if blowing out the flame of a candle, it was gone. Without a word, she stood and walked back into the bathroom, closing the door behind her.

****

Huck loaded his suitcase in the backseat of his pickup and closed the door. Sunny stood in the shade of the front porch, her head down. Mathew and Leo traded concerned looks. He'd tried to imagine what their goodbye scene would entail, fully expecting his own tears to match his wife's as they watched him drive away. Huck turned and walked back to the porch, hands tucked inside the pockets of his jeans. He offered Sunny a smile that promptly faded as tears rolled down his face. Without a word, he pulled his daughter to him. Mathew watched as they stood together, their bodies shaking as they cried tears for each other and for the loss of a dream. And though he tried, Mathew was unable to stop tears from reaching his own eyes.

"Life's a tough teacher, baby girl. It gives the test first…" Huck's voice cracked and trailed off, and he ran his hand lovingly through her hair.

"And then the lesson," she whispered through her tears.

Chapter Thirty-Four

Dear Lucien,

I should be holding you right now instead of this pen. I should be looking into your dark blue eyes, whispering secrets and singing lullabies to you. I should be laughing with joy as I watch Uncle Leo read the sports page to you in baby talk. I should be smiling with pride as your grandfather shares silly stories and his recipe for the perfect Old Fashioned. I should be filled with bliss as I watch your mother rock you to sleep. I should be spending my days and nights basking in the glow of every moment spent with you. I should be forgetting about meetings and work in general because I'm too busy being a dad. I should be filling my phone with hours of video, recording your every look and movement. I should be standing beside your crib, watching you sleep and marveling at how incredibly amazing you are. I should be joyful when your tiny cry wakes me in the middle of the night. I should be a bore at every party I attend because all I can do is talk incessantly about you. I should be rushing home from work each day because I can't wait to hold you. I should be striking up conversations with complete strangers, discussing the latest baby gadgets, and comparing brands of diapers. I should be looking into the faces of other babies and knowing with absolute certainty that you are the most beautiful of all. I should be obsessed with baby-proofing our home so that you are always safe. I should be trading financial journals for American Baby magazine. I should be checking your bathwater three times to make sure the temperature is just right. I should be rubbing a drop of your baby shampoo in my own eye first to make sure "tear-free" is just that. I should be moved by every human-interest story I hear that involves parents and children. I should be playing Peek-A-Boo with you, feeling my heart melt when you squeal with delight. I should be falling asleep on the sofa with you curled up peacefully on my chest. I should be crying when the pediatrician gives you your first shots because what hurts you hurts me. I should be writing down every milestone, knowing in my heart that you are truly advanced beyond that of other infants. I should be thinking in terms of your future instead of my own. I should be contemplating my wrath should anyone dare bring harm to you. I should be focused on your every need because they are so much more important than my own. I should be falling asleep every night wondering how I ever survived without you in my life. I should be doing all these things and infinitely more, my beautiful boy, but I'm not.

I keep hearing Uncle Leo's voice in my mind. "Some is better than none," he once told me, recalling the days he stood in the light with his beautiful young wife. I've thought a lot about the conversation we shared many months ago while I waited to find out your mother's fate—if cancer might take her from me. Will there ever be a day when I look back on the words Leo spoke to me and see the truth in them? I long for the day when I am finally able to realize that some truly was better than none, though I can't see it now. Some was not what I banked on. Some is not enough for me. I know in the deepest recesses of my heart that having you in my life, no matter how brief our time, was the most supreme blessing of my existence. But until that day comes, when I can share Leo's words with someone who aches, and speak them with complete honesty, I will fumble in the dark with my hands outstretched in front of me, feeling along the walls of my life for a light switch.

I will never forget the moment I first saw you. I have never known my heart to be so full. Perfect. That's the only word that fully describes you. Absolutely perfect. Your feet. Your hands. Your features. Everything. The nurses at the hospital gave you a bath and dressed you in a tiny white gown. You were wrapped in a soft blanket and wore a little striped hat on your perfectly shaped head when they placed you in my arms for the first time. Gorgeous. That's what all the nurses called you. But you were beyond gorgeous. I sat in a special room with you for almost two hours, just holding you and rocking you and singing Mommy's favorite songs to you. As I looked at you and studied your face, I couldn't decide who you looked like. But Mommy knew. She held you and rocked you and compared every part of you to every part of me. And that made it official. Like father, like son. Lucien Pascal Ellis. L.P. Our Little Prince. Our greatest treasure. Lucien, meaning light. And Pascal, because just as I predicted, you arrived on Easter Sunday. You truly were Sunday's Child—full of grace.

We held you all day—me, your mother, your grandfather, and Uncle Leo. Seeing the look of love in your mother's eyes as she memorized every detail of your face was the most beautiful moment of my life. And also the most heartbreaking, knowing that her hand would never caress your cheek again. Knowing that we would never again feel the softness of your skin, or drink in your heavenly scent. You were our silent little angel, and I lie awake in bed every night trying to imagine your laugh and your cry. What a symphony that would have been for my soul. But there is no music now. The only sounds around me are the sounds of my own disillusionment and your mother's tears. I feel like I'm losing her too. And I'm not ready to add her name to the list of those who have been lost. I know that with each passing year, that list will grow infinitely longer, and I am powerless to stop it. I know that one day Huck's name will find its way to the list. Leo's another. Living is not without dying. I know that. But knowing something and accepting it are two different things. Your grandfather once told me that fate has a hand in everything at once. It made sense to me at the time, but nothing makes sense anymore.

I've looked everywhere for the answer, but it doesn't exist. I've searched the moon, the sun, truth, lies, Heaven, Hell, this house, bottles of Scotch, your mother's face, my mind, my dreams, and my heart. I've screamed at the top of my lungs...and no one heard. I've thought about every moment in the light with you and your mother, and I can't let go. I can't. I don't know how. If I could just have one more day with you—just one more day. Our time together was not enough. I've searched every dark and shadowy place inside myself, trying desperately to understand, and I can't. Day after day, I try to look at this from a different angle, but it always looks the same. I've found only one thing to be true. Just one thing remains constant as I beg God for some peace of mind: this was not the race I bet on. This was not the window I stood at with a handful of priceless dreams. My race was a sure thing, and I bet it all.

I have only one wish now. One hope. One prayer. One need. Your mother is slipping away from me, and I don't know what to do or how to bring her back. I can't even imagine the physical and emotional torment she's suffering right now—but I want to. I want to hold her and love her and help her through this. And I need those things from her. But she's hidden away from the world and from me. I know it's only been two weeks. I know this will take time. But I need her. I need her like I never have before. I know she's hurting because I'm hurting. I know she's angry because I'm angry. I know she feels lost, because my life has never seemed so dark. Every time my eyes meet hers, another part of me dies. I hear her crying in the shower. I reach out to touch her, but she turns away. I wake in the night to find she's left our bed. I want to tell her how I feel, but I'm afraid it's too soon. The last thing I want to do is push her further away from me. I've never felt more alone in my life. I lost you and I can't bear to lose her too.

You have brought something to my life that cannot be described with words. The love I feel for you will never die. You are the light that will always connect your mother and me. I know that you are up above us right now, sitting proudly on a star just as a little prince should. If I could ask one favor of you, as one of Heaven's littlest angels, please shine your light down on your mother so that she may be able to once again see our path and find her way back to me.

I love you forever,
Daddy

Chapter Thirty-Five

Baby Girl,

I know you've been expecting this. I've selfishly put it off too long. These are thoughts I should have shared with you before I left. But I don't believe you were ready to hear them any more than I was prepared to say them. I've kept them hidden in the back of my mind. They've been there your whole life, collecting dust since the days after your mother died. Every parent carries these words—the ones they hope will bring comfort and understanding when their children experience life's biggest heartbreaks. It's every father's hope that he'll live out his years without ever having to speak them. Or write them. Or even think about them. But in my life, it's not to be. I don't claim them to be the most profound or the most eloquent. I only know they come from an honest place.

How does one define loss? Why do we even use that particular term? When someone loses something, don't they continue to search for it? To seek its exact location so they may be reunited with that which is missing? When we lost your mother, I looked everywhere. I searched every part of my soul and every bottle I could get my hands on. I was determined to get her back. I thought that somewhere within me I had the power to bring her back. If I just prayed a little harder. Or screamed a little louder. Or cried a little longer. But what I didn't realize at the time was that she was already there. She was there, growing and thriving every day. She was there, in the body of an innocent young girl. I wasted so many days and nights searching for something that had been right under my nose.

There are no guarantees in this life. And I know you understand this better than most. There are withered souls roaming this planet for years who neither give nor receive an ounce of joy. And then there are others. Those whose light seems to burn brightest. Souls with great gifts to share with others around them. And for reasons unbeknownst to me, these are the ones who are taken from us before we're ready. Why? I have no explanation. No rationalization. No justification. And how I've longed for those things—those answers— and so much more over the years. I'm still waiting. And I may never know. But there is one thing that time has revealed to me. And for now, it's more than enough. The days I spent with your mother, although they were mere wisps of time, were the happiest of my life and worth every tear I've shed.

I don't believe I ever told you, but LP and I are quite close. We spent months engaged in a secret exchange of life's lessons and ideals. And I want you to know that my grandson's light brightened up every room in this quiet old house. It breathed new life back into the walls and the floors and into me. I am enclosing a letter—one of many—that I wrote to LP. Again, you may think it nothing more than the ramblings of an old man, but every word comes from the place that guides my pen now. Every line is filled with love and hope—two things I pray you can still see in your own life. Should you wish to have the remaining letters, they will be here for you. They are all in a stack, tied up neatly with a light blue bow, just as your mother would have saved them. You may decide you want them tomorrow or next week. Or you may never want to see them. It doesn't matter to me. Only one thing truly matters now…that you know how much I dearly love you.

Pop

She thought she'd be a wreck after reading her father's words, but she wasn't. And now, rereading it a second time, she found she was unusually calm. His voice came through in every line. And though the letter was short by Huck's standards, he delivered a successful, honest message.

Her gaze traveled around the perimeter of their bedroom, surveying the traces of Mathew. His books on the bedside table. His running shoes beside the chair. His briefcase, unopened, on the escritoire. She wanted to find some sort of comfort in them, knowing they were extensions of him, but comfort was a feeling she couldn't embrace. There'd been a flash of it just hours before when Mathew returned home from his first day back at the office. He'd slipped into bed beside her, and after a minimal exchange, his hand found her hair. And for that tiny moment in time, everything in her world was exactly as she wanted it to be. But the morning cast a bright light back on reality, and the brief taste of solace she'd felt as Mathew's fingers moved softly through her hair during the night melted away. Even as she'd stood in Lucien's room that morning, reading the note he'd left for her, she couldn't separate herself from her pain to reach back out to him.

Glancing at the clock, she silently calculated the

time until his return. The hot shower, the coffee, and the short walk with Ivy had not been enough. Now back in pajamas, she buried herself in their bed. She held the small silver heart in her hand, rubbing it gently with her thumb and trying to remember the foreign concept formally known as happiness.

****

"You can go in now, Mr. Ellis," the receptionist said warmly.

"Thank you." He nodded.

Dr. McNichol sat behind a large desk, making notes in a folder. She waved for him to enter but didn't look up from her task. After a minute, she stood.

"Mr. Ellis, it's so nice to meet you." She extended her hand to him, which Mathew immediately accepted.

"Thank you. And thanks for seeing me on such short notice."

"Sit down, please. May I take your jacket?" She motioned to a group of oversized club chairs in the corner. They were an inviting shade of dark blue, calm and welcoming.

"No, I'm fine." Mathew positioned himself in a chair opposite Dr. McNichol.

"I bet you're the type of man who enjoys a good cup of coffee."

"That would be correct."

"Black or with cream?"

"Uh, just a touch of cream."

"Sugar?"

"Only a spoonful."

"Coming up." She pressed the intercom button on the small table beside her chair.

"Catherine, could you bring a cup of mud and a

blonde with sand? Thanks." She smiled. "Sorry. Force of habit. I was a waitress at an all-night diner back in my undergrad days."

Mathew, visibly tense upon entering her office, now released his breath. His shoulders fell into a more relaxed position. He even managed to return her smile, thankful for her engaging demeanor.

"Now then, why don't we begin with you telling me a little bit more about your phone message?"

"I didn't realize I'd said anything worthy of discussion."

"Your message sounded urgent. It was after midnight when you called."

"Well, the time was right."

"In what way?"

"When I dialed your number this last time, I didn't hang up, as I've done countless other times in the past few weeks."

"So, you've called before? But never spoke with anyone or left a message?"

"Yes."

"Why is that?"

"I don't know. Fear I guess."

"Fear of what?"

"Fear of this. Of having to do *this*." He pointed back and forth between the two of them.

"Are you afraid now?"

"No."

"There must have been some trigger that prompted you to follow through this time. Any idea what that might have been? Did something happen that suddenly changed your perspective?"

Mathew thought back to the poignant thoughts Leo

had shared in the presence of the fifteen-minute confessional timer the night before.

"I looked at the hourglass of my life and saw that the sands were disappearing quickly. I knew it was time to call."

"Well, I think you're lucky to have recognized the sign. And I'm glad you made it here today."

The receptionist tapped lightly on the door, then entered, carrying a tray. Two identical coffee mugs sat side by side, along with a plate of croissants and two linen napkins. Immediately, his mind conjured up images of Sunny and her craving for Leo's pumpkin scones during her pregnancy.

"Can I bring you anything else?" the receptionist asked.

"I think we're fine. Thank you, Catherine." She looked to Mathew for confirmation. He reached for his mug, offering a nod of approval.

She backed quietly out of the room, leaving them alone. Mathew took a sip of his coffee and wondered where the conversation would go next. He inspected the clock on the wall. Only a few minutes of his fifty-minute hour were gone, and they'd only exchanged casual pleasantries. *How long 'til we get down to hardcore business?*

"If you had to sum up your reasons for being here today in one sentence, what would it be?"

Well, she doesn't waste time, does she? Guess that answers my question. Mathew pondered her inquiry for a moment. One sentence. Could everything be summed up in one sentence? Was this another trick, like the cold questions that sniggered at him on the registration sheet he'd filled out the day before? Was he there for Lucien?

For himself? Was it about control or letting go? His life had gone off the radar and there was only one thing to get him back on track. Mathew leaned forward and looked up at Dr. McNichol with a desperate expression.

"I've lost my wife and I don't know how to get her back."

****

"Ellis Residence," Leo answered.

"I'm on my way home," Mathew said.

"How'd it go?"

"Better than I thought. Dr. McNichol is wonderful. A very sharp woman."

"That's great, Matty. I'm really proud of you."

"Thanks."

"Now listen, why don't you just let me drive Sunny out to meet you? Save you some time instead of driving back here."

"No, I really want to drive her."

"I understand."

"Has she been down today?"

"She came down for coffee and even took Ivy outside for a short walk."

"You're kidding? She went outside?"

"She sure did. It was only a couple minutes, but it's something."

"That's the best news I've heard in weeks."

"I'll let her know that you're on the way. We'll see you in a bit."

Leo hung up, feeling better than he had in days. The old man practically danced to the stairway, eager to let Sunny know Mathew was on his way. *They've both taken big steps today. Maybe this is a sign of things to come.* Carefully navigating the stairs, his concentration fell on Ivy, the dog jumping playfully beside him on every step. *You feel it too, don't you?*

Their bedroom door was closed. Leo gave it a light tap. As usual, no response. A second rap with more force produced the same result. Conferring a minute with the dog, he turned the doorknob as noiselessly as possible and peeked inside.

Though she'd showered and dressed earlier, Sunny was now back in bed. Her clothes lay discarded in a heap on the floor. The television was on, but the sound had been muted. A window across the room had been opened, and a light breeze blew the custom drapery panels in billowy ripples. Leo checked his watch. Sunny needed to be ready to go as soon as Mathew arrived. They would be cutting it close to make it to the cemetery.

"It's almost time to go, Sunny. Matty will be here in a few minutes. Let me get your clothes for you." He retrieved her now wrinkled skirt and blouse. She didn't move or respond but lay staring straight ahead.

"You want me to get you something else? These are a little wrinkled."

"I'm not going."

"You're not going?"

"Please tell him to go on without me. I just don't feel very well." She cut him off, avoiding eye contact.

Leo stood beside the bed, unsure what to do. Watching her hide away from the world was a truth he couldn't accept—not when Mathew had made such huge strides.

"But Matty is counting on you. He's been looking forward to being with you all day."

Sunny remained silent. Leo returned her clothes to

299

the empty hangers in her closet. When he entered the bedroom once more, her eyes were closed, signally the end of their discussion. Conceding defeat, the old man shuffled out of the room.

****

"What do you mean she's not coming?" Mathew closed the car door.

Leo shrugged. "That's what she said. She told me to tell you to go on without her because she's not feeling well."

"I don't get it. You said she came down for coffee and took a walk with Ivy."

"I'm just as shocked as you are. This has been her best day yet. I told her you were counting on her to be with you, but she won't budge. I'm really sorry. This must be so hard for you."

"You think I should try and talk to her?" He checked his watch.

"I don't think it'll do any good. She sounded pretty firm. And I'd hate for you to be late. If you're late, they may go ahead without you."

"You're right. I just don't understand it. She seemed okay with it this morning before I left."

"Do you want me to come with you?"

"No. I don't want Sunny here alone. You stay. I should be back in less than an hour."

Back behind the wheel, Mathew leaned into his anger. *I knew it. I knew this would happen. Grief or no grief, she has no right making Leo feel like shit. Maybe it's better this way anyway. It's not like she's offered me a drop of support. I'm better off doing everything just like I have been...alone.*

****

Standing at the window, Sunny pulled the sheers back and watched Mathew drive away. She stood frozen, watching until she could no longer see his car, twisting her mother's ring around her middle finger. After a moment, she closed the window and retreated to her writing desk and the task she'd struggled with all morning.

She stared at the blank piece of stationery, asking questions to which she had no answer. Her mind wandered, drifting along the intricate floral pattern that adorned the edge of the page. To write—to do the one thing that had always brought clarity during her pregnancy—now seemed impossible. Losing Lucien had obscured clarity and tainted purpose…and was now threatening the truest relationship she'd ever known. The point of her pen touched the surface of the paper, and she fully let go.

I'm trying, Mathew. I swear, I'm trying. And I know you're trying too. But honestly, every little thing you do for me makes it hurt more, which makes absolutely no sense. The way you bring me a cup of coffee. The way you fold and put away my clothes. The way you run your fingers through my hair in the middle of the night. All these and a thousand other things you do with love fill me with intense guilt because I am numb…and I can't give those same things back to you. I hate myself. I'm on a runaway train, and I don't see it stopping. I know you'll follow me from station to station, but my legs are so heavy I don't even have the strength to step into your arms.

For weeks now, she'd watched the world go by in a series of blurred photographs. If she could just focus on one image. Just one scene of something happy.

Something that might brush against the dark drapery of her life, letting in a little light on what used to be. She didn't feel the tears in her eyes or on her cheeks but came back to herself only when they fell onto her hands. Looking down, she blinked, causing more tears to fall, distorting the elegant graphics that decorated her stationery.

She quickly wiped the tears away. Then, as if taken over by some mystical force, she wadded up the piece of paper and crammed it in the pocket of her pajama bottoms. With a fresh sheet now in front of her, Sunny wrote the answer she'd been searching for. It had been there all the time…and it was nothing more than three little words.

I love you. I love you. I love you. I love you. I love you.

Chapter Thirty-Six

"Time's up." Dr. McNichol announced.

"It flies by, doesn't it?" Mathew stood and retrieved his suit coat from the back of the blue chair.

"You're making real progress, Mathew. I'm very proud of you. I think you're ready for a schedule change. Let's try Tuesdays only from now on. You're strong enough to drop a day."

"I'm getting promoted?" he joked.

"In a manner of speaking." She walked him to the door.

"I wish I could get Sunny here."

"You can't do it for her. It has to be *her* decision, remember? *You* were ready to go to the cemetery. *You* wanted to be there when Lucien's headstone was placed. *You* were ready. She's not. She's operating by her own hourglass."

"I know, I know. Do you always have to be right?"

"Not always, but it's good for business." She laughed.

"Have a good weekend." He swung his jacket over his shoulder.

"See you next week."

They exchanged handshakes and Mathew headed out to the car. The sun was shining, and he rode with the windows down. April showers had brought their share of May flowers and the city parks were alive with

303

greenery, blooms, and people enjoying the outdoors.

Each time he left a therapy session, it was like a rebirth. But unfortunately, the feeling was fleeting. Once the car pulled into their garage, those feelings of success and personal achievement withered. Sunny's vacant stare was like a knife, cutting away any new growth he'd experienced within the paneled walls of Dr. McNichol's office.

His subconscious redirected his route, and minutes later, he was turning into the memorial park, unsure how he got there. The traffic along the paved drive was heavy, with the sunny weather prompting many to visit their lost loved ones. Mathew followed a white convertible to the back of the park, where his baby boy waited.

The area of the cemetery known as Cherubs Garden was deserted. He stepped out of the vehicle and followed the path to a place that had become his home away from home—a concrete bench and a slab of granite on the ground—meager fixtures for the home of a little prince. Taking a seat on the bench, he stared down at the words inscribed on the marker. His eyes locked on the date. *How could something so perfect and so beautiful begin and end on the same day?* A memory slipped inside his head, and he recalled the night they'd decided on his name.

"I think you did it. This might be the one."

"It's perfect. Do you like it?"

"I love it. It's not a name I would have thought of on my own. But the meaning and everything...this is it."

"So, do we agree? Is this the name we love for our son?"

"Yes, if you're happy with it."

"I think it's meant to be."

Mathew couldn't help but smile, remembering Sunny's eyes and the excitement and happiness of that tender moment. The special times they'd shared were countless, but that one particular evening remained high on his list of the best moments in his life. He continued to study the headstone for several minutes, trying again to recreate the feeling he'd had that night at the ranch. He bent down and brushed a few blades of grass off the edge of the monument. Gently, he traced the letters of his son's name, unaware that he was crying.

Chapter Thirty-Seven

Mathew flipped up his turn indicator and eased into the parking lot, relieved when he spotted Archer's new Land Rover. To his surprise, there was an open space next to it, so he pulled in and parked. His heart pounded with nervous anticipation as he prepared to mark yet another item off his personal To-Do list: have lunch with friends.

He removed his sunglasses and turned the rear-view mirror toward his face. The dark circles that ringed his eyes for weeks were finally beginning to fade. He'd lost several pounds, but his color looked okay. He drew a deep breath and let it out slowly, focusing all his attention on a single image. He envisioned himself sitting at a table with Sunny, Archer, and Maggie, enjoying themselves just as they had on Christmas Eve. *You did it once. You can do it again.*

A few steps inside the restaurant, he spotted the Martins. They were already seated and waved him over, their faces bright with loving optimism.

"Mathew, you look wonderful." Maggie stood and kissed him on the cheek.

"Thank you. So do you." Mathew embraced her affectionately.

"You really do look good. You've been on our minds a lot." Archer shook his hand.

"Well, this was a fabulous idea. I know Sunny will be happy to see you both."

"How is she doing? Really?" Maggie asked.

"There's not been much change. But the fact that she's agreed to have lunch with us is a good sign. Actually, it's better than good. This is a huge step for her—or us, as a couple."

"When our drinks arrive, let's make our first toast of the afternoon to huge steps, shall we?" Archer smiled.

"I'll drink to that." Mathew nodded.

"Is she driving now?" Maggie inquired.

"No, she hasn't driven since before Easter. Barbara and Leo are dropping her off, then we'll ride home together."

"Has she gone to see Dr. McNichol?" Maggie asked.

"No, not yet." He shook his head, staring down at his hands.

"But you're still going, right?"

"Every Tuesday. At first, it was two times a week, but she's cut me back to one day now."

"Well, it's certainly working. You seem to be moving forward," Archer said.

"She's really helped me look at what's happened from a lot of different angles. I just can't believe it's been over six weeks now. But listen, we didn't come here to discuss my therapy. We came here to enjoy a nice relaxing lunch with good wine and good conversation." Mathew smiled at his dear friends, eager to regain some normalcy in his social life.

"Good wine and good conversation, but not good weather. This damn rain again. We could be dining out on the patio," Archer complained.

"Oh, well. This too shall pass." Mathew winked.

The waiter delivered a bottle of their finest, which they sampled and quickly approved. After a toast, Maggie gave Archer a look, which Mathew zeroed in on immediately.

"We stopped by the cemetery the other day," Archer said.

"We wanted to see if they had placed the headstone. We're sorry it took us so long to get back out there," Maggie added.

"You don't owe me an apology of any kind. I have zero expectations for you to visit. I can't even get Sunny out there."

Archer and Maggie shared a pained look.

"It's okay, really. She'll make it there when she's ready. I stop there after every appointment I have with Dr. McNichol. It's kind of my way of letting Lucien know my progress. And here I've brought us right back to the topic of my therapy. I'm so sorry." Mathew shook his head.

"The headstone is beautiful, Mathew. Just beautiful." Maggie reached for his hand.

"Thank you very much. This might sound crazy, but I'd actually forgotten what we'd selected until I saw it for the first time. I was a little out of it then."

"We don't want you to think that we've forgotten," Archer said.

"I know you haven't. But I don't want you to feel obligated to mention it every time we're together, either. If it comes up, it comes up. If it doesn't, it doesn't. I know you both care and care deeply. You don't have to make a special point." He gave them a reassuring nod.

The waiter returned, ready to take their order. Mathew asked for another minute and Archer studied the wine list, ready to request another bottle. He checked his cell phone, hoping for a text from Sunny explaining their delay. Leo was nothing if not punctual. Like Huck, he despised tardiness in all forms. *I wonder what's keeping them.* He mentally dissected the conversation they'd shared at breakfast. He'd reminded her of their lunch date, and she'd seemed genuinely enthusiastic about seeing Maggie again. Leo had been within earshot, offering to personally deliver her to the restaurant during his outing with Barbara. Surprisingly, there'd been no hesitation or reservation on Sunny's part. *But maybe that's changed. Surely Leo would have called if she'd once again had a change of heart.* It was one thing to keep him waiting, but to inconvenience their friends? Was she lying unresponsive in their bed with Leo pleading for her to get dressed? It had played out too many times before to be anything to the contrary. And with each sip of wine, his frustration grew. The waiter returned and Mathew decided to make a move.

"Would you excuse me for a moment? I want to check in with Leo. I'm sure Sunny's just running behind schedule."

"Of course. Take your time. We've got all afternoon." Archer raised his glass in Mathew's direction.

He walked briskly past the hostess stand and toward the men's lounge. He tried their home number first. *Please don't be there. Please be on the road.* But his wish was not granted. Leo answered on the first ring.

"Ellis Residence."

"She's not coming, is she?" Mathew asked.

"Matty?"

"Put her on the phone. Hold it to her ear if you have to." His tone was direct.

"What are you talking about?"

"Let me talk to Sunny." He could not hide the anger in his voice.

"She's not here. She's with you."

"She's not with me. You and Barbara were supposed to bring her here—to the restaurant to meet me and Archer and Maggie, remember?"

"She told me that she'd talked to you and that she decided to drive and meet you herself."

"What are you talking about?"

"She left here about an hour and a half ago. Said she had a stop to make and that she'd meet you guys at the restaurant."

"Oh, God." Mathew ran a hand through his hair. Suddenly, the thought of the heavy rain, coupled with the slick roads, made him feel nauseous.

"You mean she hasn't shown up yet?"

"No." Mathew's hands began to sweat.

"You want me to call the police or something?" Leo asked, his voice bordering on panic.

"No, you stay there in case she comes home. I'll go look for her."

"But she could be anywhere."

"Or she could be in the one place she's longed to be for weeks."

****

Mathew could see Sunny's dusky silhouette, seated

310

alone on the all too familiar concrete bench. The rain continued to fall but had subsided somewhat. She sat motionless, with no coat or umbrella to protect her. He pulled up next to her vehicle and sat, watching. She made no indication that she was aware of his presence. For six weeks, she'd made no indication of anything.

Seeing her there alone in the gray mist brought the haunting pictures of a nightmare back into his mind. A dream brought to life with the death of their son. The same scene now playing out in real time before him, as the windshield wipers moved back and forth, distorting her image every few seconds. His beautiful wife, sitting alone on a concrete bench, turned to stone.

He pulled an umbrella from the back seat and turned up the collar of his raincoat. Swallowing back tears, he exited the car. Walking along the gravel path, he searched his mind for the right words. The words necessary to bring her back. But none materialized.

Mathew sat beside her, shielding her from the rain with the umbrella. She neither spoke nor moved. There at their feet sat the granite reminder of the tiny life that forever changed them. Again, he studied the date. *Has it really been six weeks?* Minutes, hours, days…time had no meaning in their house anymore. They'd lived day to day, week by week, basking in the glow of each new moment. Days that brought them closer to each other and their baby boy. Days filled with letters and light.

Maybe you have to be her flashlight now. Leo's words echoed inside his head as he wrapped his arm around Sunny's shoulder. Instinctively, she stood, still silent, but not fighting. Mathew helped her through the muddy mire to his car and she leaned her body against him for support. It was the first time she'd responded to his touch in weeks. He popped open the trunk and quickly retrieved the plaid blanket, wrapping it securely around her soaking-wet body before opening the passenger side door. He waited until she was safely inside before closing the umbrella. On his way around to the driver's door, he stopped. Looking up at the darkened sky, he paused and closed his eyes, allowing the rain to wash the tears off his cheeks.

****

Sunny stared out the passenger side window, barely blinking. Tiny drops of rain sparkled in her hair. She could feel Mathew's eyes on her. She studied the drops of rain on the window and the jagged little trails they made in their random quest to join up with other droplets. Watery soldiers on an erratic and hasty path, silent in their journey and continually joined by more and more.

"We've got to get you home and out of those wet clothes." Mathew finally broke the silence between them.

Sunny kept her gaze fixed on the rain-soaked window, reaching up to trace the path of one droplet that caught her eye.

"Please, don't make me go back there. I can't go back there. I'll go anywhere, but I can't go back home."

****

It was dark when the headlights bounced off the main gate. They hadn't been to the ranch since the night they'd found out they were having a son. Mathew stopped for gas and managed to score a few essentials for them, as they had nothing but the clothes they were wearing. A quick call to Leo so he wouldn't worry was followed by a call to Archer, with a request to pick up Sunny's SUV from the cemetery. Mathew watched her through the window as he filled up the tank. Their four-hour journey had felt more like eight. Sunny's silence was deafening, compounded by the argument he held with himself the entire way there.

She surprised him by carrying a few bags of groceries. Her hair was almost dry now, but she still remained in damp clothes, and the plaid blanket hung limply around her shoulders. Mathew went directly to the closet in their bedroom in search of something dry. He found an old Texas Longhorns t-shirt and some sweatpants, along with a pair of fuzzy wool socks in the dresser. *These will have to do.*

"I found some dry things for you to put on. It's not much, but you really need to get out of those damp clothes." He pulled the blanket from her shoulders, letting it fall to the floor.

A heavy silence hung between them as they stood face to face, almost touching yet miles apart.

"Why don't you take a shower and I'll get a fire going. All right?" He looked into her eyes.

With a nod, she disappeared behind the bedroom door. Mathew grabbed a few logs from the back porch and busied himself with building a small fire. It was unseasonably cool outside for May and within minutes, the glow of the flames on his face made him feel better. He returned to the kitchen, organized the groceries, and poured them each a glass of wine. Back in front of the fire, his mind tumbled through the day, and all its unexpected twists. *Sunny can't hide from me here. It's time to get everything out in the open.*

Mathew was deep in thought when Sunny returned,

baggy clothes hanging on her frail frame. She'd dropped double the number of pounds he had. Her face was painfully thin and pale—almost unrecognizable.

"I poured us some wine."

"Thank you." She picked up the glass and curled up on the opposite end of the sofa.

"Feel better?" he asked.

"Much."

They sat in silence, without touching, drinking wine and watching the fire. Husband and wife...mother and father...total strangers. Mathew's heart beat a cautious cadence as he gathered his thoughts. The words were there, but saying everything he felt took a certain level of courage. *What would Dr. McNichol say?* Without a word, he reached out for her feet and lifted them onto his lap. To his surprise, she didn't protest. Socks removed and tossed on the floor, his hands moved across her feet. To feel her skin again, after weeks of distance, was an answered prayer. His fingers traced the lines of her toes. *Lucien had your toes, Sunny. Our baby boy had your beautiful, beautiful toes.*

So many wonderful moments in their marriage existed without words or conversation of any kind. This was not one of them. The clock on the mantle moved time forward in the tiniest of increments. After sitting in silence for close to twenty minutes, he could stand it no longer.

"You really scared us when you didn't show up for lunch." He continued to rub her feet with a soothing touch.

Sunny remained stoic and silent.

"Sunny?" He stopped and held her feet tightly in

his hands. "Did you hear what I said?"

"Yes," she whispered, her gaze still frozen.

"You could at least answer me." He looked directly at her, but she avoided his stare. The light of the fire shined in Sunny's eyes, but nothing more. "Sunny, are you gonna answer me?" His normally understanding tone was observably turning to one of annoyance.

Her focus shifted from the fireplace to the glass of wine in her hand. She mumbled something to herself, shaking her head with an aggravated expression.

"You know what? I've got a better idea. Don't answer me." His tone was firm. "I don't want you to answer me. You know what I want? I want you to yell at me. Scream at me! Throw something—break something. Hell, I'd love for you to tear this whole place apart. Just do one goddamn thing to show me that you still have a heart beating inside you!"

He hadn't meant to, but it was too late. The calm tone he'd promised himself he'd maintain was gone. Weeks of walking on eggshells around her. Days and nights spent living alone. He couldn't do it another day.

Sunny jerked her feet from his grasp and slammed the wine glass on the table. Mathew was quick, catching her hand before she could escape.

"Let go!" She tried to wrestle away from him.

"No! I'm not letting go! Your answer to everything is running away. You've been running for weeks and it stops now!" He held fast to her wrist.

"Mathew, let me go!" She struggled against his grasp.

"No! I'm not letting go until you look at me. I mean *really* look at me, Sunny. You haven't looked at me in six weeks! You haven't done a damn thing in *six weeks*!"

"That's because *my* heart stopped beating six weeks ago!"

"And so now you're just giving up, is that it? You're quitting? Is that what you're telling me?"

"You don't understand." She looked away.

"I don't understand? *I* don't understand? I understand that every day you break off another piece of my heart, Sunny, and there's not much left. It's almost all in a box buried with Lucien. But I kept one little piece—one tiny, little piece for you with the hope that maybe, just maybe, you'd be able to plant a seed in me and help it grow back. But every day, you just kill it off. Every time I hear you crying in the shower, every time you cry out in your dreams, every time you slip off by yourself. You're killing yourself, you're killing me, you're killing us. The *us* that you were so afraid of losing. You're killing it! You! So, if this is your way of telling me your life is completely over—"

"I don't know what I'm telling you because I don't *feel* anything anymore!" She shouted back at him. "I felt it all. Everything, Mathew, everything for nine months, and then it's all just ripped away. I did everything I was supposed to do and now it's gone. How am I supposed to feel? You tell me! Because that part of me—the part that feels—that part is gone!"

He grabbed her hand and placed it over his heart, holding it firmly against him. "Can you feel this? Can you? Do you know what this is? This is my heart. It's the same as yours. It's broken, just like yours. We're victims of the same disease but you don't see it! We're suffering the same affliction, only I've decided to fight, and you've decided to give up."

"How would you know what I've decided or what I feel? You don't know because you never felt him move inside you!" she shouted again.

"You think that just because I'm a man or that I wasn't the one to carry our baby, *that* somehow makes me immune to the pain? 'Cause if that's what you think, then you don't know me. You never knew me!" Rage rose inside him, and he resented her for it.

"Well, I'm sorry if my grieving bothers you…" she snapped, jerking her hand away from him. "You didn't buy a book on how to grieve for a dead baby, Mathew. I guess I'm not doing it right."

"I have tried to be there for you from the moment we lost Lucien. You keep pushing me away, and I don't know what to do or how to make you stop. I want to hold you and make it all go away and I need those things from you, Sunny. I need to feel that from you too. You're not the only one here!" His angry words bounced off the cabin walls.

"What do you want from me? You want me to say it? Huh? Is that what this is all about? Fine, I'll say it. It's my fault. Lucien's dead and it's my fault. There. Are you happy now? Feel better?"

"My God! Is that what you honestly think? You don't get it, do you? Just listen to what you are saying! This isn't about pointing a finger. You can't honestly believe that I hold you responsible for this." His heart hurt like never before. Her words stung his soul and pierced him to the point of tears.

"Our baby died, Mathew! Our precious baby died!" She cried out as tears flowed freely down her cheeks, her body shaking uncontrollably. "I don't know what you want from me. I just don't know what you want from me." Her last words were mere whispers—and maybe, a plea for help.

For the first time since they'd given their son back to God, she completely let go and fell against him. Her tired body felt lifeless in his arms, and together they sank to the floor. He held her for a long time, with only the sounds of their collective tears and the crackling fire around them.

You're still with me. You're still in there, full of hurt and anger and fear. All real feelings and proof that you're still here. And I promise to be right here with you. We will get through this, Sunny. Just don't give up. Please don't give up. You're strong. You're the strongest person I've ever known.

"Losing Lucien is the hardest thing I've ever been through. I don't want to lose you too. I can't make it in this life without you." He squeezed her tightly.

"I am so sorry. He was your son...and I...and I..." Her words stalled.

"It's okay. It's okay." Gently, he rocked her back and forth.

"I didn't know that he...if I'd...if we'd just gone to the hospital a little earlier..."

"I never want to hear you speak those words again. It was an accident. An *accident* and nothing more."

"I know you love him as much as I do. I just don't know what to do, Mathew. I just feel lost."

"Then tell me what I can do to bring you back to me. I need you. I need you more than I've ever needed anyone. I'll do anything. Just please come back to me. I don't want to do this without you." He combed his fingers through her damp hair.

"I can't do this again. I just can't. Please don't

make me. If you really want to have a baby, then maybe I'm not the person you should be with."

"Oh, Sunny…" Tears slid down his face. "How could you even think that?"

"I don't know. I'm just so afraid. I know how much you wanted this, but I'm just not that strong. I know you think I am, but I'm not. Not for this. I can't do this again. And it scares me to death that you might…or that I might be keeping you from something you want and need."

"But I love you. God, I love you more than I ever thought I could love someone. You are my whole life. Without you, I have nothing. And I felt this love for you before Lucien—before we even got married. Having a baby or not having a baby won't change how I feel about you. I don't have to be a father to feel like a complete man. I became a complete man the day I fell in love with you."

She reached and took his hand. Bringing it to her face, she held it quietly against her cheek. Beyond the layers of hurt and loss, he could see it—the tiniest sparkle in her eyes. His gaze moved to her lips, wet with tears. Lips he hadn't kissed since the night before Lucien was born.

"I love you so much, Mathew," she whispered.

"And I love you. More than you will ever know."

****

They spent the night in front of the fire, holding each other. The softness of every look and touch they shared as their bodies reconnected brought them back to the place they cherished most—a place that had grown dark with curtains drawn up tight to conceal all light. Prayers of thankfulness filled him as he held her in his arms. The joy of once again feeling her skin, tasting her lips, and drinking in the very essence of her being. It wasn't about satisfying his flesh. It went beyond desire and longing. She was his well—the only thing to restore his thirsty soul.

The flames died down, leaving only orange embers to light the Great Room. The cabin was quiet and for the first time in weeks, Mathew anticipated a night of true, restful sleep beside his wife.

"Mathew?"

"Yes?"

"I'm so sorry I made you doubt my love for you. I've never stopped loving you. I knew I was slipping, like I was watching myself from outside my body. I was yelling at myself to wake up and come back to you, but the deepest hurt in me kept me a prisoner. I was frozen."

The words fell from her mouth with a soft certainty that he hadn't heard in weeks. This was the Sunny he needed. The woman who shared her deepest emotions with him, giving him the courage to do the same. She'd stepped back on their path, healing him and quieting his fears.

"I don't ever want you to stop thinking about Lucien. I won't. He'll always be a part of us. The stars are a little brighter tonight because our Lucien—our Light—is shining down on us. Remember what The Little Prince said?"

"I just wanted so much to be his mom." Tears once again formed in her eyes.

"You were his mom. You *are* his mom. You took care of him, protected him, and loved him as only a mother can. In fact, I can prove it. I'll be right back."

Silently, his shadow moved across the walls of the Great Room, disappearing behind the door of their bedroom. He returned within a minute, and slipped back under the blanket beside her, flipping on a tiny flashlight.

"I want to read something to you."

He was holding a wrinkled piece of paper, looking at her with the sweetest expression. With the same honest tone that brought endless comfort, he read the words she'd written months before.

Well, it's getting late, and I should probably turn off the light. Your father is lying here beside me, sleeping peacefully with a smile on his face. I know what he's dreaming about...his little angel boy. Or girl. Either way, you're an angel to us. I want you to know something right from the start: I promise to always be completely honest with you, no matter what. There have been things in my past that have been painful and ugly and have led me to make some poor decisions where trust is concerned. I don't want there to be any secrets between us. And I want you to know that you are loved beyond measure by so many people. Your father has taught me so much about love and trust—the most valuable lessons I've learned to date. I want to share all that and more with you. That's what family is all about. Love and trust.

"Only a mother could write something like this, Sunny." He handed the letter to her. "We may not have Lucien anymore but there are two things that we do have. The two most important things we can share— and that's love and trust."

"Where did you get this? I threw this away."

"No, you didn't. I found it. I found all your letters.

I've been carrying this one around in my wallet. I read it every day hoping that someday the woman who wrote this would come back to me."

"Oh." She tried to look away, but he caught her chin, turning her face back to his.

"I can't for the life of me figure out why you'd want to throw them away?"

"I couldn't look at them."

"But these letters will connect you and Lucien forever. Every thought and wish you had about him and us is there in your letters. Don't throw this part of us away, Sunny. Your letters are your legacy to our son."

"It just hurts too much."

"It hurts because it was real. It can only be real if there's a chance you'll get hurt. There will be days when you feel the pain so deeply, but I promise that I'll be here with you. And I'll need you to pick me up on *my* dark days. Some couples never even get the chance to experience what we did. We stood in the light for a little while...and some is better than none." Mathew remembered the honest words that came to him from Leo.

"What did you do with your letters?" She looked up at him with glassy eyes.

"You know about my letters?"

"I accidentally stumbled across them."

"Oh." Mathew was unsure what to say.

"They made me laugh and cry. All your fatherly advice. They're beautiful. They're just beautiful, Mathew."

"I meant every word. Every single word."

Sunny looked down at the wrinkled paper in her hands. "You saved them all? All my letters?"

"Every one of them." He nodded.

"You know, you've given me some special gifts, but this—this one means more than any of them. I have cried so many tears over the loss of these letters. I wasn't myself when I threw them away. I wasn't thinking."

"It's okay. I have all the letters and they're safe. I even have the letters from your father and Leo."

Sunny offered her first smile in weeks. "Grandpa and Uncle Leo. They loved him too, didn't they?" Her voice cracked.

"Yes, they did. Very much." He wrapped his strong, protective arms around her. "Our baby was precious and perfect, and we all loved him. We'll always love him."

The room quieted again and within minutes he found himself once more on the threshold of sleep.

"I was so afraid that I would never hold you again," he whispered as he drifted.

"Just don't let go. I need you, Mathew."

Chapter Thirty-Eight

Mathew sat up in bed, rubbing his tired eyes and listening. Their bedroom was dark with only the muffled sound of Ivy's breathing in the air. A check of the clock, along with a familiar pain in his heart, confirmed his worst fear. With a heavy sigh, he fell back in defeat against his pillow and stared up at the ceiling. Just a few hours before, his confidence was rock solid, with the need to search for Sunny in the hours before sunrise now over. Mathew swallowed hard. The tiny bit of growth they'd cultivated at the cabin the night before had withered away in just a day.

Was she sitting in the rocking chair studying the black and white images of his ultrasound pictures? Had she fallen asleep on the floor beside the crib amid a collection of cherished children's books? Perhaps she found the box of letters and was now fighting her way through every emotional line. Though he'd staggered down the dark hall from their bedroom to Lucien's room many times, he suddenly felt weak.

He made his way into their bathroom. A splash of cool water on his face and a quick sip from the tap was followed by a look in the mirror. A good, long look. *This is reality. And reality is the only thing that's going to bring her back. Real life. Real feelings. Real love. Like Dr. McNichol said—Sunny's operating by her own hourglass. There's no speeding up time.*

As quietly as he could, he made the fateful journey down the hall. His legs were much heavier this time, with the harsh realization that their return to happiness would take more than just one night in each other's arms. The door at the end of the hall seemed to drift further and further away with each step. He pushed it open, his eyes widening with surprise to find the room empty. A feeling of relief washed over him, and he continued on downstairs. He found Sunny asleep on the couch, a book balancing on her lap. The serene look on her face triggered a smile on his.

His gaze moved to her hands for a minute, noticing for the first time the absence of her mother's ring. Was it a sign or merely an oversight? He'd been hurt too many times to allow himself to read too much into it. His gaze traveled down the length of her body, stopping at her feet. *Lucien's toes.* Unable to resist, Mathew sat down gently on the edge of the sofa and rubbed her feet with a soft touch.

"You never could let me rest, could you?" she whispered before opening her eyes.

"Are you okay?" he asked.

"I'm fine." She gave a slight nod.

"When I rolled over and you weren't there…"

"You thought the worst?"

"I'd be lying if I said otherwise."

"Mathew, I can't guarantee those nights are over. I just can't think that far ahead."

"I understand."

"I walked down to Lucien's room. I stood at the doorway for a long time, you know, trying to decide if going in would…"

"You don't have to explain. And don't feel like

you have to hide it from me either. I just want you to promise me one thing."

"What's that?"

"Don't try to do this on your own."

"I know," she whispered, avoiding his eyes.

"Sunny?"

"Yes?"

"I love you." He squeezed her feet between his hands.

"I know you do. And that's made all the difference."

He turned his attention to the book in her lap. Their entire love story began because of a conversation about books. While it might have gone unnoticed to most, seeing his wife with a book in hand filled him with hope.

It was one step closer to the real Sunny.

Chapter Thirty-Nine

Dear Pop,

Do you remember Libby? That raggedy stuffed kitty I insisted on dragging all over creation? Of course you do. I'm sure there were times that you cursed that poor cat's existence as you spent many a bedtime searching high and low for her, knowing I would not fall asleep until my hands were wrapped securely around her. I've often wondered what happened to my dear old friend. I like to think she found her way into the arms of a loving child. Or maybe, like the Velveteen Rabbit, she became real. I guess it doesn't really matter where she is, only that I remember every stitch of her little golden body, every secret we ever shared, and the way she made me feel when I held her. She added a unique color to the canvas of my childhood, creating a layer that changed me forever.

I remember the night you tucked me in with the sad truth that my precious Libby was gone. I can still see the look in your eyes as you moved your hand gently through my hair. I understand now how hard that must have been for you. You've always wanted to shield me from pain. You've always tried to protect me from the ugliness of the world. You've always shown me the one thing that every human desires and needs as much as breath itself—unconditional love.

It was those same eyes that stared down at me on

Easter morning, as you stood bravely by my hospital bed. I couldn't acknowledge it then, and it's so fresh it pierces my heart still, but seeing your eyes and feeling your arms around me allowed me to fall away with the assurance that you would catch me. You've always caught me. And I know that as long as you're able, you always will. That's what fathers do—the good ones, anyway. I always felt your love. I know I always will.

I don't quite know how I did it, but I have surrounded myself with loving, gifted men who are much better writers than I am. The feelings and emotions you expressed to me in your letter have haunted me for days and days. And it's with your honesty and Mathew's support that I now find myself sitting in a place I couldn't have imagined just a few weeks ago. I wandered off the path for a long time, but today I will plant my feet solidly back upon it, hoping one day I'll be strong enough to make this journey again.

I love you the most,
Baby Girl

"You can go in now," the receptionist announced.

"Thank you."

Standing on shaky legs, Sunny quickly stashed the notebook and letter in her tote bag. She crossed the waiting room, stopping to take one last breath. Her heartbeat increased and the place inside her that once housed a little prince was now home to a thousand anxious butterflies. One hand rested warily on the doorknob while the other disappeared inside her pocket, rubbing the tiny silver heart with a gentle touch. *I can do this.*

Dr. McNichol looked up from behind her desk as

the door to her private office opened.

"Good afternoon. I'm so glad you're here." Her greeting was genuine, and she stood, offering a handshake and a smile.

"Good afternoon."

"Right on time. Please, come in and make yourself at home." The doctor pointed toward the blue club chairs.

"Thank you."

"Coffee?" Dr. McNichol asked, making her way to the comfy seating area.

"I don't think so."

"You sure?"

"I'm fine, really."

"Catherine makes a mean cup of hot cocoa too, complete with a dash of almond, if you're interested."

Sunny couldn't help but smile, immediately put at ease by the woman sitting directly across from her. Though they'd never met, Sunny felt a strange connection to her—the woman who'd help rebuild the person she loved most. For weeks she'd shared hours of intimate conversations with her husband, yet Sunny felt no pangs of jealousy. Many times, she'd imagined him sitting in her office, reliving the scenes of an Easter morning that brought both immense joy and indescribable sorrow. And now, after much soul searching, she found herself in the very same chair where her husband sat week after week. Though she'd debated and questioned this meeting for days, he'd helped her find the strength to pull back the curtain that hid her deepest pain, allowing the first real rays of light back inside.

"A dash of almond?" Sunny raised an eyebrow.

"You know Mathew–he's a stickler for detail." Dr. McNichol grinned.

A word about the author…

Suzy England fell in love with fiction the minute she picked up her first Judy Blume book in third grade. A retired elementary educator and native Texan, she lives in Houston with her husband. She loves to brag about her two adult children and is always dreaming of her next travel adventure. Suzy is the author of THE WEEKEND (Silver Phoenix, 2019), CHASING MR. CROWN (a Wattpad Paid Story, which has amassed over 2 million reads), and PERFECT (The Wild Rose Press, 2023). When she's not writing, she's binge-watching British television, listening to true crime podcasts, or cheering for her alma mater, The University of Texas at Austin. www.suzyengland.com